# belmondo
# style

ALSO BY ADAM BERLIN

*Headlock*

# *belmondo style*

## Adam Berlin

ST. MARTIN'S PRESS ❧ NEW YORK

www.stmartins.com

Library of Congress Cataloging-in-Publication Data

Berlin, Adam, 1966–
    Belmondo style / by Adam Berlin.—1st St. Martin's ed.
        p. cm.
    ISBN 0-312-31923-1
    EAN 978-0312-31923-6
        1. Greenwich Village (New York, N.Y.)—Fiction. 2. Belmondo,
Jean-Paul, 1933—Influence—Fiction. 3. Criminals—Family relation-
ships—Fiction. 4. Fugitives from justice—Fiction. 5. Marginality,
Social—Fiction. 6. Fathers and sons—Fiction. 7. Single fathers—
Fiction. 8. Teenage boys—Fiction. 9. Gay youth—Fiction. I. Title.

PS3552.E724837B45 2004
813'.6—dc22

                                                        2003066790

First Edition: April 2004

10   9   8   7   6   5   4   3   2   1

To my mother and father
and my brother David

WITH WARM THANKS TO:

Robert Lescher, my agent, who always reads my work
carefully and treats me with care

Keith Kahla, my editor, whose thorough and insightful
comments made me see this book anew

Linda Bailey for her continued and steady faith in me

—Do you believe in love?
—It's the only thing one can believe in.
—What is your greatest ambition?
—To become immortal, and then to die.

from Breathless

PART ONE

*breathe out*

# I

MY FATHER WAS A PLAYER.

Sometimes, the next morning, the woman sitting at our breakfast table would talk to me like she knew me. Maybe she thought a maternal show towards his kid was the way to win my father forever. It wasn't. My father would tell whatever woman was sitting there, her legs crossed, usually, coffee cup in her hand, usually, that he had to get me ready for school and what could she say to that? I always got myself ready for school, but the line was perfect. Not delivered mean or impatiently, just as a matter of fact. So the woman would go into my father's room, take off his bathrobe, get dressed in her own clothes, now wrinkled and looking very much like last night's outfit, and she would leave. Some of the women kissed him good-bye in front of me and if the kiss went on too long I would watch my father's hands gently push them away. His hands could go very gentle when he wanted them to. Some of the women scribbled a phone number down or put a business card flat on the table with a hopeful click of paper against wood and told my father to call and he'd smile that small smile of his that was more in his eyes than his mouth like the world was a game.

I was a perfect prop for his lifestyle, but I wasn't a prop at all. Not really. I'd get ready for school. He'd make his bed. I'd gather my books and he'd walk me to school when I was very young and then, when I was older, he would walk me to the subway, kiss my cheek, tell me to have a good day.

A line of women. That's how I pictured them, a long line stretching from the front door of our walk-up apartment and down the stairs and out, along Bedford Street until it hit Seventh Avenue and then downtown, the bodies diminishing in size and disappearing into the horizon. The World Trade Centers had once broken the view, holding solid, looking like two steel pillars thrust into Manhattan to keep it from floating away, but they were gone. The horizon became both more open and less open and my father continued to meet women.

We started that January together, a new year and a new morning. I had been at a friend's house for a party and a bunch of us had spent the night drinking alcohol snuck in from various parental liquor cabinets and smoking stolen packs of cigarettes on a Park Avenue terrace. My friend James Worthen was a rich kid and his parents let him roam freely, didn't complain when smoke came out of his room or when the noise of teens jostling for prime floor positions, an excuse to tackle and horse around, became too loud. The Worthen apartment was a duplex with an actual spiral staircase and a wrap-around balcony on the top floor that offered relatively unobstructed views of the East River on one side and Central Park on the other, the tops of trees looking foreign in the middle of concrete and brick. In the summer, in full bloom, I always thought they looked like the heads of broccoli. That January there were no leaves, only branches, almost the color of concrete but not quite, retouched by the shadows they cast on the hard ground below, creating their own lighting effect. We drank and talked and watched the New Year's ball drop on TV and talked some more and made some prank phone calls to revelers too drunk to hang up immediately and a few of the guys hooked up with a few of the girls. I spent the end of the night listening to James. I wasn't interested in what he was saying, but I liked his voice. It was deep and soothing and I just took his voice into my head, the sound, not the words. His voice made me want to close my eyes and go to another place.

In the morning, on the walk home, my legs were heavy. I stayed in shape between cross-country season and track season by running the streets of Manhattan, but that morning I was tired.

My father was sleeping on the couch. The wastebasket had been pulled next to him, a plastic bag from D'Agostino's stuffed inside in case he puked. I hated his hangovers, but it was New Year's Eve. Everyone had a right to be hungover. I walked quietly past him, past his bedroom where the outline of another body lay, and into my room. I closed the door and slept until the afternoon. When I got up, my legs rested and springy, my father was sitting on the couch, watching TV, the wastebasket back in place, the plastic bag removed. I didn't even have to look. I knew the woman was long gone.

"How was your New Year's eve?" I said.

"My New Year's eve was a lot of champagne."

"You never drink champagne."

"I drank champagne last night. I drank champagne all the way to midnight and then all the way after midnight. It was good champagne."

"Are you hungover?"

"Completely. And my lungs are killing me. I hate when I smoke cigarettes. How was your night?"

"I didn't smoke."

"Good boy. Did you drink?"

"Just a little. I was more exhausted when I came home than anything else."

"The Worthens didn't tuck you in after the ball dropped?"

"I never even saw them," I said. "They were at some black-tie gala."

"I've never been to a New Year's Eve party where black tie was required," my father said. "Maybe next year I'll put away the jeans and T and do it in style."

I had seen my father wear a tuxedo only once, to the sweet sixteen of a classmate of mine. The party was at the Plaza and I knew he'd like the atmosphere so I convinced him to go. From my table I saw my father moving from his table to the bar, walking his trademark walk, shoulders slightly swaying like he could kick anyone's ass if confronted even if he was dressed formally. He walked like a fighter, but gracefully too, and he looked tough and refined at the same time, his blond hair cut short, cheekbones visible from working out, push-ups and pull-ups and runs along the river. Sometimes in the winter, between running seasons, we ran together along the Hudson if he hadn't already run while I was at school. The girl sitting next to me was also watching my father walk. She watched him order a drink from the bartender. She watched him lift the drink, which I knew was bourbon. She watched him walk back to the table and smile at the woman to his right, a woman I had never seen before and, I guessed, my father had only met that afternoon. The girl at my table didn't stop looking.

"You know who that is?" I said.

"Who is it?"

"Jared Chiziver."

"I thought your name was Chiziver," the girl said.

"It is my name," I said.

"What is he, your older brother?"

"He's my father."

6

"Really," she said and she looked me over to see if I had what he had, if I was at least starting to develop what he had. We were built alike and we even looked alike, a little, although my hair was brown and my eyes not as narrow, blue not green, but I could tell the girl didn't see it in me, not the part of it she had been watching, and so she turned back to my father and I ordered another ginger ale from the waiter standing at attention in white gloves.

My father pressed his eyes, the hangover set in his crow's feet that became defined after a night of drinking. The New Year's Eve champagne had done a number on him.

"Are you hungry?" I said to my father.

"I must be. I lost everything I ate at the party."

"Booze and then beer, nothing to fear. Beer and then booze, you're gonna lose. What's the story with champagne?"

"Good champagne," my father said.

"Okay. What's the story with good champagne?"

"Good champagne has a story all its own."

"You still had the wastebasket at the ready."

"I'm always prepared," he said and I left it alone.

My father hit the remote and the channel changed. A long shot of last night's Times Square, thousands of revelers acting happy for the camera.

"Happy New Year," my father shouted.

"Happy New Year to you too," I said. "I'm starving."

"Is that your resolution?"

"Very funny."

"Come on, we'll go down. What are you in the mood for? Pizza? Chinese food? Whatever you want."

"You're in no shape to go out," I said.

"I can go out."

"You don't want to go out."

"Not really, but I should probably eat something."

"We can order a pizza from Lombardi's."

"Call up. Get a pie with the works. Get two pies if you want. We can have a New Year's Day feast. Start the year off right with mozzarella and Italian sausage on top."

My father stretched. He arranged himself inside the pair of sweats he wore to bed when he slept alone. I called up and ordered two pizzas, one with mushrooms and sausage and one with anchovies. Sometimes I was the one doing everything, like I was the father, like I was holding down the job and making the adult decisions, like what kind of pizza to order, but I wasn't. I always knew he was there for me, would protect me, and he gave me everything I wanted that he could afford. He didn't have much, but he always had enough. He always kept that balance. And when he introduced me, usually to a woman, he always held my shoulder in his strong hand and said *This is my son, Ben,* and I felt how much I was the son.

The voice at the pizza place asked if I wanted the pies delivered. I said I'd pick them up. I could run down to Lombardi's and back and save a few tip bucks. I was fast. I was only a sophomore, but there were already college scouts checking me out, standing around the inside of the track with stopwatches of their own, and I knew that some school would offer me a free ride. My father didn't exactly have a kitty tucked away for my education. He had never even finished school. I'd already read more books than my father, but he had lived more than me. Jared Chiziver had lived more than most men, real-life living, and his real stories, when he told them, were not fabricated. Just as his walk was no longer fabricated. He had probably tried the walk on for size when he had been younger, younger than I was, younger than sixteen, and the walk had fit. Walk the walk.

I ran. I did my schoolwork. My father taught me other things.

# 2

THE FIRST TWO WEEKS OF JANUARY WERE WARM, BUT PEOPLE still wore their heavy coats. Winter coats made things difficult. In other seasons pockets were more visible. My dad hated winter. He hated the cold. His hands had bad circulation and he never wore gloves so when he was walking he'd constantly be blowing into his hands. Smoke came out between his fingers and his eyes were always moving, past the smoke. That's how he looked in the winter, his fedora pulled low covering his blond hair, his hands cupped around his mouth and nose, his eyes surveying the scene.

The city, crowded during the morning and evening rush hours and during lunch, was my father's office. My father was a pickpocket. He made his living as a petty thief and he never really hid that from me. I knew more about what my father did than my friends knew about their fathers. It always amazed me how little most kids knew of their parents' work. As far as they were concerned, their parents went to an office somewhere, spent the day away doing something, came home. My father had no set schedule. When we needed money he would get money. He called it a Spartan existence. He called it living off the land. The land was not green pasture or densely populated woods. My father's land was concrete. He walked the sidewalks plowing fields of pedestrians, separating wheat from chaff, money from man. As a kid I saw all of my father's criminal tricks. Manhattan was one big treasure hunt and we often ate for free, saw movies for free, went shopping for free, and to get cash my father stole people's wallets.

We were able to live in the city, eat three meals a day at home if we wanted, live fairly comfortably, even take a trip to Florida every summer, all on a pickpocket's salary. My father told me there were two kinds of stealing. There was big stealing and little stealing and in reality, even though big stealing was romantic and even though people claimed that a big heist was the way to go, a one-shot fantasy deal, big stealing landed you in jail while little stealing did not. My father had been in jail just once, just over the weekend, but it hadn't been for stealing. A jealous husband had confronted my father and my father had confronted him back, broken his rib, a punch to the body a safer punch for my father's hand, and he was arrested. The husband was a low-level politician who didn't want his wife's affair making the papers so the charges had been dropped. My father's fingerprints were on file but he had no record, and when he worked, as far as I knew, he never made mistakes.

My father always wore a coat when he worked. A light raincoat in the summer as if he expected it to drizzle all the time. A long winter coat when the weather turned cold. He bit his nails short. When I asked him about his nails he said he had started biting them when he was a kid and had never stopped. It was one of the few details he told me about his childhood. He said he didn't know what could concern a kid so much to make him that nervous. Maybe he'd forgotten what it was like to be a kid even if he was still a kid in many ways. When my friends came over they loved my father.

Women and kids. Only men disliked him. And, I assumed, the people he stole from.

I didn't bite my nails. The nervousness was in my stomach. Before a race I sometimes threw up. I'd walk to a place where no one could see me, away from the track or near some trees during cross-country season, and I'd pretend to stretch, my back turned to everyone before I puked. I was nervous some days when I came home from school and my father wasn't there. There was always the chance he'd get caught. I never told him I was concerned, afraid I might jinx his run of luck. My father didn't believe in luck. With his nails bitten short, short to the point just before bleeding, the nerves almost exposed, he had complete feel. Even the finest silk pocket touched ever so slightly could be felt and his success was based on practice, skill, making no mistakes. In that, my father, Jared Chiziver, felt he could control his life.

I felt the most control when I ran, but even then I wasn't in full control. During a 3200-meter race, I was going stride for stride with an opponent from Humanities High School. I was hanging back with him and I knew there was enough breath in my lungs and enough strength in my legs to pull away in the last two hundred yards. I would start my kick and win the race. One of my teammates was a new father. His one-year-old kid and the mother of his baby, still his girlfriend, still a kid herself, were there to cheer him on. The child had been a complete mistake, but like many city kids he felt a baby was something to define him and so he and his girlfriend were trying as best they could to bring the kid up. I was running hard. I was starting to make my move. I lifted my legs, increased my stride, pumped my hands harder, started feeling the freedom of speed that I waited for, that I kept for races, my reward for holding the kick when I wasn't racing, when I was just putting in the miles, preparing for when it was time to really run. I was running hard, starting my sprint, my body filling with freedom and then this kid, this kid that had just learned to crawl, came crawling out of the crowd. I jumped to avoid him. My foot slipped, I fell, scraped my knee, watched my opponent move ahead of me to the finish line and the baby kept crawling and crawling across the track before his mother snatched him up. I finished the race in third. It was impossible to control everything. There were parts of life that just happened, that just were.

It was a warm January, but it was still January. My father walked the streets in his long coat looking for tourists who carried cash. When I came home from school, my father was usually home, and if he'd just come back from work, he'd be counting the money at our kitchen table. Ones and fives and tens and twenties and some- times, on good days, there would be six separate piles, fifties and hundreds. He wasn't overly neat in most things, but this was his work and my father took pride in his work. He kept his own wallet full of cash and put the rest away in the cabinet under the bathroom sink, behind toilet paper and paper towels and soap from the Miami hotel where we stayed, the Holiday Inn South Beach, soap we took from the maids' carts and stockpiled in our bags. My father didn't hide the money from me. I had no set allowance, but he gave me twenties to carry in my own wallet. He never wanted me to be broke if I came upon a good time. Of course, my good times were different from his. I didn't need money to take a woman to a bar. He was a player and I had no desire to play like that. I didn't need money to pop into a movie during the day, something my father of- ten did. I was in school. And of course I didn't need money for a cab ride home, getting out of a neighborhood fast, hit and run. I spent my money to keep up with James Worthen and his Park Av- enue friends, which really didn't take that much. We'd go out to eat or go to a party or hang out in Central Park and I'd wait for the quieter times when James would speak quietly and I could just listen to his voice.

Two weeks into January and my father was at the table counting money. I put my book bag in my room and came back to the kitchen, had a glass of milk and some chocolate chip cookies, a wholesome tableau except for the row of other people's bills on the table. I didn't talk while my father counted. I read some of the newspaper until he was done. He filled his wallet, slid two twenties at me across the table. I thanked him and he smiled. He put rubber bands around the stacks of bills and brought the money to the bathroom. He came back, poured himself a glass of milk, took a cookie from the Chips Ahoy bag.

"Good day?" I said.

"Christmas is over."

"Bad day?"

"Not that bad. Some thin wallets in Grand Central and some slightly thicker ones on the street."

"I got a ninety-two on my Political Science test and an A on my English essay."

"Excellent. What did you write about?"

"This book we've been reading. *Things Fall Apart*. By Chinua Achebe."

"Never heard of him."

"He's African. He wrote about the fall of a strong man in Africa. There was a pretty good part in there about wrestling, how he was a good wrestler, but I guess wrestling doesn't count for much when the people attacking you have guns."

"The great equalizer," my father said and took another cookie.

"Everything we read in this class is about oppression. It's a little annoying."

"Not if you're the oppressor."

"How much fun can that be? I mean, you can only ruin some-body's life for so long before it gets boring."

"Then you move on," my father said. "You get tired of oppress-ing one people, you move on to another people. There's plenty of people in the world to oppress."

"Well, we're reading about most of them."

"You got an A. That's the main thing."

"The main thing is that Ms. Scalato didn't give us any home-work tonight."

"The new teacher," my father said. "How's she working out?"

"She's enthusiastic. You can tell she's new."

I asked my father if he wanted more milk, closed the carton, put it in the refrigerator. He'd bought me one of those magnetized po-etry sets and right next to the fridge handle was one of my poems.

> hot food for delicate whisper
> feed my hungry bowl
> the earth is his sullen drunk
> a deep ditch, a rare hole

I didn't know what it was supposed to mean, but I'd put it together, along with some other stupid stanzas, and my father got a kick out of reading them out loud whenever we were having an argument and he wanted to break the tension. How could I respond to my own line about hungry bowls? We didn't argue much. He let me do whatever I wanted to do and he trusted me to do the right thing.

He also trusted me not to steal. Long ago he had made me promise not to do what he did and I'd kept that promise. My father felt there was a difference between me walking out of a restaurant without paying the bill when I was with him and me walking out on my own. He wanted better for me. The way a father who works as a janitor wants his son to stay away from mops and cleaning agents. I guess my father wanted me to be the kind of man he would steal from. He pictured me grown up, wearing an expensive cashmere coat in the wintertime, my wallet thick with hard-earned cash.

"So do all the boys still have a crush on Ms. Scalato?"

"Almost all of them."

"It doesn't hurt to be good-looking if you're a teacher."

"It also helps to be smart," I said.

"I never thought of that. Are you meeting your friends tonight?"

"I've got trigonometry homework and psychology. What about you?"

"I don't know. I'll probably take a walk. I'm feeling restless."

Restless. That's what he always said. *I'm feeling restless.* It was his euphemism for *I'm going out to meet a woman*, but he didn't say that. I sometimes wondered what he'd been like at my age, if he was scoring with girls then, if he talked about it with his buddies like my friends did when they screwed a girl, describing what their pussies smelled like, how they moaned, what they said. They all talked and they all listened to that talk, focused on that talk as if there was a secret there, or the answer to a secret. I pretended to listen, pretended to care, but I didn't. When they talked that way it was like a movie scene I didn't believe.

I guessed my father didn't talk. I thought of my father as a private kid, like me, only tougher than me. He rarely talked about his childhood and when I asked him pointed questions he gave vague answers. He'd moved to New York young. He'd learned some things. I stopped asking when he clenched his jaw, cutting off the past.

My father's favorite stories were movie stories. Movies were his one great love besides women and when I was a kid he'd tell me the most elaborate stories, which, I later found out, were movie plots. I would be watching an old film with my father and suddenly, even though I had never seen the film before, I recognized the characters and the action. Sometimes I preferred the way my father told the story to the actual film. He cut the bad scenes, highlighted the good scenes, zoomed in and out like a deft cameraman to heighten the conflict, the resolution, the message. His favorite films were the ones without a clear moral. He wouldn't talk about those, not right away. We'd walk out of the theater together and he'd just nod his head.

I watched TV while my dad showered and shaved for his restlessness. I could smell his shaving cream. I could hear him humming a tune. Smoke from the hot water came out the open bathroom door. I heard him walk into his room, his bare feet on the wood floor. I knew how he looked without turning around. Towel wrapped around his thin waist. Hair still wet. The boxer's roll of the shoulders even as he walked inside our apartment, bathroom to bedroom. He would dress and come out looking fresh and striking. It was hard to believe he was my father. He smiled his smile, his eyes full of the night ahead, really looking forward to his adventure, the same adventure he never seemed to tire of, a woman, somewhere, out there, to be found and entered. It was more than the sex. I knew that. Even if I didn't know much.

"Anything good on?" he said.

"Not really."

"Crap TV will make it easier to do your homework. No distractions."

"Have fun," I said like I was the father. "Don't stay out too late."

My father said good night and walked out the door. I heard his footsteps, springy on the stairs, and then the city was before him.

# 3

I WAS MY FATHER'S ONLY MALE COMPANION AND I BELIEVE he genuinely enjoyed my company. I knew his low-key sense of humor, when he was being sarcastic, when he was poking fun. I knew his over-the-top pranks as well, his large sweeping gestures. He spent much of his time entertaining me and I laughed genuinely. I didn't have a mother. My father evaded my questions about her, kept his answers vague, the way he stayed away from all past specifics. The future. The past. All my father focused on was the present and perhaps that was why he loved movies so much. It was two hours of present. The movies could be replayed and replayed, present upon present, a constant now.

I was more of a planner. As a runner I had to plan. Preparation was part of running and if my legs didn't have the miles in them, then I would never win the race. If I was to afford the cashmere coats my father envisioned me wearing, I would have to work for them, and that took preparation too. My father saw no point in preparing too much for anything and it was more than just the obvious you-can-die-at-any-time cliché. He said the now was all that mattered. Look at the movie stars. The ones that had been hand-some on screen grew into old men. They could reminisce all they wanted, but the reality of now was that the stars of yesterday were old. My father felt it was better if they didn't grant interviews or play old men in movies. That way the only image preserved would be the image of their highest now and in that they would achieve youthful immortality. I believe that's what my father wanted. To be young forever. His body was almost as young as the bodies in my school. Before gym class, as we stripped in the locker room, or be-fore track practice when we had to put on our uniforms, the bodies I saw were often beautiful, but not like my father's body. He had no fat. He had strength. He had the boy and the man in his body and that was why both girls and women looked at him, watched him walk, sometimes made fun of his trademark strut, but were attracted to it nonetheless. My father said the winners were winners now. The beautiful were beautiful now. The young were young now. The old-timers could talk about their glory days, but it was only talk.

The line of women was a present line. When the now was over the women were sent out of our apartment, or my father, more of-ten, walked out of theirs. The future. The past. None of that con-cerned my father.

If I were to learn about my past I would have to go somewhere else for the information and while I thought of it sometimes, thought of tracking down where I came from, I never pursued it. In that way I was all now as well, just like my father. We had a history together, but our times together were very present. He entertained. I laughed. He smiled his eye-smile. I smiled back. He said a movie line. I said the next line. Immediately. So I never fully felt the need to track down my past. I was happy with my father.

Of course, there were times when I craved to know where I'd come from, from what woman I'd been born. She must have been special to my father, if only for a while. I daydreamed about her, made pictures of her that melded into one picture of her, a distant fairy-tale of a picture that was somewhere between cartoon and photograph. I never described the picture to my father to see if what I pictured and what was real resembled each other. That was part of our deal, a silent pact, yet as binding as my promise not to steal. I didn't ask questions that made my father clench his jaw and he gave me enough love to fill that hollow place in my past.

There was no snow on the ground. It had snowed once and melted, before New Year's, and there was just a dusting of sand where the trucks had moved through the streets. When I came home from school my father was watching a tape of *Bad Day at Black Rock*, a classic, the one-armed Spencer Tracy tracking down the truth about a small-town murder. It was the end of the movie and Tracy was getting back on the train, his work done, riding off into the sunset, a victorious loner with a war wound. That was his past and he had moved on, but in the film he was all present. On film, he would always be the same Spencer Tracy stepping up on that same train riding off into that same sunset.

"Did you run yet?" I said.

"Not today. You want to go?" His eyes were on the TV.

"It's a nice night. Not much of a wind."

"Look at him heading out," my father said. "Now that is a real movie star."

"Better than Bogie?" I said.

"Better than Bacall."

"Better than Belmondo?"

"No one is better than Belmondo."

We both moved our thumbs across our lips the way Jean-Paul Belmondo did in *Breathless*, our all-time favorite movie. We had seen that movie many times. We always moved our thumbs across our lips when it was done. My father even wore a hat like the one Belmondo wore. Belmondo in *Breathless* was my father on film. A petty thief who gets by. The only difference was that Belmondo had fallen in love in the movie and my father continued to play and play. Maybe my father wished for someone that could hold his attention for more than a night, but in truth *Breathless* was a two-hour movie, and so the love affair was only that long in real time too. My father could do two hours. I saw my father in Jean-Paul Belmondo and of course he saw himself. Movies, especially *Breathless*, were the closest things we had to a history. In the repetition, in seeing that movie over and over again, in moving our thumbs across our lips like Belmondo, over and over, we had a past. The movie itself was in the present. *Breathless* was about a man who lived for now.

"I'll run," my father said. "Streets or river?"

"River."

My father removed the disk. Renting movies was one of the things he paid for outright, as if movies were above taking.

"Do I need a jacket?"

"Just a couple of sweatshirts," I said.

"I'll try to find some clean ones."

"We can do a laundry after we sweat up our clothes."

"A man with a plan," he said.

My father went into his room to change and I went into my room to change. I double knotted my running shoes, stretched my thighs and calves. My father didn't stretch before he ran, just after. He did some sit-ups and push-ups on the floor and stood up.

"Let's go," he said.

We went down, jogged to Christopher Street and then west to the West Side Highway, jogged in place as we waited for the light. The light changed and we crossed the highway.

My father didn't run the way I ran. His right foot jutted slightly out and his stride was not as long as mine. He'd never been taught how to run the way my coaches had taught me, and his walking style infiltrated his running style. His feet were a little heavy on the pavement and his shoulders a little bunched up. What looked strong and even graceful when he walked did not translate well into running. My father didn't care that his form was poor. He cared that his legs were strong, that he had his wind, that he felt young. Only when he sprinted did his legs open up and then he looked like a runner, his head held high, his arms pumping. My father was a vain man, but it wasn't a distasteful vanity. He was proud of his looks, but he wasn't just looks. Even Jean-Paul Belmondo caught himself in the mirror sometimes and stopped and stayed looking. That was part of his charm.

We ran along the highway and again, more like the father than the son, I let my father set the pace and stayed with him. When he slowed slightly, I slowed, and when he caught his second wind and picked up the pace, I picked up the pace with him. He breathed just a little harder than I did. I knew how to glide over the pavement, keep my legs up, my balance slightly forward to keep me moving forward, my posture open so that my lungs could get the most out of each breath. We passed all the other runners.

"Catch the turtles," I said, which is what my coach said.

"Nobody beats us," my father said. "Not even the turtles."

"We are invincible."

"We are mighty."

We ran to Stuyvesant, where I went to school, and past Stuyvesant and around the Hudson River Park. It was a beautifully landscaped park for New York City, not overly manicured, wildflowers in the summer and marsh grass and large cattails, their brown-furred heads offsetting the different greens. During the fall and winter the grass was fenced off. Sometimes whole flocks of Canadian geese grazed before they continued their journey, south or north I didn't know. There was no snow, no ice, just hard pavement and an overcast sky before us. Without a chop, the river looked like slate. A ferry from New Jersey docked, sending black smoke towards us, and my father must have gotten a gulp of it since he started spitting. If something from the city went into his mouth, a particle of soot, an exhaust fume, even the smell of paint, he would try to spit it out. The Statue of Liberty did not look that far away in the fading light. We got to the stairs near the Museum of Jewish Heritage and ran up and down ten times. My father threw some punches at the air. I kept my hands above my head, clasped behind my neck, elbows out in a butterflied V so that all the weight would be on my legs. We ran to Battery Park and turned around.

The wind was against us on the run back and it was cold.

"How do you feel?" I said.

"I'm fine. Just a little frostbitten. I stopped feeling my feet a mile back and I'll probably lose a couple of fingers. Other than that, I'm fine."

"You're cold blooded."

"I'm warm blooded. I'm hot blooded. That's why I'm cold."

"You have thin blood."

"Did they teach you that in science class today?"

"I'm not taking biology this year."

I pictured the oxygen in my blood, feeding my muscles to keep me running all night. I listened to my father breathe, his breath a little heavier than mine.

"Do you want to see a movie tonight?" he said.

"I have to finish a research paper for history that was due last week."

"Finish it then. We'll go on Saturday. We'll catch a matinee. I'm feeling restless."

"Run it out," I said, but I knew he wouldn't.

My father picked up the pace and I went with him. We rounded the grass and ran toward Stuyvesant, the orange bricks lit up against the dusk, and then we hit the straightaway, a full mile back to Christopher Street. There weren't many runners out. Most people ran during the first good days of spring and the last good days of fall and stayed away from the summer and winter extremes. They had no discipline. I liked that my father ran at all times. In the summer he ran with his shirt off. In the winter he wore layers of sweatshirts and blew into his hands, and when it was very cold he wore socks over his hands to keep them warm. We sprinted the last quarter mile. His stride opened up and he looked like a runner. I never passed my father on the sprints even though I felt the power in my legs. We ran through the mile marker, our finish line, and stretched on the rail that separated land from river. Across the Hudson, Jersey was lit up, but it was nothing to the view they had, Manhattan at night.

Two women walked over to the railing to look at the river. In the afternoons the gay crowd hung out, men with men, women with women, boys with boys, girls with girls, and there would always be music and the smell of pot in the air and kisses of friendship everywhere. I never really paid attention to them. They were there, part of the scenery, but lately when I finished my run I would stretch out longer, watch them move, listen to them talk, listening for a secret, or the answer to a secret, while easing the muscles in my legs. I wasn't sure if the two women were gay. Maybe they were just friends, taking a walk, looking for some quiet away from the streets. One of the women looked us over and kept her eyes on my father. He was stretching out his calves.

"That looks like it hurts," she said.

"It does hurt," he said.

"Aren't you cold?"

"I'm cold and I'm hurting. Basically, I'm miserable."

The woman laughed and so did her friend.

"I'm sorry to hear that," she said.

I looked at the woman. I looked at her friend. Her friend was not as good-looking. She just smiled and watched and I stood there, stretching out my calves, and watched.

"So what brings you out on a miserable evening like this?" he said.

"We wanted to get some air."

My father took a deep, exaggerated breath, then mock-coughed.

"Nothing like it," he said. "Fresh and delicious."

"And what brings you out?" she said to me.

"I wanted to run."

"Look at those legs," my father said. "Those legs are going to the Olympics one day."

"They are?"

"Show them some leg," my father said.

I lifted my sweat pants and showed them my calf.

"Very nice."

"We're professional athletes," my father said.

He was leaning back against the railing and he puffed his chest out when he said that.

"We're professional Olympic athletes," I said.

"There's no such thing," the woman said.

"Sure there is," my father said. "Professional baseball players go to the Olympics. And you know those Russian athletes get paid to compete."

"That's true. So what do you play?"

"I'm a professional athlete," he said. "Let's leave it at that."

My father was leaning back on the railing, his legs bent, his back straight. I knew what was coming. He moved away from the railing, but he didn't straighten his legs. His body was completely crooked. He started walking like a cripple, like his legs had been broken years ago and had never healed. He looked ridiculous.

"I'm a professional," he said.

The women started laughing once they knew it was a joke. My father walked in a palsied circle. He leaned back against the railing, his legs still bent, natural for leaning but not walking, and relaxed into position, his chest puffed.

"Yes," my father said. "I'm a professional athlete."

"I'll have to look for you on TV."

"Look for me in the movies," my father said.

"Is that what you do?"

"No, I just watch them. I'm going to the movies tonight as soon as I straighten my legs out, take a hot shower, and get rid of this misery. My son has declined my invitation."

"This is your son?"

"That's me," I said.

They never thought I was his son. I was either his younger brother or just a kid he was hanging out with. That's what I was in many ways, a kid hanging out with my father, and that's what he was too sometimes, a kid hanging out with his kid.

"So are you up for a movie?" my father said.

"What movie?" the woman said.

"I always decide when I get there. Get a feel for what the crowd is excited about."

"No you don't."

"Yes he does," I said.

"Really?" she said and smiled and then the look happened, the way it always happened, my father just watching her, the smile in his eyes changing to another look and the woman stopped smiling and looked.

"I could see a movie," the woman said.

"Good."

And just like that she became part of the long line, the newest member, the most recent, the now.

She gave my father her number and he said he'd call her in an hour and we walked away, up Christopher Street, home.

"You have homework to do, right?"

"I have that paper."

"Well then. We'll go to the movies on Saturday."

"A man with a plan."

"She seemed like she had a sense of humor."

"Sure," I said.

"We'll do laundry tomorrow night. We're good for another day at least."

We were on Bedford Street. My bed was parallel to Bedford Street. That's how I remembered it as a kid.

"Besides," he said, "we're professional Olympic athletes. We can wear whatever we want, clean or dirty."

"Is that your resolution?"

"It's a new year," my father said.

The wind picked up, pressing against my side. I wondered if I was blocking some of the wind for my father. He lifted his hands, brought them together, blew into them. I saw his fingers, nails bitten even and short, and between his fingers came the smoke, there for an instant, then disappearing, then there, with each breath. I waited for his next breath. It came. I turned my head before the smoke went away.

# 4

THE DAYS STAYED WARM FOR JANUARY AND THEN, AS IF LOW-pressure systems and arctic airflows had synchronized their entrance with the calendar, the city became frigid on February first. I woke after midnight and was freezing. My dad had been restless and had gone out. I listened, but couldn't hear a woman on the other side of the apartment so I guessed he had gone to her place unless they were sleeping. I usually didn't even wake up when he brought a woman home. I was so used to the opening and closing of doors, the sounds of sex, that they had become white noise, as unspectacular as the other city noises, sirens and gunned engines and drunken kids coming out of bars at four in the morning with so much energy they had to scream.

I got up, took a leak, shivered. I took two blankets from the closet, put them on my bed, and bundled up, fetally, to keep warm.

A car drove by. The engine's sound was clear, amplified by the cold. Then Bedford Street went quiet. Over the Christmas break, free from school, wandering Manhattan, I had suddenly seen the city in a different way and maybe it was because the people in the city seemed to see me differently. I had grown. My face had come together in a way that was more young man and less kid. I was looked at on the subway, and I was fascinated by my own face in the reflection, the windows made into mirrors by the tunnel's darkness. Of course, the change had been gradual, but I had solidified into something else and there would be no more days when I would regress, when my lines would go blurry, when I would just be a cute child. I took the subway to school and it was me in the window, I knew the face, but it was not the me I remembered. Sometimes I took me by surprise. I was checked out on the street. Even when I ran people looked at me differently, beyond my speed. The look was close to the look my father received. The eyes that stared did not linger as long, were not as sure, but they were stares akin to how people watched my father. The difference was that I was sized up while with my father it wasn't about sizing up at all. A glance at Jared Chiziver was all a person needed. Not even a glance. People were aware of him before he was even focused upon. His fighter's walk opened up a room. I heard the conversations at our table when they stayed for coffee. Women would invariably ask where my father came from, their own eyes narrowing when they asked. It wasn't about geography. They wanted to know where he had come from as if he had been sent from another place. By the time this question was asked, my father was beyond caring. He'd heard it all the night before, when he'd been restless, when he'd been hunting down the now, and in the morning the now was over. The restlessness, along with his sperm, was depleted. He'd tell the woman that he had to get his son ready for school.

I had always been a good student, but after Christmas break I was not completely there. The teachers' voices were background noise to my thoughts. The bell would ring and I would be hard and I would have to pick up my books and press them close to me so that no one saw. The other kids joked about this when it happened to them. Not while they were hard, but after, as if relating the experience, as if making a joke out of it for others, sharing the joke, it was nothing embarrassing, just something all boys went through. They said they had a big roll of Lifesavers in their front pocket. They said they kept their school lunch in their pants. They said they could hang their book bags on it so it was a perfect tool for school. They didn't know the line about the pistol in your pocket, Mae West practically winking with her voice.

I slept badly. Cold. Then sweaty. Then cold again. I curled tighter and tighter until I gave up and got out of bed.

I walked past my father's room. The door was open. He was out. In some bedroom somewhere in the city. I didn't understand it, but I didn't ask. Some mornings he would walk in, a bottle of chocolate Yoo-hoo in his hand to soothe his hangover and I recognized the empty-tired I felt at the end of a hard race, but his seemed a used-up empty while mine was about winning, or at least trying to win.

I walked to the living room and drew back the curtain. The sky was just starting to lighten, beyond the street light, and the edge of the building across the street looked particularly sharp, clean. I checked the clock. It was almost five. I had two more hours before the alarm went off for school. I stretched out my legs. Sometimes early-morning runs were the best, or late-night runs, past midnight or before five, when the city hadn't really started yet. There was a different energy when the streets were almost empty and it didn't matter if the lights were green or red or if I ran in the middle of the avenues. There were no people, no cars, no exhaust fumes cutting into whatever pure air was left in Manhattan. Running along the river, with the river right there, I imagined some sort of natural filtration system working, air skimming over water, that made what I breathed more clean. I put sweatpants on and a thermal top and a hooded sweatshirt to look rough enough and went down.

The air was crisp. I took an exaggerated breath and felt the cold, sharp angles in my lungs and then the angles disappeared, melted with the warmth of an exhale, the heat from my body pushing out the cold that had come from outside my body. I ran west.

There was one person out, covered in a blue tarp, sleeping on the sidewalk. The top of his head almost touched the steps of a brownstone. He was wearing a Yankees cap with a *World Champions* insignia stitched into the side. I thought how if I were homeless I would try to get to Florida before the days went too cold, but I knew that was a stupid thought. The homeless were crazy or poor, or crazy and poor. Their scavenged money went to food and booze, not bus tickets. Their existence was Spartan in the worst way. Sometimes my father gave the drunks money. Only the drunks. And only men. He said that most people empathized with women more, assumed their lives were harder, that they were less self-sufficient, that life on the street was more dangerous for them, which it probably was. My father felt for the men. The drunk men. They would sit on the subways and yammer about the fight they'd almost been in or the success they'd almost had or the woman they'd almost married and their eyes would be lit from the booze, back in that moment, replaying the best now of their lives even if it had been embellished through years of drunken repetition. My father would hand them a couple of bucks. Just to test my father, I asked him what he thought they would use the money for. I was his son, after all. I had to ask the questions, even if the harder questions were never answered. So I asked the now-question about the drunken men. My father said he knew what they would spend it on, but a gift was a gift and it was none of his business. If they could afford a drink to keep them going, to keep them talking, to make them feel the high like they had once felt the high or thought they'd felt it, then that was fine. Next to the homeless man's Yankees cap was a bottle. Perhaps he'd fallen asleep dreaming of a time and place that was warmer than a city sidewalk, where his blankets had been wool instead of plastic.

I ran to the West Side Highway. I saw a car's headlights approach too fast and then it passed. I ran across the highway. The lights on the Jersey side of the river were still on and the sky was starting to brighten, still a dark blue but with the faintest wisps of gray clouds that would turn white with light. There were no runners. No walkers. No rollerbladers. Only me. Part of me wanted to start running hard. When it was morning and the energy was in my legs it felt like I had to release the energy and move. But I had slept badly. I could taste the tired in my mouth. I forced myself to run easy.

Stuyvesant was ahead. Even in the dawn the bricks looked golden, a fine city school for the best and the brightest. Lately, I wasn't the best or the brightest, not at all. I did my work without ambition. I hung out with my friends without interest. I ran hard some days, less hard others. There was no consistency or concentration. I was restless, but not my father's kind of restless. I was my father's son, but not my father at all. I would get a hard-on during class and my mind would go far away and I wondered if anyone could tell.

It was a mile to the school, painted white lines demarcating the distance from Christopher Street to Stuyvesant. The quarter-mile mark was in front of the FedEx garage. In the morning a long line of trucks departed with their urgent packages and in the evening they returned empty. I could no longer look at a FedEx truck without seeing the arrow in the design, a white arrow of space between the capital E and the small X. My father had pointed it out to me. A woman had pointed it out to him, probably a designer of some sort. He asked if I saw the arrow and I said I didn't and he showed me where, traced the arrow with his finger for me, and now that was all

I could see when a FedEx truck drove by. An arrow moving forward. It was too early. There were no trucks. No arrows. Just me running. Forward.

The half-mile mark was well past the garage. To my left, the highway, a paved river that ran straight and quiet. To my right, the Hudson. There was not much chop, just a little going out and suddenly I was aware, by seeing the chop, that there was some wind at my back. I ran a little harder, took advantage of the wind's push, knowing on the return route I would have to move my arms against the wind and push myself. The Statue of Liberty was lit. Her robed body strong and solitary, more gray than green in the morning light, not yet surrounded by tour boats and the ferry shuttling people between Staten Island and Battery Park. The torch was lit brightest, as always.

The three-quarter mark was in front of the boathouse where kayakers gathered in the summer, tipping their red and yellow boats for practice. Stuyvesant took over the horizon. There were no students around and it could have passed for another kind of building, not much different from the luxury apartments that surrounded it. I pictured the janitors inside, cleaning out the bathrooms, sweeping the halls to get ready for the surge of kids and all of their adolescent insecurities, the pushing and pulling and flirting and screaming and the occasional fight, a rare thing in such a good school, one of the reasons kids wanted to come to this school, a high test score the needed ticket to escape other city schools where kids walked with box cutters and switchblades and sometimes guns and where hired security stood watch at the entrance.

My school days had always been easy. I was a bright kid so the teachers liked me. I could run so the coaches liked me. I got along with the smart kids and the jocks. In most ways I was a model student. My father was not a model man. He was not a model parent, not by standard definitions. He didn't believe in rules. Rules, he felt, were made to keep steady people feeling steady, responsible people feeling responsible, mannequins who didn't really live. He trusted me to live. In life. In school. When I showed him my report cards he told me he was proud and to keep doing what I was doing. He knew I was a better student than he had been so any academic advice would have been hypocritical.

When I was in seventh grade my father attended his first parent/teacher day. Maybe he wanted to show me that he understood the significance of junior high. The next step was high school, where grades would count, which would lead to getting admitted to a good college, which would lead to a good job, a logical progression my father had avoided. Maybe he came because he had a late date and was just killing time before he went out. If I had been doing poorly, he might have been on top of me, but he left me alone since I was doing well. That was his way of letting me grow up. He joked that anything I needed to know I could learn in the gutter, and the rest wasn't worth knowing.

I pictured my father smiling to himself as he listened to my teachers describing their pedagogical techniques. My history teacher was a young woman named Ms. Stein. When she finished her talk and the other parents walked out of her classroom, my father stayed behind.

The next morning Ms. Stein sat at our table in my father's bathrobe, drinking a cup of coffee, her hair disheveled, looking too young to be a teacher. She was more uncomfortable than I was. I asked how she had slept. I knew it was cruel, but I didn't like that she knew my father's business and that she'd spent the night in our apartment. I felt angry at her and sorry for her at the same time, but the anger won out so I asked how she'd slept. I was thinking of the word *fuck* when I said *sleep* so it came out mean. Ms. Stein turned red, looked away, said a quiet *Very well, thank you.* I asked her if she wanted some cereal. She said *No thank you.* My father came out of the bathroom and when he saw the two of us sitting there at the table and realized what he had done, finally realized it by seeing the two of us together, he started laughing. Sometimes when my father laughed I couldn't help laughing too. He stood there laughing and I started laughing, the milk from the cereal bubbling out my nose. Ms. Stein just sat there, red-faced. My father said the usual, that he had to get me ready for school, which sounded so ridiculous that I laughed harder. I laughed so hard my father couldn't help laughing harder. There were tears in our eyes. Even Ms. Stein had to smile at the situation, beyond her red-faced embarrassment. When we composed ourselves, my history teacher got up from the table and went into my father's bedroom to dress.

I guessed my father's women could go three ways. They could go bitter once they realized my father would have nothing to do with them after a night. They could stay steady, be cool and neutral, which was truly rare but was the right way to go, it seemed to me. These women had spent a night with my father and had lived as much in the now as he had. I heard the moans. I heard the breathing when I cared to hear. If they had some perspective on life they could easily accept the night as a good night out and move on. The third way was the saddest. Some women hoped for more. My history teacher hoped for more. She was a history teacher, after all. I became a sort of umbilical cord connecting her to my father, the kid in the middle, a student in her class. I knew she liked my father and she would ask after him sometimes. Even as a seventh grader I had been good at coming up with vague answers to keep my father's distance sacred. Ms. Stein gave me A's on everything, so I stopped working. I was too young to care about integrity, if that was even what was involved, and old enough to know that when someone gives you something for virtually nothing that you should take it, no questions asked, not even of yourself. Maybe that was one of the lessons my father taught me.

The mile mark was right in front of the school. When my father and I ran we took a right and kept running, all the way to Battery Park, but I was running alone and it was early. I would have to be back here soon enough.

The light was coming out. It had come out a lot in the last quarter mile, as if the sun, following me, had decided to finish with a sprint. I touched the one-mile marker with my foot, turned and ran back toward Christopher Street.

# 5

THAT EVENING I GOT A PHONE CALL FROM MY FATHER. IF HE
wasn't home in the morning he was home in the afternoon, and if
he wasn't home when I came back from school, he was home soon
after. I'd hear him walking up the stairs, hear the key in the lock, the
squeak of the hinge as the door opened. He was often singing *la la
la*s to some tune. It was his background music. The same way Belmondo sings as he drives the stolen car at the beginning of *Breathless*.

I picked up the phone before the machine clicked in. My father
asked how my day at school was. He asked what I planned to do the
rest of the night. I knew when he was just asking and not listening.
I kept my answers short so he could say what he had to say. My father knew what I was doing. He stopped asking questions and told
me that he was staying out and would be back the next day. He
asked if that was okay. I said it was okay. He asked if I was sure. I
said I was sure. He told me to take whatever money I needed to get
whatever I wanted to eat and he'd see me tomorrow. In the pause I
tried to hear where he was, but I couldn't hear anything. It was

quiet so I knew he wasn't calling from a payphone. I asked him if he was in trouble. My father laughed. He said he was fine.

My father gave me a number to write down just in case of an emergency. I knew it was a woman's number. I had never done that. Written a woman's number down where my father was staying. I had written many numbers down, women giving me their numbers on the phone to pass on to my father. Sometimes they wondered aloud who I was, who was staying at my father's house. A kid's high voice when I was younger so they mistook me for a daughter and lately, with my voice changed, wondering whether my father had a roommate or if Jared Chiziver was just saying it wasn't him, declining them politely. He rarely gave out his number, only sometimes when he was drunk.

My father asked again how school had been. He wasn't really listening. He said he'd see me soon.

I liked the evenings with my father even if we just sat around and watched a movie or hung out talking while we ate dinner. He always had a story about his day. Something he'd seen. Someone he'd *taken* from, the word he used instead of *stealing*. A celebrity sighting. A presidential entourage of limousines. A suicide lying under a sheet. A brawl between cab drivers. An apartment fire. An arrest. He could pretty much tell the crime by looking at the person being handcuffed and the way the cops behaved. My father told a great story. He didn't skimp on the setup and he pointed out details I would never have seen. He used his hands a lot, made gestures, made faces to look like the person he was describing, changed his voice. It wasn't fake or showy. He just automatically slipped into the role. I think that's what made him a good thief. He was a chameleon. His looks made him stand out, but he could become the exact person the other person would trust. He plugged into what people wanted and gave it to them. It was part of his charm with women too. He could listen very well, or at least pretend to. He could ask the right questions to make them think he cared.

My father was staying out. Two full days in a row, something he'd never done before. I didn't feel like sitting around the house by myself.

I called James Worthen to see if he was home. He usually had a bunch of friends at his house, friends from his neighborhood who went to private schools. James wanted to go to a public school and when he got into Stuyvesant his parents agreed to let him go there. His parents pretended that their kid was a tough kid, a real street-smart rebel, when they spoke about him to their rich neighbors. James said he didn't want to break their little working-class fantasy so he never let on that Stuyvesant was as safe as any private school with a pricey tuition. James answered his cell phone on the fifth ring. I could hear some kids in the background talking about lighting up. He told me to come over. I caught the subway to Forty-second Street, took the shuttle across town, took the Lexington Avenue local uptown.

The Upper East Side always felt like a completely different city. I'd grown up in Manhattan and all the neighborhoods had a city feel that connected them. There was a smell in the air, an attitude in the people, a noise in the background, an aura of possibility, a grit that was actually visible on your skin at day's end, tactile pieces of the city and all it meant. If dust was mostly composed of dead skin, city dust was made of something stronger, the slight decay of brick and mortar as well as flesh. But unlike lives, the city could renew itself. New buildings constantly replaced old and the street drills could be heard all over the city all the time, breaking something down to build something up. I knew all the neighborhoods and each neighborhood had its own distinguishing characteristics. The angled, tree-lined streets of the West Village where we lived. The claustrophobic streets of the East Village where people wore clothes that were really costumes and where artists pretended to starve. The brownstones and restaurants of Chelsea where gay men cruised the coffee shops. The lofts and galleries of Soho, broke painters selling their wares next to street vendors. The more desolate streets of Tribeca where celebrity spottings were easiest, familiar faces tucked under baseball caps, eyes hidden by tinted sunglasses. The apartments and bars of the Upper West Side, the masses holding briefcases by day, transforming into drunken revelers at night. The posh offices and posher stores of Midtown, executives and tourists crowding the streets, where my father did most of his taking.

The Upper East Side was different. It was too quiet, for one thing. It wasn't the kind of quiet that was punctuated by cars like some of the other neighborhoods. The buildings were tall and clean. The avenues seemed wider and maybe that dissipated the usual ricochet of sounds. And the people all seemed rich. There was nothing of the fighter in them, nothing that was part of the city I knew. Everything was a bit of a fight in New York. Getting on the subway was a fight. Bumped shoulders, hard stares, bodies pressed close. When my father walked he looked like a fighter approaching the ring. He faced the city head on, walked forward, forward, ready to deliver body shots and do whatever damage he might have to do to a city that always won in the end. Where James Worthen lived it was clean, calm and, most of all, safe. His parents were loaded. That was what money was, my father said. Protection. Money was a moat that surrounded them, kept them insulated, and while their castles were turretless, the high apartment buildings with doormen at the ready were no different from guarded havens.

The 6 local train stopped at Seventy-seventh. Not many people got off with me. The Upper East Siders were either at work, still in suits and ties, protected in other buildings, or traveling above ground, taxicabs their mode of transportation. Most of the people on the 6 line stayed on the subway past Seventy-seventh. They rode uptown to where uptown became the opposite of what uptown meant, way uptown. Rough streets. Rough people. Potential violence on every corner.

The doorman in James's building, spit and polish in a green uniform, recognized me, but he got on the intercom anyway. James gave him the okay and the doorman sent me up. The elevator was spotless. The brass was newly polished. The carpeting vacuumed. Even the sound of the air was fresh, vacuum-packed. I rang the doorbell. The cook let me in. I walked past the kitchen, a wide open room the size of our apartment. On a cutting board were chopped carrots and celery. Steam came from a pot on the burner. Something smelled delicious.

James and two of his friends were in his room. Hunter was a year older than us and his claim to fame was that he'd slept with his math teacher freshman year. He was a good-looking kid in a preppy way, thin lipped but good teeth. His father was a lawyer. Hunter was popular, but I didn't understand his appeal. His face was uninteresting, no features to focus on, and his voice never took me to another place. Tre was our age. His father was a major executive at ABC. Tre was a skinny kid with bad acne on his forehead, but he was fearless. I'd seen him fight bigger kids for making fun of his zits. He lost most of the fights, but he fought and so kids were less likely to make fun of him. Tre was also funny. He made up jokes that sometimes ended up on the Internet. He smoked nonstop when he was outside of school and was known for rolling the tightest joints. James was sitting all the way back on his bed. He looked tired, his lids low. His eyelashes were very long.

The four of us hung out talking. They asked what was new and I told them nothing. I asked them what was new and they told me nothing. They started talking girls. Hunter was close to banging a black chick. Tre called her a luscious Nubian princess with nipples the color of dog turds. Hunter told Tre to shut up. I wondered what kind of woman my father was with, what kind of princess he had picked up for more than a night. It was always a night. I once asked him why he never went out with women for more than a night at a time, why he never dated the way other people did. He told me that most people had one big story. One story per person. A life-philosophy story. And if you went out on a given night and you listened closely, the person would reveal that one story, a distilled version of everything lived. A longer relationship might bring out other stories, but not the best story. And there was so much repetition. He said it was like a movie. The sequel never lived up.

"When I get done with her, I'll be the Nubian king," Hunter said.

"When you get done with her, your dick will be the Nubian jester," Tre said.

"King."

"Jester."

"I'll be the king of fucking Africa."

"She's hot," James said. "She's definitely hot."

Tre pretended to jerk off, pounding his fist against his pants.

"That's about all you're getting," Hunter said.

I didn't feel like listening to their talk anymore.

"I'm hungry," I said. "You guys want to get something to eat?"

"I don't have any money on me," Hunter said.

"I'm busted too," James said. "My allowance is out for the week. And if my grades keep falling I'm going to lose my allowance for the year."

Rich kids were always pleading poverty as if it were a badge of cool. My father and I weren't poor, but next to these kids we had nothing.

"Let's go to a restaurant anyway," I said. "We'll hit and run."

"You mean eat for free?" Tre said.

"It's easy."

"It's easy as long as the waiter's one of those little stubby guys with stubby legs so he can't catch our sorry asses. We're not all stars on the track team."

"Have you done it before?" James said to me.

"I've done it."

"Not with me."

"I've done it. It's something to do. You guys are always hungry. I'm hungry now."

"What if we get caught?" James said.

"What if we don't?"

We got our coats and took the elevator down. When we reached the lobby Tre hit all the elevator buttons. James told him to cut the shit out, it was his building, he had to live here. Tre said he was deeply sorry. He lit up a Camel unfiltered.

We chose a Greek diner on Third Avenue. A diner was easier, more appropriate for four kids hanging out after school than a regular restaurant. We ordered burgers and shakes and since we were running out on the check anyway we ordered slices of oversized diner cakes for dessert. We watched the waiter open the revolving glass case. He cut off hunks of lemon meringue pie, chocolate cream pie, coconut layer cake. The three of them couldn't stop laughing, which was not the way to do what we were going to do. My father taught me the importance of a poker face, of drawing no attention, of pretending that the bill would come and we would pay like honest patrons, round it out with a generous tip. The waiter delivered the desserts and walked away.

"So how are we going to do this?" James said.

I looked to make sure the waiter was out of earshot.

"It was my idea. I'll be the last one out. We'll get the bill, put a few bucks down under the salt shaker and if the cashier asks, I'll say the money is on the table. When you're on the street just walk. Act natural. If someone comes out, start running."

"I knew I should have quit smoking this morning," Tre said.

Hunter's cell phone went off. He answered it and talked low-key. It was obviously a woman. He feigned boredom. He made a face at us like it was just another chick he could take or leave, fuck or not. He said maybe he could meet her tomorrow. He told her he was going to rip off a restaurant like he was a seasoned thief. I was glad he was talking low, monotone. It was stupid talk and if it had been an old-time movie his stupidity would have brought him down. Character was fate, in Hollywood and in life. He got off the phone.

"You want to be the last one out?" I said.

"It was your idea," Hunter said.

"My idea was to eat for free and not get caught. Sometimes you talk too much."

"What the fuck, man."

"What the fuck yourself."

"What's gotten into your friend?" Hunter said to James. "He sounds like he's got a dick up his ass."

I looked at Hunter. Looked at his plain face. Focused on his plain features. Quick-studied him to see if he was quick-studying me. He was just talking. I looked away.

"What's up?" James said to me.

James liked Hunter. Hunter was the ladies' man that James hoped to be. And he was an upper classman with all his little stories of experience, which were not worth distilling into one big story.

"Nothing's up," I said. "He's talking like he's a seasoned veteran. Maybe he has a better idea of how to walk out. Maybe he wants to make an announcement to the entire restaurant when the check comes. So, Hunter, was the girl impressed?"

"More impressed with me than she'd be with you."

He was just talking. I looked away.

We ate the oversized pies. My lemon meringue wasn't that good. The meringue was hard and the lemon didn't taste like real lemon. It was time to go.

"All right," I said.

"Hold on," Tre said and shoveled the last pieces of coconut cream into his mouth.

"Are you ready?"

"You're in charge, big man," Hunter said.

I looked at Hunter. I nodded my head for myself like my father. I looked at the waiter and scribbled fake cursive in the air. The waiter started to write the check. The busboy cleared the plates. The waiter walked over and put the check on the table closest to me. I reached for my wallet. It was my idea. I could spend a few bucks as a decoy. I slipped five singles under the salt shaker.

"All right," I said again.

I kept my eyes calm the way my father did. I kept my breath even and low like when I was about to pass someone in a race. If the other runner heard me breathing hard he would try to stay with me. If he heard nothing, if he thought my lungs didn't have a care in the world, he gave up right there.

Hunter and James filed out of their side of the booth and Tre fell in behind them. I was last. Three runners ahead of me, but I had the wind. They were laughing like idiots and then they were out the door. The cashier didn't say a word. I was too angry to be nervous and I was aware how calm I was. I would have to remember this before I raced in the spring. If I was angry enough I wouldn't be nervous and maybe I would run harder. I would pretend that the other runners were my enemies and in many ways that was the truth. There could be only one winner per race. I got to the door. Calm and easy. My hand on the door. Pushing it open. Out.

The three of them were already sprinting down Third Avenue. Three guilty kids. I walked. I walked and waited for the shout. I walked almost hoping for the shout. I wanted an adrenaline rush, but it never came. I wanted what they didn't. The three of them were far ahead, blocks away, and I saw them cut into a street, one two three so it was only me on the avenue. I walked to the subway, the downtown side, walked down the steps, disappeared.

# 6

THE NEXT EVENING AT 7:18 MY FATHER WALKED IN. I HEARD him hang up his coat and hat and walk to my room. He looked a different kind of handsome when he was tired. His eyes were more sensitive and he smiled more, as if the world were a little heavier and he was reassuring me that everything would be fine anyway. His hair was disheveled even though it was cut short, pressed down in places, sticking up in others, like his head had been rubbed and rubbed.

"What's the good news?"

"No news," I said.

He moved his hand over his cheeks. He needed a shave.

"You didn't throw a party? You had the place all to yourself."

"What kind of party?"

"A party. I don't know. A slumber party. You could have invited James over. You usually go to his house. A change of scenery is always good."

"You know about those. Speaking metaphorically."

"Thanks for clarifying that. What's wrong?"

"Nothing's wrong. I'm bored."

"A bored person is a boring person."

"I guess I'm boring."

My father turned around and walked out of my room. I heard him put on his coat and hat. I heard him open the door and close it, lock it. He even walked down a full flight of steps. He could be very dramatic. Then there was silence and I could picture him standing there on the landing waiting for the perfect moment when the quiet would make me wonder whether he really had left. Then I heard his footsteps coming up and up, the key in the lock, the door open. He hung up his coat and hat and walked into my room and smiled.

"Take two," he said. "From the top. What's the good news?"

"No news."

"How was your day? I mean, how were your days?"

"My days were fine."

"Excellent. Wonderful and exciting, I hope."

"Not as exciting as yours," I said. "That was a record for you. Staying out two days and two nights with one woman. I'm assuming it was one woman."

"It wasn't a record. You forget that I had a whole lifetime before we were introduced."

"The good old days."

"I didn't say that. These are the best days."

"That's because they're happening right now."

"That's not the only reason. I have you. You're my record. Sixteen years."

"Sure, Pops. You could have had a whole different life without me."

"When you call me Pops, I just melt," my father said.

"You could have had a different life."

"I like this life. I like coming home and seeing you. I love coming home and seeing you. I was gone for two days. That's all. Two days and two nights. I was having a good time and now I'm back."

He was leaning against the doorway and I focused on how his body cut the space. Head tilted. Arm raised. The white paint of the hallway lightest in the V between his extended arm and the line of his neck.

"You make her sound like my competition," I said.

"Not at all. You know that."

"So what is she like?"

"She's just a woman I met. We got along."

"You got along for more than a night. That's not like you. I don't know what you do when you go out, not exactly, but I know she had to be special."

My father looked at me. He kept his arm where it was, the V-shape steady, the light the same, but there was a shift in shading. Perhaps he had moved his head forward just slightly to see me better. He studied me and I could almost feel how my face had changed, as if my bones had further solidified into their more adult configuration by my father's recognition. I flushed. I knew my father had suddenly seen me as more than his son. It was a flush of excitement and even power. I was someone in my own right and so my take on his life was something to consider, one man to another, or at least one man to an almost-man.

"Well," my father said and he held my eyes because he knew I could hold his back, that I could face him that way. He was letting me know that he understood that I understood that he was seeing me in a new light. It wasn't all thought out that way. It was just a glance. But I had lived with him so long, all my life for me, most of his adult life for him, just the two of us in a small apartment with no one to dilute the concentration, that our glances were clearly understood. The layers and the patterns of our days together, of our relationship, circled in on themselves at that moment until it became a tight ball, the edges clear and the center hard. He nodded his head. He let me know.

"Well," he said again. "You're right. She was special. I haven't met someone special in a long time and she was that. She didn't repeat herself once in the two days. The second day was as fresh as the first."

"Would she repeat herself on a third day?"

"I don't know. I'm hoping not."

"Could you buy milk with her?"

"What does that mean?"

"Could you go to the the store and buy milk with her? Could you do something that mundane and domestic and still keep it fresh? That would be the test."

"Very good," my father said looking at me, tired-eyed but focused. "That would be the test. So where did you get so worldly? Have you fallen in love?"

"Never," I said.

"Well you know something."

"I don't know that much. What does she do?"

"She works in a dairy. She makes milk."

"Really. What does she do?"

"She's a photographer. She does some freelance work for some magazines and she had a book of photographs published."

"Did you see it?"

"I did. They're all photographs of dead people."

"What made her choose dead people?"

"I don't know," he said. "I guess she likes still-lifes."

"Very funny."

"Now she's working on not-so-still-lifes. She's photographing criminals."

"How does she know they're criminals?"

"She goes to the courthouses, watches the trials, and takes photographs during the breaks."

"They let her do that?"

"I bet they let her do most things."

My father rubbed his face again. His eyes broke with mine and he went someplace else for a moment and then came back. I sometimes tried to imagine where my father went. In his head he had to have so many memories. I guessed that where he had just gone was very recent. Not some long-ago encounter, not some fleeting face, but the woman he had been with for two days and two nights and who might interest him for a third. I wondered if my mother had interested him for days on end. If the two of them had gone to the store to buy milk only to fall in love all over again.

"Is she a good photographer?"

My father laughed.

"Is she?" I said.

"Wouldn't that be terrible if she wasn't? What if she showed me her work and it was pure crap? I guess if I hated her photographs I would have walked out the door, but I couldn't have hated them. She wouldn't be who she is. Yes. I think she's good. I think you'd like her book."

"Does she know what you do?" I said.

My father looked at me, so easy for him to look straight on. He had taught me to keep eye contact. He taught me practical lessons, day-to-day life lessons, to be well adjusted or at least seem so. I was to be polite with people. I was to hold their eyes. I was to learn more about them than I revealed about myself. I was to trust no one but family and my father was my only family. The last was a hard lesson, but all big life lessons are big because there's a price attached. I paid with a cynical attitude at a young age.

Lately, things didn't matter that much to me. I had broken a promise I'd made to my father, but that's not what I'd been thinking about. I was thinking I cared about things less and less. I'd walked away from a friendship, even if it was not a deep friendship, when I'd walked out of the diner and into the subway, and I didn't care. They were easy come, easy go, friends, not family. They didn't know me anyway.

"She knows I don't work a regular job," my father said.

"Does she know what you do?"

"She'll never find me in court to take a picture of me. How's that?"

"You told her."

"I told her in a vague sort of roundabout offhandish obscure way."

My father was smiling, trying to move me away from the subject, make it into a joke.

"How could you trust her?" I said.

"I knew she wouldn't judge me."

"Did she photograph you?"

"Why are you asking that?"

"She's a photographer."

"She took some photographs. She was just fooling around."

"Photographs of you doing what?"

"I wasn't taking anything. I didn't have my hand in someone's pocket while I smiled for the camera. Don't worry."

"I'm not worried."

"I was walking down the street and she ran ahead of me and turned around and took a few shots."

"Did she ask if you minded?"

"I didn't mind."

So my father, who looked like an old-time movie star, who hated the stars who stuck around too long after they'd lost their virility, who lived for the now in all ways of his life, had someone to immortalize him, at least with a photograph. I didn't know this woman. I wondered if she knew my father at all. I wondered if she held his eye, or if she needed to hide behind a camera to look closely. And I wondered if my father would forget about his life lesson on trust. Maybe he'd been wrong about the lesson. My new face, my new status, my almost manhood could put him and his philosophy into question. He dropped his arm. The V shape disappeared.

"Let's get something to eat," he said. "I'm craving pasta. I'm craving some linguini with pesto at Trattoria Spaghetto. How does that sound?"

"I guess you don't want to talk about her."

"When we start buying milk together I'll talk. How's that?"

"Have you ever bought milk with someone?"

My father held my eyes. It was a question that held another question. I was asking if he'd ever bought milk with my mother. He'd left me alone for two days and I'd had time to think about my past.

"I buy milk with you," he finally said. "Let's go."

I let it go. It was part of our deal. I went into my room and put on a hoody sweatshirt and my down jacket over that. I heard my father walk into the kitchen. I heard him counting out money. He had mixed business with pleasure. My father put the money away and put his coat on. He was about to shut the light in the kitchen when he stopped.

"Look at you," he said.

He put his hand flat against the top of my head and moved it across to him. He pressed his hand to the line just above his eyes. I was almost as tall as he was. In my bulky jacket I looked like I weighed as much as he did.

"I still have a few more inches to go."

"You have plenty of time to get those inches," my father said. "Longer legs will mean longer strides. You'll wipe out the competition."

"Fast as a gazelle."

"Fast as a gazelle chased by a hungry lion."

My father pretended to charge me. I opened the door and ran

down the five flights of stairs and my father locked up and ran down the stairs behind me.

There was no line at Trattoria Spaghetto. I ordered penne ortolana. Since I'd been a kid my father let me order for myself. I was comfortable in restaurants, another life lesson my dad had quietly imparted. I was comfortable in most adult places. My father ordered the linguini with pesto and a side of broccoli, garlic and oil to share. He ordered a beer for himself. I said I'd have water. My father passed me the basket of bread and I ripped off a piece. The bread was from Zito's, a half block away on Bleecker Street. The workers there had never changed. They just grew older. One man, senile even when I was a kid, still did what work he could, dragging crates of loaves by a rope and muttering curses about this fucking bastard and that fucking bastard. His world was peopled by fucking bastards. My father filled a small plate with olive oil, added some hot pepper, dipped his piece of bread.

"So what did you do last night?"

"I hung out with James. We got something to eat."

"How's he doing?"

"He's fine."

"I hit a little jackpot on the way home. I was taking the One train and this guy got on at Forty-second Street. He was wearing a Showtime Boxing jacket and a Caesar's Palace cap. What does that tell you?"

"Port Authority Bus Station. Atlantic City. Gambler."

"Exactly. He wasn't crying so I figured he might be one of the lucky ones. He had his wallet in his front pocket and it was bulging. It was wedged in so tight I thought I'd have to use a Jaws of Life to squeeze open his pocket. You know that track switch right before the subway hits Thirty-fourth Street?"

"The one that almost bounces you out of your seat?"

"Best track switch in the city. The train hits the switch, I practically body slam the guy, take his wallet, smile when he gives me a dirty look, and get off the train. He didn't even put his hand on his pocket to check."

"How much?"

"Three thousand and change. I wonder how many hours he spent throwing dice to make that. The guy was so oblivious I could have taken the Showtime jacket off his back."

The waiter set the bottle of Moretti on the table. My father looked at the label and drank.

"Good beer," he said.

"When did you start?"

"When did I start what?"

"When did you start taking from people?"

"When did you decide to start giving me the third degree?"

"Since you left me alone for two days. When did you start taking?"

"Is that a moral question?"

"It's a practical question. We were talking about family histories in English this week."

"The class with your good-looking teacher."

"Ms. Scalato. So when did you start?"

My father narrowed his eyes. He was getting into character.

"Is this off the record?" my father said, a major crime figure being interviewed by a crack reporter.

"Strictly off the record," I said, falling into my character so we could play the scene.

"You know that whatever I say cannot be used against me in a court of law."

"This is just between us. Strictly confidential."

"All right then. It all started when I was born."

"Really," I said, breaking the part. "I'm serious. Tell me."

My father took a long swallow of beer. He put the bottle down. "Okay," he said.

I held his eyes the way he'd taught me to.

"The first thing I took was a candy bar. The infamous candy bar. I'd bet the house that candy bars are the most frequently stolen items in the world. Every great criminal, every diabolical mastermind that ever lived must have started by stealing a candy bar."

"What kind of candy bar?"

"Good question. It's all in the details. If you gather enough details you can figure out the man. If you get enough details you can figure out your father."

My father smiled and I shook my head. He really was the kid sometimes. When I shook my head that way, aware that I was shaking my head, aware of my movements the way my father was, I felt like I was the father and he was the son. Shaking my head. A father impressed by his kid. Impressed but not wanting to admit it blatantly. Like the kid had done something bad, but good too. The goods and the bads.

In ninth grade I had taken an essay test, one of those in-class exams so the teacher could gauge who was getting too much outside help with homework. I was writing the conclusion, about to tie my ideas together, but I blanked on the words *advantage* and *disadvantage*. So I wrote the *goods* and the *bads* instead. I knew it sounded stupid, but I couldn't come up with the words I wanted until I'd already handed in the exam. When I got the exam back the teacher had circled the words in red ink and written a sarcastic *Excellent Vocabulary* in the margin. I showed my father the exam because I thought it was funny. Whenever there was a situation that had advantages and disadvantages we would say the goods and the bads.

"The candy bar was a Milky Way," my father said.

"Very symbolic."

"Why is that?"

"The Milky Way. A cluster of stars. When you take you're the star."

"How do you come up with these things?"

"Fast as a gazelle."

"I don't think any candy bar ever tasted as good as that first one I took. That was my first crime."

*Crime.* He had never used that word before. It was always *taking*. It was always *work*. It was always *little stealing*. *Crime.* Blunt and bad. Serious in my father's mouth.

My father nodded his head for me.

The waiter set the plate of sautéed broccoli between us. My father speared a stem with his fork and ate it. He did everything cool. Like his walk, his movements must have been practiced at one time and then they'd become natural. I speared a stem also, but it didn't look as good.

"And then what? What did you do after that first candy bar?"

"I took more candy bars. I was the kid in the candy store without any money and it didn't matter. I moved from Milky Ways to Cadbury chocolate bars to the really good stuff. Godiva. Teuscher. I hit the best candy stores in the city and got my fill of designer chocolate. I could fit five chocolate truffles in my coat pocket without crushing a single one of them."

"Trick of the trade."

"It's all in the details. Then I started taking other things. I'd eat for free. I'd take small things like radios and calculators and sell them on the street."

"You never felt guilty?"

My father looked closely at me, the way he'd done in my room.

"Guilt is a waste of time," my father said. "If I felt guilt I wouldn't be able to do what I do."

My father kept his eyes on mine.

"What did you do?" he said.

"Nothing."

"Something happened. It wasn't just that I was out with a woman for a couple of days."

"A woman," I said. "A nameless woman."

"To protect the innocent," my father said. He forked a spear of broccoli, put it in his mouth. Food always looked more delicious when he ate.

"Is she innocent?"

"She's innocent and corrupt. Just like me. What did you do, Ben?"

"Who said I did anything?"

"You did. You're showing your guilt."

"How? We're not playing poker."

"No we're not," he said. "I taught you how to keep still in poker."

"I'm not showing anything."

"You're asking questions. People ask questions because they're curious about something personal. Or they ask questions so they can eventually do their own telling."

"I'm just asking."

"You never asked when I started stealing before."

"I'm curious."

"And?"

"I'm just curious. Sometimes I'd like to know about my family history."

"And?"

"And nothing."

My father kept his eyes steady on mine.

"I walked out of a diner with some friends yesterday," I said,

My father put his fork down. He drank his beer. He wiped his mouth with the back of his hand. He was always leaning forward, forearms on the table, but he leaned forward more now and his eyes had no smile in them. They were almost sleepy, and I knew this was how his eyes looked when he did his work.

"Was it their idea or was it your idea?" he said.

"It was my idea."

My father looked at the beer label. He turned the bottle in his hand. He looked back in my eyes.

"You broke your promise," he said. "I told you never to take anything. I do the taking. You don't need to take."

"Aren't kids supposed to follow in their father's footsteps?"

"Not mine."

"Why not? Is that guilt or am I just asking a selfish question?"

"Listen, Ben. I know you're a smart kid. I know you can banter with the best of them, but I'm not going to debate you on this."

"Why not? Don't fathers want their kids to follow in their footsteps?"

"You know the answer. You know I want better for you. That's all."

"Because what you're doing is immoral?"

"At the count of ten," my father said.

He started counting down the way he used to do when I was a little kid and we were in a restaurant. He called it magic-ing the food. I was always impatient for the meal to arrive. He would get down to two and one and suddenly the waiter would appear and set the plates on the table as if on cue. My father's voice was cold. He wasn't counting down for food. My father was angry and the counting allowed him to let the calm come back. He got down to two. He got down to one. Had I been a stranger he wouldn't have counted.

"Eat your food," he said.

The plates were in front of us. I'd hardly noticed the waiter.

We ate without talking.

I finished the penne ortolana, chunks of eggplant and mozzarella cheese. I could feel the carbs filling my leg muscles. Maybe I would run tonight. Running alone, just for practice, gave me time to think back on the day. I wanted to go over the look my father had given me in my bedroom like looking at me for the first time, not like a kid at all. Maybe when I was done thinking I would time myself on the last mile, see if I could break my personal best.

"Was the penne good?"

"It was," I said.

"Good. Do you want some dessert?"

"No thanks."

"Promise me you won't steal again."

"You steal."

"I take enough so I don't have to spend my life at a job I hate. I'm just spreading the wealth a little. I'm feeding off the land."

"So that's your life philosophy?"

"No, it's just what I do."

"That's a philosophy," I said.

"All right. Then that's my philosophy."

"So why can't I adopt it?"

"You can come up with your own philosophy."

"What if I like yours? I think wealth should be spread around. If I had to work in McDonald's my whole life, stealing would be justified."

"You don't have to work in McDonald's," my father said.

"Neither do you."

"I'm talking about you. You don't have to work in McDonald's. You don't have to work in Burger King. You don't even have to work here at Trattoria Spaghetto. You'll do well in whatever you choose to do, you understand? You don't need to take the way I take. Rebel against me. Rebel against your father. Do better than your parent. That's what kids are supposed to do. That's the American dream."

"So I can wear a cashmere coat and spread my wealth the other way."

"Exactly. Only you'll be aware that there are people like me on the street."

"You never were caught? Not even when you were a kid?"

I knew my father didn't like to talk about his past, but I also knew he would answer my questions to stop the conversation about stealing.

"I did it as a joke at first," he said. "I used to pickpocket kids in school just for fun. I took their wallets and I gave their wallets back to them. It got so everyone in school knew they had to keep an eye on me when I was around them, which is what I wanted. I wanted them to be aware of me and then if they felt nothing, I knew I was good. I got good. Then I moved out into the world."

"The world. Free to do as you please."

"Be as sarcastic as you want. We're free enough to have a nice dinner, free enough to live in Manhattan, free enough to spend time together, more than any father and son I know. We're free to live for the moment. Like in *Breathless*."

"Belmondo got caught."

"At the end of the movie."

"Isn't that what you want? To live life like it's a movie?"

"What's gotten into you?"

"Tell me."

My father moved his hand over his face and leaned in even closer.

"You're close," he said. "I want to live life like it's the beginning of a movie. Before the movie turns stale."

"So you want to live life like the beginning of *Breathless*?"

"He's singing at the beginning of the movie, isn't he? He's in the car he's just taken and he's singing. Right?"

"Right."

"Sounds like a philosophy to me," my father said.

It sounded like a kid's philosophy, but maybe I didn't know enough to judge. Maybe it only seemed like a kid's philosophy because it was pure. Maybe that was what everyone strove for, a certain purity, and for my father that purity came from the thrill, so maybe it wasn't a kid's philosophy at all. Maybe a kid's philosophy was about safety. Kids left safety and eventually ended up making their own safety, cashmere-coat safety. My father made my life safe. He wanted me to continue to be safe. That was natural for a father, but for himself he was willing to risk. He was willing to steal small, to live for the moment. Like *Breathless*. Like the beginning of *Breathless*. It was just a movie. At some point, we all tell ourselves that as we sit in the theater, usually at a disturbing point. *It's just a movie*. At the beginning of *Breathless*, Belmondo sings. At the end of *Breathless*, he's running for his life. His pure, all-or-nothing philosophy may seem young, but it ends in a very adult way.

"Yesterday when I took from the diner I just kept walking," I said.

"You didn't run?"

"The guys I was with think they're so cool, but they ran as soon as they were out the door. I was the only one who walked. You taught me well."

"Learn some other things from me."

"I do."

"What have you learned?" my father said. Now he was asking the questions.

"You taught me how to act with confidence. When I become confident inside, life will be easier."

"You should be confident inside."

"I am. In some ways."

"The goods and the bads," my father said.

He finished his beer. My father paid the bill, left a generous tip as he always did, spreading the wealth to the working class as best he could.

We walked out to the street. My father cupped his hands over his mouth and we headed home. He stopped in front of the candy store on Bleecker Street. He told me to hold on for a second. I stayed on the sidewalk. He went into the candy store and pretended to look over the headlines of the newspapers. I turned from him to look up Bleecker. Right before Christmas, trees for sale lined the sidewalk and made the air fresh, the pine needles and sap from the sawed-off trunks cutting the pollution. It was a clear night and I could almost smell the evergreens even though the season was over, even though the trees had all been dumped somewhere, hopefully a forest like the one where they'd been cut from.

My father came out of the candy store. We walked home. On the way his arm reached toward mine as if he were passing me a baton in a relay race. He placed the Milky Way in my palm.

# 7

I KNEW SHE WAS THE ONE AS SOON AS I SAW THEM TOGETHER. She was the kind of woman a man could give his life for, at least in the movies. Even I knew that. She and my father were sitting on the steps in front of our apartment building. She was smoking a cigarette and laughing an open and innocent laugh and my father was clowning for her. He must have been telling her one of his stories. I heard her say *Stop, stop* and then she laughed and laughed some more. I stopped a few yards away from the steps. They didn't see me.

My father was always aware of all that went on around him, that was part of his job, but he was completely focused on her. She had dark hair, so dark that I didn't think sunlight could sink in, only reflect off. Her hair covered her face when she laughed and she would lift her head and brush it away. She wore jeans and a black leather coat with a fur collar, the sash tight around her waist, and her body looked thin and strong and graceful. She had perfect posture even as she sat. Her legs were long, kicked out almost like a boy's in front of her. I stood there and watched the charmer that was my father and the woman who had charmed my father. She tapped out two cigarettes, smooth, and gave one to my father and put one in her mouth. She had movie-star moves of her own. It was slow motion, their gestures. All the time in the world.

My father took her lighter, lit her cigarette, lit his own and they seemed to inhale and exhale at the same time, the tobacco smoke mixing with the cold air smoke and the smoke vanished and there they were. It was all clear. My father held the cigarette tight in his fist. He lifted his other hand and pressed his thumb against his lips and moved it across like Belmondo. She smiled. It was clear she'd already seen him rub his lips. It was part of the code between them, a code that had obviously been established in a few short days. Belmondo's move was part of our code also, but their code held more mystery than the code between a father and his son.

There were times when I felt older than I actually was. Seeing them, standing back and seeing them, I knew my place in the world in relation to her and in relation to him. She would be the one for my father, if there could be a one, and he wasn't even fighting it. I suddenly saw how honest my father was to his gut feelings. He didn't hit and run and hit and run with all those women out of ego or some past damage. He had genuinely not been interested in any of them and so he hadn't seen them again. The distilled essence of those women was good for a night. This woman was worth more than a night. She was worth a night and a day and another night and another day, sitting on Manhattan steps, smoking a cigarette, moving a thumb across her own lips, and my father was oblivious to the world around him and to his son standing a few concrete sidewalk-squares away.

I walked forward. I entered their world. My father put his hand on my shoulder and smiled.

"This is my son, Ben," he said.

She put out her hand, her short nails painted blue, the color the girls were wearing at school. She had a strong handshake and her hand was warm.

"Hello," I said.

I held her eyes and she held mine easily and I knew she'd learned this on her own and not from my father.

"So," she said. "So. So you're Ben."

"I'm Ben."

"I'm Anna."

"This is Anna Partager," my father said.

"You only lied to your father once," she said and her eyes were still on mine.

"Only once in my life. I walked out of a diner without paying. That was the once."

It was strange, but I didn't mind that she knew. I had resented her before I'd met her, this woman who had kept my father away, but there was something about her that fit. She wasn't trying to impress me. She seemed natural and if it was an act, she was acting perfectly. My father's hands went to her, but not to push her away, and when he touched her arm it seemed natural also. I was happy that my father had found someone to talk to. With me he talked about almost everything. Almost. I was still sixteen. Even if I was newly older in his eyes.

"So will you lie again?" she said to me.

"Not to my father."

Anna laughed and my father laughed and they both took hits off their cigarettes. It still felt like a movie, the lines better than just how-are-you lines, the pauses between the words full of meaning, the glances as strong as close-ups. I felt like taking a cigarette and lighting up too just for show.

"Ante up," she said.

"Excuse me?" I said.

"Your poker face is just the way your father described. You keep your mouth very straight like he does. If I photographed you I bet you wouldn't even smile for the camera."

"I bet you're right."

"Smile with your eyes and you'll be famous."

"I'm not looking for fame."

"I figured that out already," she said and laughed. "You don't pose like most teenagers. When people, young people especially, find out I'm a photographer there's all kinds of posing going on. They think they'll be the next supermodels until they find out what I photograph."

"You photograph dead people and criminals. I've heard about you too."

Anna looked at my father. I noticed that her mouth parted, just slightly, when she looked closely at him. The part was not so much that you could see her teeth, but just a sliver of darkness, almost like a challenge. If you could figure out the darkness there, you could figure out what she was thinking, the mystery behind her mouth and behind her eyes that were more green than blue.

"My father always looks like he's posing," I said. "But it's natural."

"I figured that out too."

I looked at my father. He seemed content to sit there and watch us. Anna took a hit off her cigarette.

"Why are you photographing criminals?" I said.

"Because they have something in their eyes. I used to think that maybe it was in their eyes because I was putting it there, that my knowing they were criminals changed the way they looked, the way I perceived them. But there's something in their eyes, different things, depending on the crime."

"You can see the crime in their eyes?"

"In their eyes. In their body language. You can see if it was a crime of passion or a crime of irresponsibility or if there is no humanity there whatsoever. Then their eyes really are closer to dead people's eyes."

"So that's the connection."

"That's the connection."

"What's your book of photographs called?"

"It's called *Half a Dead Man.*"

"Why just half?"

"The first corpse I ever photographed had been cut in two by a subway. That started me off. So. So I started taking shots of people who were dead because of the city in some way. Victims of crime, subway accidents, drug overdoses."

"Sounds like a lot of fun."

"It is," she said and laughed. She had an easy laugh. I looked at them sitting there, my father's hat pushed back and Anna Partager's fur-collared coat, sash pulled tight, making them look like from another time. The gray sky added to the effect. It was more black and white than color.

"It's the last laugh," she said.

"As long as they die laughing," my father said.

"Is that how you'll die?" she said.

"I don't think about dying," he said. "You know I never plan ahead."

"I thought we had plans for this afternoon."

"That's not ahead. It's this afternoon."

My father put out his cigarette on the step. It was cold, but he didn't blow into his hands.

"Put your books away," my father said to me. "We're going to take the ferry to Staten Island."

"What's in Staten Island?"

"Nothing. We're just taking a boat ride."

"Shaolin."

"What?"

"Shaolin is Staten Island. Boogie Down is the Bronx. Boogie Down Bronx."

"Top of the food chain Brooklyn," Anna said.

"She knows," I said.

"What's Manhattan?" my father said.

"Manhattan is Manhattan. Manhattan is the Big Apple."

"Word up," my father said and folded his arms like he was just another gangster rapper wearing a fedora.

"Why do you want to go to Staten Island?"

"It's a nice day for a boat ride," Anna said. "It's always good to do a city something."

"You must not be from around here."

"I'm from around here now. I like to look at the city from a newcomer's perspective. I might see something I've never seen before."

Her mouth had parted slightly.

"She's right," my father said. "Come on, Ben. Come with us. We'll go to Lombardi's for pizza afterwards."

"Ante up," I said.

Anna laughed. It was a great-sounding laugh. It was almost hysterical really, her eyes thinned out and her mouth was wide open and it was a real laugh, a head-thrown-back laugh, not put on at all. My father was smiling, watching her.

We took the subway to South Ferry. We went through the turnstiles and waited for the boat. The people waiting were different from Manhattan New Yorkers. Their faces were less striking. People in the city had a fashionable look just from being in the city, but Staten Islanders looked more Middle America, as if there might be farms across the bay. There wasn't anything graceful in most of the faces. Jared Chiziver and Anna Partager stood out. I watched the faces watching them.

The gate opened and we walked onto the ferry. I looked at my feet crossing the line, one foot land, one foot boat, and I knew, not in a concrete way but just knew, not about what, not about why, just knew there was no going back, not for any of us, that the boat might dock, that the boat might return, but a line had still been crossed, or would be crossed. My father walked a little ahead and we followed. The seats were filling up. We walked to the front deck and the three of us leaned against the steel rail and waited for the passage to begin. The torch on the Statue of Liberty was lit, an orange flame against the pink sky, the symbol of America right there. The green of her robe rose above the water's gray chop. I was seeing her like for the first time. Like a newcomer. Like I had not passed her a thousand times as I ran along the Hudson.

My father blew into his hands. Anna took his hands between hers and blew into them. He let himself be taken, warmed by her, not pushing her away at all. They looked so comfortable that I was comfortable. There seemed nothing out of the ordinary that they were acting like kids on a first date, flirting, focused. I couldn't stop watching them. We were the only ones on the outside deck, but they wouldn't have cared if everyone on the boat had been watching. They were doing it for themselves, really doing it and not performing. The boat started to move. It cut the water white. The world seemed to fall away.

*"There's a deep dark mystery about the sea whose gentle, awful stirrings seem to speak of some hidden soul beneath."*

My father had lowered his voice to capture the deepness and the darkness.

"Herman Melville," I said.

"He knows his father's lines."

"He knows Melville's lines," Anna said. "So was that from the book or the movie?"

"I only do movies," my father said.

She looked away from my father and down at the water.

"It is mysterious," she said.

He made a howling sound, like the wind, like a ghost, like something mysterious, like a great white whale would rise at any moment from the depths.

"Stop," she said and laughed.

"He does sound effects too," I said.

"He's a one-man show."

"No," my father said. "We're a two-man show. We were a two-man show. What do you think, Ben? Can we add a third member to the cast?"

He was watching me closely. He wanted me to approve.

"Sure," I said. "We can give her a trial run."

"Anna Partager," my father said stretching out her name. "We hereby declare you the newest member of the Chiziver Players."

"I'm honored," she said.

"The honor is ours."

"Well. Well, I'll try to uphold my responsibilities."

"No responsibilities," my father said. "Once they come in, there's no more fun. There's no more freedom."

And as if on cue the boat sped up. The water whirled and spread. The air pressed against our faces. The engines were loud, pushing us forward.

"All right," my father said to the speed.

It was getting dark to our left, night coming early, but the winter days had gone over the hump, a minute increase a day, all the way to summer. I liked the long nights of summer best. That's when possibility was always in the air, especially in Manhattan, especially the older I got. I admired my father because day or night, short or long, there was always adventure. The way we were lined up at the front of the boat we could just as well have been on a cruise ship headed to exotic points south and not just across the bay to Staten Island.

# 8

SHE WAS THERE THE NEXT MORNING. I DIDN'T SEE HER, MY
father's door was closed, but I could hear them talking quietly, and
I could hear her laugh. I wondered what they were talking about,
what jokes they had invented for themselves, threads of inside refer-
ences that provided a foundation for a new relationship. I had never
had a relationship like that, I was still too young, but I knew from
watching my father that it was not just about sex, not at all. He
could find those other connections so quickly. There were times
when I saw him with a woman, at the beginning of the night if he
had just met her, when he amazed me. He made them feel special
almost immediately, listened to them, decided which threads to
draw out, to quietly play with until a warm cocoon was spun and
they trusted him completely. I could only imagine how close Anna
and my father had become in a few days.

I took a shower, poured my cereal, sat at the table and ate. I kept
the radio volume low. A bomb scare had closed the Holland Tunnel. A fire in the Bronx had killed two people. There would be another appeal in the Abner Louima case, the police department

holding out on paying for damages. Some cops had taken Louima into custody and had literally shoved a plunger up his ass. His rectum had been punctured. He'd bled internally. The cop that had held the plunger was doing a thirty-year term in jail, but Louima wanted his monetary compensation and why not? He would always be known as the man who'd had a plunger shoved into his asshole. That was the kind of damage that deserved some serious bucks. The weather said another cold front was moving through.

I finished my cereal, tipped the bowl, drank the sweet milk, put the bowl in the sink, brushed my teeth, heard Anna laugh behind the wall, say *Stop, stop* and laugh some more. I picked up my books and left.

It was cold. I bunched up my fingers in my gloves and walked to the subway. The number 1 local going downtown was crowded. A lot of suit and ties. A lot of students going to Stuyvesant. Sharon Lee was sitting with her head bent, poring over a calculus text. She was a year ahead of me, but we sometimes sat together at lunch. I felt like talking to someone, like I'd had a drink. When my father was restless he drank. Maybe he wouldn't wake up with so many hangovers now that he'd met Anna. Maybe he'd go for weeks at a time without red eyes, a pounding head, a hollow stomach craving meat to slow his heart. I went over to Sharon and pushed her book with my knees until she looked up.

"It's you," she said and smiled. "I was wondering whose legs those were."

"Big test today?" I said.

"Actually I have two big tests today. One in calculus and one in physics."

"I'm sure you're ready."

"I'm sure I'm not. It doesn't matter. I got early admission to MIT."

"Congratulations. That's great. You can fail your tests just for the fun of it."

"If I fail, I don't graduate."

"Then get a D minus. Nobody gets D minuses at Stuyvesant."

"That's why they're at Stuyvesant."

The train stopped. People got on. The train started. The doors between cars opened and some kids I didn't recognize walked by, jeans hanging low on their waists. They pushed through the people, but no one said a word. They pushed by me, shoulder against shoulder, three in a row, the last kid practically shoving me, my knee hitting Sharon's calculus book hard. Other kids hated the kids from Stuyvesant. They thought we were protected in there and so here, in the subway, we were unprotected, fresh meat, just a bunch of pussies to fuck with. I glared at the back of the last kid's head.

There wasn't much I could do anyway. There were three of them and one of me and they were bigger than I was and inside the confines of a moving subway car I was stuck. There was no place to run. There was no place to hit and then run. They would have moved around my father. He was that kind of man with that kind of aura. Like in the movies. All the leading men were tough guys no matter how androgynous male leads were becoming. When the climax came, and almost all movies climaxed in violence, the leading men kicked ass. The door between the subway cars closed and the three kids were gone.

"D minus students," I said.

"Idiots," Sharon said. "I hope Boston is more peaceful."

"MIT will be great. I bet it's beautiful."

"It is. Even the subways are nicer in Boston."

"You went there already?"

"My parents took me around to different campuses this summer. We visited Harvard and Brown and the University of Pennsylvania.

MIT's on the river and there's grass and trees and everyone seemed genuinely friendly."

"Just wait. I bet you'll miss the subways. I bet you'll miss these punks walking through."

"Not me. I never liked New York."

"Really?"

"Really. We moved here when I was eleven because my dad got a good job. I always wanted to get out. Don't you?"

"Not really. We go to Florida every summer and I'm always happy to come back to New York."

"I can't wait to get out."

"I think I'd get bored anywhere else. I love being anonymous so Manhattan is perfect. This city is big enough to get lost in."

"Why do you want to get lost?"

"I don't know. Sometimes it's nice to be a stranger in a familiar place."

"Well, next time I'll pretend not to recognize you."

"I'll be me and me incognito at the same time."

The train stopped. It started. Sharon closed her book. The next stop was Chambers Street, our stop. We got out and walked together, past BMCC where the college kids went, their conversations more street than anything we heard at Stuyvesant. Students were hanging out on the basketball court that connected the college to our school. Lit cigarettes. Hawked-up phlegm, spit. One guy drank what looked like a forty-ouncer from a paper bag, getting a quick beer-buzz before the first bell rang. We walked into Stuyvesant and suddenly the noise of outside Manhattan, cars and sirens and construction and the under-rhythm of all the voices echoing off the skyscrapers, turned to the inside noise of school where the echoes off the corridors were more pronounced, a quick bounce off metal lockers and cement walls before falling flat on the linoleum floor that looked freshly polished. I said good-bye to Sharon. I congratulated her again on her acceptance to MIT.

I walked to the junior corridor to my locker, put some books away and walked to my homeroom. The corridors were filling up. The boys yelling out their usual vulgar greetings, pushing each other forward, checks and slaps and punches with friendly intentions. The girls walking in packs, holding their books with both hands in front of them, laughing, seeming to have more time to get to where they were going.

I sat in my assigned seat at the first lab table. Mr. Beyers, our homeroom teacher, taught chemistry, and so we started each day surrounded by beakers and Bunsen burners, inhaling sulfur. Someone would always light up a Bunsen burner or try to mix compounds to make an explosion or a stink bomb until Mr. Beyers told the whole class to cut the crap and took attendance in his military monotone. I'd had him for chemistry during sophomore year. He was a strict teacher. His wife was a guidance counselor and a very sweet woman and I wondered how the two of them fit together, what common ground they had invented. A chart of the periodic table filled much of the front wall. Bold squares. Thick letters. As if those elements held the key to all the answers.

Announcements were made. Starting time for the basketball game. A Yearbook Club meeting. Names of students who had to report to the principal's office. The bell rang and we had five minutes to get to first classes. My first class was trigonometry. I did the assigned problems quickly and William Mena and I started talking track in low voices. He was a solidly built kid who threw javelin. He'd come in third in the all-city tournament and after that his nickname was Spear. Spear said he'd been training hard in the weight room. I said I'd been running nights mostly, filling my lungs with freezing air so that when spring came I'd have nerves of ice. I didn't tell him I'd walked out of a restaurant and found a new calm. Spear said his lungs were already ice, hard ice, that even a javelin couldn't puncture them. I told Spear he needed to prove himself with a ten-mile run in arctic temperatures. Spear made a muscle for me and said he never needed to run. His bicep was cut, round and hard. I didn't touch it.

Time was up on the math problems. A few volunteers started writing their equations on the blackboard. Different shaped bodies. Different handwriting. Only one correct answer per equation. I drew a Nike sneaker at the top of my notebook page, colored in the winged insignia, added sparks coming out the back to make it seem like the speed of light was possible.

English was next. The corridors were packed. Some couples walked by holding hands. One couple made out against the lockers, a public display of affection that was more about display than affection. I nodded and said heys to the people I knew. *Hey. Hey. What's up? Hey.* And the greetings came back. *Hey, Ben. Hey. What's up? Hey.* It was scintillating conversation, the hallways of Stuyvesant a hotbed of back-and-forth banter, an exchange of big ideas from the future stars of America about Hey. Ms. Scalato, the pretty one, the new one, the one all the guys said they would fuck if they could fuck one teacher, was sitting at her desk looking over her notes. She had a black skirt on and a black top that hugged her curves and showed enough cleavage that someone would eventually drop a pencil in her direction so that it rolled to her feet and she'd have to bend down to pick it up. Russ Keedy said he'd caught a nipple shot of her, had seen the pinkest nipple he'd ever seen during the first week of school when the weather had been hot and her dress had been light.

Ms. Scalato didn't open things up to discussion right away. She was a better teacher than that. She lectured during the first part of the class, sometimes through most of the class, and she was always prepared. New teachers were usually the best that way. They weren't into a routine, so what they said was not overly rehearsed, and they still cared. She was disappointed when class discussions fell flat, when we were not as enthusiastic as she was about worldwide oppression, the basic theme of her course. It was a new unit, Literature of the Holocaust, and she told us to imagine being singled out as Stuyvesant students, which wasn't that hard to imagine. She told us to imagine being forced to leave the different neighborhoods where we now lived. She asked if we believed we would persecute someone just because we were told to. Some students said they would never follow such orders, adopting a holier-than-thou attitude. Some said it was human nature to follow. One student said that only rats and humans killed their own for no reason. Another said it was the adults' fault, that people our age would never do such horrible things. I raised my hand. I said people our age were worse than anyone. We were cliquish and mean spirited and if someone didn't fit in he was ostracized. All you had to do was stand in the hallway and listen. This one was a loser. That one was a nerd. This one was a faggot.

"Damn," someone said at the back of the room.

The class laughed. I felt the heat in my face. It had just come out.

"Which one are you?" someone else said.

I sat there looking at my desk.

"Loser, nerd or faggot?" someone said. "Or all three?"

I was looking at my desk. Ms. Scalato was trying to quiet the class.

"Faggot," someone yelled in back and kicked his shoe against the wall, a pretend-cover for the word said so clearly.

"Faggot," someone else yelled, mock-coughing into his hand.

I clenched my jaw. I made my face expressionless. For a moment my eyes blinked and blinked again and then I kept my eyes steady and looked up from my desk.

"That's what I mean," I said.

"Excellent point, Ben," Ms. Scalato said. "And if I hear another word out of anyone, I'll personally make sure that student is suspended from school."

I waited for a kick, a cough, the word. Quiet followed quiet. I kept my eyes steady until the bell rang, the class emptied.

Ms. Scalato was looking at me. She said she'd really liked my last paper on *Things Fall Apart*. I looked her in the eyes the way my father had taught me to do and told Ms. Scalato that I had better get going to my next class. She smiled a young smile and looked away.

Phys ed was next. I changed in the locker room. Depending on the day the place smelled either musty or sickeningly sweet from the cleaning agents they used. The guys were horsing around. Talking shit. Talking girls. James Worthen was in my class and he was telling someone how he'd walked out of a diner, making it seem like he'd been the leader.

"Nothing like eating for free, right, Ben?" he said.

"Right," I said.

"The food always tastes that much better," he said for everyone.

"I've never seen you run so fast," I said.

"That's why they call it eat and run."

James knew he was full of shit so I didn't say anything else. The other kids wanted to know what he'd eaten and James embellished the menu, his voice not quiet at all, not worth getting lost in. His Upper East Side crowd was just so much talk, so much exaggeration, and his two floors of luxury apartment didn't impress me. If my father saw James Worthen's father walking around Grand Central, he'd take his wallet the same as any other man's in a cashmere coat. I closed my locker and walked away.

The Stuyvesant gym was state-of-the-art, long wood floors, brand-new basketball hoops, a volleyball net set up at the far end. We stood in a line while Mr. Nadel took attendance. They called him one-nut Nadel because he'd supposedly lost a ball in the Vietnam War, but it was just a rumor and I didn't think anyone had seen his balls or ball. He had three red kickballs by his feet so I knew we'd be playing Bombardment. I would have preferred to stretch out, run laps around the gym, get lost in my own world until we had to shower and change.

We counted off by twos and walked to our respective sides of the gym, half the gym really, another class on the other half. Mr. Nadel placed the three balls across the center-court line, walked to the side, blew his whistle and the game began. It was a game with few rules. You whipped the ball as hard as you could at one of your opponents. If the ball hit him, he was out. If he caught the ball, you were out. If you hurt the person, you were a hero.

The three balls bounced and skidded. Some of the guys had great arms and it was tough to dodge, let alone catch, the ball. The guy next to me was hit in the leg and he limped off to the sidelines to wait for the game to end. A guy on my team readied himself to whip the ball and didn't see another ball coming at him. He took it in the head and looked dazed for a moment before he walked off to the sidelines, out. James Worthen was on the other team. He threw the ball at me. He had a pretty good arm, but I was quick and got out of the way. I retrieved the ball, threw it at him. He jumped over it. The guy next to me tried to catch a ball, but it came at him too hard and bounced out of his hands. There weren't many people left. James had two balls. He passed one to the guy next to him. They both focused on me.

"Don't ostracize Chiziver," someone yelled from the sideline. "Hit him."

Ostracize. It was the word I'd used. I looked to see who it was. There were a couple of guys in my phys ed class from Ms. Scalato's class. I turned back around. It was too late. One ball hit me in the chest. One ball hit me in the balls. I doubled over, forced myself to catch my breath. I stood up and kept my face expressionless and walked to the sideline.

I stood there. I watched the game end. James Worthen and two of his teammates were left standing, victorious. Mr. Nadel blew his whistle and lined up the three balls along the center-court line and blew his whistle again.

Before I went to the cafeteria, my hair still wet from the showers, my balls still sore, I went to get my trigonometry book. I had a free period after lunch and always did my math homework during that time. I was hungry. The cafeteria was serving lasagna, which was actually one of the better meals. The junior corridor was packed. It was the equivalent of lunch hour in the city, the time my father worked. The more people, the easier to jostle them, pick their pockets. Stuyvesant's students were restless to eat, but they were also restless to hang out, stretch their muscles and their voices, free from sitting at a desk and having to concentrate.

I walked up to my locker. Someone had written FAGGOT in graffiti letters. The A and the O looked like boxes. I wet my hand. I rubbed off the ink. The side of my fist became black.

# 9

UNLIKE MOST MOVIES, *BREATHLESS* REMAINED. MY FATHER could be influenced by a coming attraction or a few opening minutes of another movie, and he'd passed these movie-feelings down to me, the high I felt when the movie started, the music, the rush of images, but *Breathless* touched my father the whole movie through Eighty-nine minutes. He knew the length exactly. Maybe my father had been like Belmondo before he'd ever seen the movie, but in many ways the character was my father and my father was the character. I'd once looked up the biography of Jean-Paul Belmondo. He'd been a respected actor. He'd been a tough guy. He'd even been a boxer, probably rolled his shoulders in real life the way my father did.

The movie rubbed off on me too. There was something right about the all-or-nothing philosophy for a teenager, perhaps especially for a teenager. Kids don't think of repercussions, especially when in love, and that is Belmondo's downfall. Without love he could have carried on. With love he worries about the moment with her and about nothing else. When he is shot, he isn't watching his back. I hadn't been watching my back when I spoke in class. It seemed so stupid that anyone cared. Liking a boy was no different from liking a girl. Not the liking part. The part that counted. I was no different. I didn't act differently. I wasn't a cliché. I didn't revolve my whole life around sex the way so many kids did. But I had always watched my back. Kids judged harshly even if there was nothing to judge. I wanted my life to be easy.

It was supposed to snow later that night. My father had called from Anna's apartment to say he'd be staying there if that was okay and I said it was fine. I felt like taking a run. I wanted to go over some things. And I had an English paper to write for Ms. Scalato's class that I'd put off all week. When my father and Anna were around I didn't seem to get any work done. The sky was thick when I'd left school and I could tell the weatherman wasn't going to be wrong about the snow. I laced up my running shoes, double-knotted them.

To change the routine I ran through the streets, uptown instead of downtown. When too many cars were coming at me, I switched to the sidewalks and wove around the people, skimming their winter jackets or the bags they held, pretending I was a pickpocket dodging pedestrians as the cops chased me and then when the sidewalks opened up I was just a runner again, just me, which is what I was, part of what I was. There were patches of ice so I couldn't dig my feet into the pavement for a real sprint. I skimmed the concrete surface.

The gray sky seemed close, tenable, a few inches from the Empire State Building's spire. I ran across Forty-second Street, the Chrysler Building a straight shot to the right, its spire ornate and thin, a dangerous spear for wayward birds. I ran through Times Square, the lights and the people distracting me, running in place at the lights and then forward to Central Park, stopping right before the park, turning, running back downtown on the far west side, the avenues less crowded. I crossed the West Side Highway and ran along the Hudson toward Christopher Street.

It was late and cold and I liked how empty the riverfront became at night. It was a different kind of anonymity from the one I felt on the crowded streets. There was no one to even look at me.

I finished the run with as much of a sprint as I could. The cold made my lungs burn, but I was in shape and my stride felt easy and long. I slowed, walked, put my hands on my head to expand my chest, open my lungs. I'd heard it was good to walk after a run to avoid getting blood clots. It was probably just a rumor, but I always walked a little anyway.

I went over to the rail that bordered the river and held on while I stretched my calves. I lifted one leg at a time onto the rail and stretched my thighs. I stretched my hamstrings and made circles with my foot to loosen my Achilles tendons. I saw someone walking towards me, the bulk of a down jacket outlined by the dark.

He came closer. His pace was slow, but not self-conscious at all. He didn't seem to care that I was looking at him. He was about my age, maybe a year older. He had dark hair and a full mouth and eyes that looked very calm. His lips looked pink, almost red, even in the faint light from the highway, as if the blood had been sucked to their surface. He stopped and looked at me.

"Do you always run at night?"

"Sometimes," I said.

"I've never seen you before."

I had seen this scene played out on Christopher Street, on the piers, and sometimes in movies as I sat next to my father. A shiver started in my stomach, but not from the cold.

"I'm usually out later than this," he said. "I got an early start tonight. It's supposed to snow."

"It feels like snow," I said.

He smiled and looked me over. I put my hands in the pockets of my sweatpants.

"I did see you once," he said.

"You did?"

"You were running with a very handsome man. But I liked the way you ran better. You run like a natural."

"Thank you."

"Who was the man you were with?"

I knew what he was doing. He was asking questions to make sure, and asking them in such a way that I wouldn't run off. He had such calm eyes. If he didn't get the answers he was looking for he would probably just smile and tell me to have a good night and walk on. His lower lip was a little chapped, but his mouth looked like it would be warm.

"He's my father," I said.

"Really. I can't even imagine taking a run with my father. I can't even imagine taking a walk with my father."

"We're very close."

"Would you like to finish up my walk with me?"

I breathed out.

"Where's the finish line?" I said and he smiled.

"I usually walk to that big building over there where they keep the snowplows. Then I cut into the city."

"They'll be using the plows tonight."

"We better hurry before they run us over," he said.

I walked next to him. My hands were still in my pockets. I hadn't stretched enough, my legs felt tight, but it was easy to follow him. His voice was calm when he spoke and I didn't have to pretend to get lost, to go to another place.

"I'm Michael," he said.

"I'm Ben," I said.

88

In the building where they housed the plows a yellow light flashed as one of the trucks pulled out. There was a mountain of salt behind it.

"I guess we're too late," Michael said.

He stopped walking. I stopped walking. He moved his face to mine. I stayed there. He put his mouth on mine, soft. We kissed like that, lips on lips, and I could feel the softness of his mouth and the rougher line where his lip was chapped. The shiver in my stomach was there. The way I knew it would be, only more. It was real. It was really happening. He put his hands through my hair, his hands over my neck and down my back, pressing one vertebra at a time. He pressed his crotch against mine. He moved his hand under my sweatpants and took me in his hand and moved his hand back and forth, gently, and then harder and I could hear my breath change and I breathed out and it was real and I closed my eyes and just held him close and I came.

I listened to my breath slow, slow against his shoulder.

"Did that feel good?" he said.

"It did," I said.

"You feel good," he said.

He took my hand and moved it under his own pants and I moved my hand over his cock. It was smooth and hard and it felt like mine. It was like touching me, but it wasn't me and I listened to his breathing for clues of what felt good for him and then I felt him press into my hand and I moved my hand faster until I felt the warm come shoot over my hands and I moved more slowly until it was all out of him and I listened to his breath slow.

"Did that feel good?" I said.

"It did," he said and smiled, the two of us using the same lines.

It had started to snow. Just a few flakes coming down. My come was now cold. We walked back toward Christopher Street without touching, but I felt close to him anyway.

"It's really snowing," I said.

"It always gets warmer when it snows," he said. "It's like the city becomes insulated."

There were no runners around. Nobody. Just the steady noise of the cars on the highway and the plows pulling out.

"This is where I live," I said, looking up Christopher Street.

"You live on Christopher Street?"

"I live near it."

"My parents wouldn't even walk down this street," he said. "Little do they know that their own son fits right in on Christopher. You're lucky. Your parents actually live here. That must make things easier."

I didn't say anything. My father didn't mind walking down Christopher. To him, it was only a street. To him, I was only his son. I didn't think my father knew.

"Will I see you again?" Michael said.

"Where did you come from?"

It was the line many women used in the morning with my father and I knew the same admiration was in my eyes as I looked at Michael. The chapping on his lower lip had disappeared.

"I told you," he said. "I walk here sometimes. I told you I saw you and your father running."

"Where do you live?"

"East Side," Michael said. "I live near Gramercy Park. When my parents come home from work they're always screaming at each other and I always feel boxed in so I like to walk. And the pier is good for people like us."

"I just run here," I said.

"Not anymore," he said.

He kissed me on the mouth, fast, and said he better get going. He asked if I wanted to meet again. I checked my watch. It was eight-twenty. I'd met him around eight. Twenty minutes. I said I would be at the same place in two days, on Friday night, at eight, and Michael said he'd try to make it. The light changed. The traffic on the West Side Highway slowed, stopped. He touched my arm and started walking downtown. He'd said he usually cut into the city, but he walked back along the river instead. I crossed the highway to Christopher Street. It was snowing more heavily now, the flakes taking up space under the streetlight, swirling.

I went home and tried to concentrate on writing my paper. I finished it as best I could, but I couldn't stop thinking about Michael. I had changed my clothes, but I hadn't showered. I wanted to still be there in some way, slightly sticky, my skin smelling of sweat but also sperm, now dry. I wondered if my father showered off Anna. He showered the others off. As soon as he came home or as soon as they left he was in the shower. We went through a lot of soap. With Anna he looked unshowered sometimes, his five o'clock shadow moving into six and seven o'clock, his hair a little wild. I was almost sure he wanted to keep her smell on him. I wondered if when Belmondo is killed, her smell is still on him. At the end of *Breathless,* when Belmondo is shot in the back by the cops, he runs slower and slower and then he falls in the street. Jean Seberg runs after him. She looks down and he looks up and he says, *You are really . . .* but he doesn't finish the line. His eyes close and his head falls to the side and he's dead. She moves her thumb across her lips. Looks at the camera. Turns around. The word *Fin* appears on the screen. *The End* in English. As a kid, I thought it was fin, like a fish fin, until my father told me it meant The End, which didn't make sense to me since The End was two words, but I accepted his explanation, accepted whatever my father told me. I wondered if my father would accept this.

My father never talked to me about sex. He could have, but he assumed I didn't need the talk. He knew my friends went out, that they probably had sex, that they probably talked about it. It wasn't like we were protected. In New York City everyone knew practically everything from early on and if I'd had a question about sex my father would have answered it. He sometimes joked that anything I needed to learn I could learn in the gutter and if it wasn't in the gutter it wasn't worth learning. No one really used the word gutter anymore. It was one of his old-fashioned words.

I hadn't needed to learn it. I had known for a long time. Different. But not different at all. The kiss had solidified something, like my face had solidified, the bones coming together in a certain way that would never change.

I looked out the window. The snow was thick and the trees were coated, brittle branches now softened. The sidewalks were all white. New York City always looked clean after the first snowfall. Then the cabs and buses would turn it to slush and the plows would salt and gravel the streets until they were brown and muddy. But it was clean now. It was white even in the dark. The snow was sticking and maybe tomorrow they'd call off school. I got under the covers.

I couldn't stop thinking of him. I was hard and I touched myself the way I had touched him. At night I thought about boys from school, boys in my class, or boys that I saw in the hallway. The way a certain boy moved. The way a certain boy stood at his locker, not aware that I was watching him, and in that he was alone with me, me watching him. The way a certain boy laughed, his mouth open, his eyes bright. Now I thought of Michael and it wasn't all made up. I had felt him. His hand had been on me and my hand had been on him. Skin on skin. It had been real. It was real. It was like a movie I had been part of, but it was real and the dried sperm was still on me, was really there, and I moved my hand faster and faster.

# IO

MY FATHER AND ANNA CAME BACK TO THE HOUSE AROUND noon. I'd woken at seven, looked out the window, listened to the news on the radio, heard that school was cancelled, and fell back to sleep. When they came in Anna was laughing her open laugh and I could hear the low sounds of my father talking.

I stretched in bed and felt rested, more rested than I'd felt in a long time. I heard that guilty men slept soundly once they'd been caught. I didn't feel guilty. I hadn't been caught. It had felt innocent and a trace of the feeling remained, like a piece of chocolate stuck in my teeth long after the bar has been devoured, an actual piece of the sweet still there, to be played with, dislodged, a freed dark sliver resting on my tongue and slowly dissolving, the urge to swallow it checked, forcing myself to let it stay there, stay slow, even though last night seemed far away.

I got up and looked out the window. The city was white. There were tracks in the snow, tire and footprint and dog print. A man walked by with a hood covering his head. The sidewalk across the street had been shoveled, but the sidewalk in front of our building wasn't. The super didn't care about keeping the place up. He wanted everyone out so he could redo the rooms, jack up the rent. I went into the kitchen and my father was sitting at the table, leaning back in the chair with his legs kicked out, watching Anna at the stove. I'd seen women in the apartment cooking breakfast before, but only when my father was about to guide them out the door.

"Let me check for bedsores," my father said. "I see you're taking full advantage of your day off."

"I think I needed it. I was out cold."

"Good afternoon, Ben," Anna said.

"What are you making?"

"Pancakes and eggs and bacon."

"A lumberjack breakfast," my father said. "As soon as we heard it was a snow day we thought we'd pretend we were in New England. I was going to wake you in a minute."

"Is sunny-side over okay?" Anna said to me.

"Sunny-side over is great. I smell cinnamon rolls."

"You smell correctly," my father said.

Anna flipped the bacon. The grease sputtered.

"She's a great cook," my father said. "I get gourmet meals every day."

"Don't listen to your father. I don't cook that much. I grew up with cooks so I usually just eat."

"I love a woman who eats," my father said. "I love a woman who goes to a restaurant, orders everything she wants and then has dessert even if she's full. Never trust a woman who doesn't eat."

"I suppose I'm very trustworthy then."

"It really snowed last night," I said.

"Almost a foot in Central Park according to the weather," my father said. "We saw one guy skiing up Seventh Avenue."

Anna took three plates from the cupboard as if she'd been cooking breakfast in our apartment forever.

"The bacon's almost done," she said. "Why don't you pour yourself some juice. I hear you don't drink coffee."

I went to the refrigerator. My father patted my back as I passed him. He was always physical with me, but he also wanted me to know that I still had his attention, even with this woman in our lives. He looked genuinely happy. His eyes seemed rested like he'd had a full night's sleep, a row of full nights. He didn't have to say he was restless, go out to some bar, drink, meet some woman, sleep on some strange bed. I wondered if he ever slept well in strange beds, or if he slept well in his own with a stranger. I wondered if he ever woke up not knowing where he was and if that bothered him. Sitting at the table, he looked more peaceful than I'd ever seen him, the lines around his eyes almost nonexistent. I sat down. The sound of the popping bacon fat was a perfect complement to the cold outside, the cold floor against my bare feet. I was starving.

Anna removed the strips of bacon and let them dry on a paper towel she'd placed over a plate. She cracked eggs in the grease, one-handed, like a professional cook in a diner. The eggs sputtered and settled. In another pan she flipped pancakes.

"Nothing better than a snow day," my father said. "A free day off. We'll go up to Central Park, take some sleds, hit some hills."

"We don't have sleds."

"We'll find some."

"Do you have syrup?" Anna said.

"Vermont Maple," my father said.

He sometimes walked through the farmer's market in Union Square and took provisions. There was always something good to eat that my father brought home from his walks. Chocolate from Teuscher's or Godiva, easy to pocket when the stores were crowded. Sweets from Taylor's that were displayed above the counter, brownies or giant chocolate chip cookies or mudballs, laced with rum. Cupcakes from the Magnolia Bakery, chocolate-

and pink- and yellow-topped, easily accessible when the help was frothing up cappuccinos for paying customers. From the farmer's market, fresh breads and fruit and jams and pure Vermont Maple Syrup, like the jug my father was getting from the refrigerator. It was a free horn of plenty. It was the working man's due, according to my father, which was ironic since he really wasn't working unless you considered that getting his due was his work, was his full-time job. It was little stealing, not big stealing, not greedy stealing. He believed his little stealing was justified when people like James Worthen's parents could live in an uptown duplex while we lived in a relatively beat-up place. He never complained. He just liked to spread the wealth. He made sure to point out that we were doing well, very well, compared to many. Manhattan was the ultimate capitalist town. Its economic striations were clear, the lowly browns of the underlayers highlighting the wealthy greens of the upper crust, that thinnest layer, but also the most visible in the Porsches and Jaguars and Mercedes and penthouse apartments with doormen at the ready to protect the rich from the masses. In Manhattan my father felt justified doing what he did.

People could judge him as a petty thief, but I never thought of him that way. I could define him as a petty thief. But I never judged him as one. He was not greedy. He only took enough. Real Vermont Maple Syrup was as extravagant as he got.

Anna filled the three plates with eggs and bacon and pancakes and brought them to the table. She sat down next to my father and he kissed her on the mouth. They didn't care that I was watching. I thought of the kiss I'd had. I hoped he wouldn't judge. He rarely judged others. He never used the word *faggot*. Even when we ran past the men and women hanging out at the pier he didn't say anything about them. He didn't need to. I think my father honestly believed in a to-each-his-own philosophy. The only thing he judged was movies. He either criticized them when they were poor or praised them when they were good. I also assumed he judged women. In my memory, they had all failed after a night. He was gentle with them, but he let them go. He hadn't let Anna Partager go.

The eggs were delicious, cooked in the bacon grease, and the butter melted on the pancakes, golden and perfect. My father kept telling Anna how great everything was.

"What do you two usually do for food?" she said.

"I cook sometimes," my father said. "A lot of pasta. I'm great with the boiling water and spaghetti and Aunt Millie's tomato sauce. I think Aunt Millie is our favorite relative. We get a lot of takeout. We go out to eat quite a bit."

"Is he a good cook?"

"I love my father's cooking," I said. "He even makes his own sauce sometimes. He uses the recipe from *The Godfather*, the one Clemenza shows Michael."

When I said the name Michael I felt my face flush so I kept talking fast.

"It's just before Michael kills the two men in the restaurant and chooses his father's way of life."

"He regretted that choice," my father said.

I sopped up the last of the yolks with the pancakes. I thanked Anna for the meal. She held my eyes and I noticed hers were more green than blue in the light and a little crazy. It was the way my father's eyes went sometimes when I could tell he just didn't care about consequences, when he talked about something he'd done that would be so absurd for most people, but was just a joke for him. She liked me, I could tell, and her eyes said she didn't care that she liked me, didn't care in a good way, wasn't worried about the consequences. It was so different from the other women who pretended to be maternal with me or friendly in a peer kind of way, with the obvious agenda to impress my father. Anna was not trying to impress. Maybe she really was the most trustworthy woman he had met. She seemed to have no ulterior motives and so she didn't have to give a damn. One of my father's favorite movie lines was *Baby, I don't care*, a line Robert Mitchum said in the movie *Out of the Past*. Mitchum was right up there for my father, especially in his early movies, my father said, just a notch below Belmondo. Anna didn't seem to care. She seemed comfortable. She'd made our kitchen her own, but it was just to cook breakfast.

"You haven't had a snow day in years," my father said.

"Three years. It was because of ice last time, not snow."

"We never had snow days," Anna said.

"Anna grew up in St. Martin. On the French half."

"What's the other half?" I said.

"One side is Dutch," Anna said. "One side is French. My father owned a restaurant on the French side."

"That must have been great."

"It's a beautiful island, but growing up there was strange. I always felt like an outsider. I spent a lot of time alone and I swore that when I was old enough I would never live on an island again."

"This is an island."

"The island of Manhattan is not a Caribbean island. One bridge or one tunnel and you're free."

"You're free on this island," I said. "You're anonymous."

"That's my boy," my father said.

Anna ate the last triangle of pancake and put her fork on the empty plate.

"You finished," my father said to her. "Now I trust you."

"Perhaps you're mistaken," she said.

"I don't think I am. Once we see how many cinnamon rolls you eat and how well you sled you'll be fully trustworthy."

"Your requirements are a little skewed."

"A graceful slide down a hill, a delicious lumberjack breakfast, what else is there?"

"Morality. Goodness. Wisdom. I can think of many things."

"I'll stick with breakfast," my father said.

"Oh boy."

"I'll stick with the simple things."

"Simplicity I'll accept," she said.

"Okay. Sledding. Breakfast. Simplicity."

"My favorite photographs pay attention to the simple details. An eyebrow or a wrinkle or the curve of a knuckle. You can read a person's life in a knuckle."

My father made a fist and put his fist on her plate.

"What do you see?"

"Stop," she said and laughed.

"Come on, tell me."

"I see the knuckle of a man with skewed requirements."

"Simplicity," he said and lifted his fist off her plate. "That's why I like your photographs and your eggs. And my knuckles. I'm no artist, but I think there's a little bit of art to what I do."

My father nodded for himself, then wiped off his hand. I wasn't sure how much she knew. She knew he picked pockets. He'd said as much. I wondered if my father had walked out of a restaurant with her yet. If he'd gone into a store and left with some merchandise. If he'd explained his philosophy on little-stealing. If he'd let her try on one of his coats to make her feel what it was like, coats with deep pockets that hid what he took. And I wondered if she'd let him photograph her, if my father had looked at Anna through the lens like she looked at him.

"When my son runs he pays attention to the simple details, to what makes a stride a perfect stride. That's why he wins."

"I don't always win."

"Nobody always wins," he said.

Anna got up and went to the kitchen counter to ice the cinnamon rolls. I watched her hand on the knife, swirling the white icing, easy and perfect. When she brought the rolls to the table they looked like they'd been arranged for a commercial. It was easy to see that her father owned a restaurant. When I'd left the diner it was easy to see what I'd learned.

A muffled ring went off and Anna walked into the living room to get her bag. She walked gracefully, her posture upright and her strides long, almost like she was slow-motion running. It was a different grace from my father's walk, his springy, full of power about to explode, hers long and fluid, as if the energy was even.

"Could you buy milk with her?" I said.

My father looked at me. He knew I wasn't being sarcastic. He knew all of my inflections, every tone I had. He had been there when I was a baby, colicky and coughing, he had learned all of my noises, when I wanted food, when I wanted to be played with, when I wanted to be set free to crawl around, my past the only past we discussed, my past with him.

"Maybe I could buy milk with her," he said.

"I'm happy for you."

"You've grown up in the last few days."

"You've been gone for days at a time. You can see the change more clearly when you come back after a while."

"So that's it," he said and smiled the soft smile that was all in his eyes.

We heard Anna punching in the numbers on her phone, saying *Yes, yes, yes*. She walked into the kitchen and took the pen by our phone. She jotted down a number, said she really appreciated it and hung up.

"There's a dead man in the subway. On Twenty-eighth Street. The one line on the downtown side. I have to go there."

"Talk about connections," my father said.

"I have a friend in the transit authority. I acknowledged him in my first book and he always keeps an eye out for me. I'm thinking about a second book so I have to take some shots."

"Another *Half a Dead Man?*"

"Perhaps. I have to go."

"Want some company?"

"If you'd like to come you're welcome. It's pretty horrible sometimes."

"The horrible details of death," my father said.

She took her camera from her bag and checked how much film she had left.

"Can I come?" I said.

"It's up to your father."

"Are you ready?" he said.

"I've never seen a dead person before."

"I haven't seen many myself."

"I'm ready," I said.

We all put on our coats, fast, and went through the snow, down to the 1 train. Anna kept walking to the edge of the platform to see if the train was coming. My father leaned against the wall, blowing warmth into his hands. I had butterflies in my stomach, like before a race, but I wanted to see this. The train finally came. At Fourteenth Street the conductor said the train would be running on the express track because of a police investigation at Twenty-eighth Street.

"Stupid," Anna said. "We should have caught a cab."

Her eyes were clear now, very clear, and her easy laugh was gone. This was her work. My father never laughed before he took. I never laughed before a race.

We followed her out of the subway car, up the steps of the station, into the cab she hailed. We slid up Sixth Avenue. Banks of snow lined each intersection. At Twenty-eighth Street there was a parked ambulance and three police cars. My father paid the driver, tipped him well. We almost never took cabs. We followed Anna down into the station. There were people waiting outside the turnstiles. Cops were standing along the platform. Anna ducked under a turnstile and flashed a press pass, and my father followed her and I followed him. He had taught me to always look like I belonged so I put on my best press-face, whatever that was. No one said anything to us. Just outside the last subway car a stretcher rested on the floor. We walked into the car. Anna was already telling the police officers she was from the Associated Press. Her camera was out. They didn't stop her.

A man was sitting there. His face was white. His eyes were closed. He still held a plastic shopping bag in his hand and through the D'Agostino's logo I could see a box of Wheaties, Breakfast of Champions. I wondered how long he had sat there going back and forth, uptown and downtown, until someone noticed that the man was sitting too still. He was fascinating. He was gone, really gone. It was that easy.

Anna started photographing his hands. Simple details. His hands, relaxed-looking but stiff, the knuckles telling of a lifetime of whatever work he did, the box of Wheaties that would never be opened, never be eaten, no more breakfasts, no more pouring cereal into a bowl, filling the bowl with milk, quickly dipping in the spoon so the flakes stayed crisp. None of that. I walked out of the subway car. I walked to the end of the platform and puked on the tracks. No one saw me. I waited outside the car until my father came out and then Anna, her camera in her hand. We followed her out, up the stairs, into the street. It was cold. It was too cold to just stand there, but that's what we did.

"The party's over," my father said.

"No more parties for him," Anna said.

"Did you get some good shots?"

"I won't know until I develop them. I think so. He had wonderful hands. A scrape against his knuckle that looked fresh, the last scrape he'd ever have. That's reality. I loved the Wheatie's box in the plastic bag."

"The last breakfast. Not even. The last breakfast that got away."

"How long do you think he was dead?" I said.

"Two hours," Anna said. "Two or three."

"How do you know?"

"There was still some give in his hands. The bag slid a little when I was photographing it."

"He just looked like he was sleeping."

"Maybe he was," she said and smiled at me. "It's strange, isn't it?"

"It's so final."

"The book is closed," she said. "That's what I try to capture. That the book is closed."

"Not just half a dead man," my father said. "A whole dead man."

"That's the new title," she said and laughed. "That or *Half a Dead Man: The Other Half.*"

"Or *Three Quarters of a Dead Man*," my father said to keep her laughing, loving her laugh, loving the way she said *Stop* before she laughed some more, and for me he placed his hand on my shoulder and squeezed it to let me know everything was fine.

I thought how my father must have seen more dead people than he'd let on. He took his hand from my shoulder and blew into his hands. Nails bitten. Smoke.

# II

I STRETCHED OUT MY LEGS FOR THE THIRD TIME, PRETEND-
ing I had just finished my run and just needed to loosen my muscles
before I went home and that I wasn't waiting for anyone. The cold
days and the snow had changed the Hudson River. There were
large blocks of ice against the pier, looking like remnants of Arctic
glaciers traveled south, stuck here before a warm day freed them to
flow past the Statue of Liberty and out to the Atlantic. The chunks
had spaces between them, cracks, a jigsaw puzzle of ice. Even in the
dark I could see how heavy the pieces were. I hoped he would
come. I couldn't stop thinking about him.

I stretched some more. I was always warm after I ran, but the
cold air was taking over. I saw a figure in the distance, but the figure was running and I watched until the shape became clearer, a
woman running with a Walkman over her hat, her eyes looking
ahead, mouth open, breathing too hard, struggling. I stretched some
more. I had spent two days waiting for this moment and I wondered
if he had as well. I wondered if I was just another kid he'd met,
charmed into kissing, touching, or if I was more. If I was closer to

all the women my father met and left or if I was closer to Anna, something about her that kept my father seeing her again and then again, a row of days. I wondered how long the ones who weren't chosen thought about my father. He made no promises. But in the morning, before he quietly sent them away, I often saw betrayal in the way they looked at him and in the way they asked if he would call. As I waited there in the cold I felt some of that, a disappointed anger that had started to turn inward. I knew that I should leave and yet I couldn't leave.

I stayed there, pretending to stretch, until I started to shiver, until one figure approached, became defined, passed, and then another figure and then another and then I saw the outline approach more slowly, a walker, not a runner, the bulk of a down jacket. It was him.

I did a final stretch and turned from the river. He was smiling, his straight teeth visible in the dark, his lower lip chapped.

"I'm glad you're here," Michael said.

"I almost left."

"Some shit went down at my house. I couldn't get away."

"You need to take up running," I said. "It gets you around a lot more quickly."

"Do you always run?"

"I run track and cross-country for school. That's why I'm out in the snow."

"I never played any sports. I mean, when I was a kid I played sports, but in junior high I started hanging around the drama club kids."

"So you act?"

"No. I don't do much of anything."

He took off his gloves and reached out his hand and took mine. He warmed my hand with his two hands.

"Your hands aren't that cold," he said.

It was good to feel his touch and to hear his voice. He had a very soothing voice, low and relaxed like he'd never been confused in his life. I wondered if he sometimes felt more adult than his parents. A final chill went through me, to my shoulders and up to my head, and then I didn't shiver anymore.

"Should we find someplace warm to go to?" he said.

"I'm not exactly dressed to go out to dinner," I said and smiled to let him know it was a joke. I didn't know him, and he didn't know me.

"You live around here, right?"

"My father might be home."

"You can check. And if he's not home I can come up."

"Do you do this a lot?"

"Do what a lot?"

"Meet people like this?"

"I meet some guys. If I didn't like you I wouldn't have come back, especially on a cold night."

"It's not that cold."

"I would have come back anyway. How's that? You're new at this, aren't you?"

"Good guess."

Michael smiled and stopped rubbing my hands.

"I'm a good guesser," he said. "That's okay. I'm glad you're new at this. Some guys I see are already so jaded it's not any fun. It's like a routine for them."

"Are you jaded?"

"Not right now."

"I think growing up in the city makes everyone a little jaded."

"Well, I'm not jaded now. I wanted to see you."

"Good," I said. "I wanted to see you too. But you knew that. You're a good guesser."

We walked to the highway and waited for the long light. Cars sped by. I could see some of the drivers looking at us. Maybe they knew. Maybe they thought we were just a couple of high school friends taking a walk. The light changed. We crossed the street and walked along Christopher. I usually turned right on Bedford. Michael pointed to The Cupping Room, a place I often passed but never went in. He said they had good coffee there. I told him I never drank hot drinks. He said he wanted some caffeine so we walked down Hudson and went in. They had all kinds of sandwiches and pastries on display and if my father had been with us he would have had easy access to plenty of food. The man behind the counter looked us over. He looked like an actor. He liked us right away. I always passed for straight, but next to Michael my camouflage was gone. It was gone for a moment in school and someone had written FAGGOT on my locker right after. Now it was different. Now I wasn't alone. Now I was with someone who didn't seem to care about camouflage and it made me not care. When he touched my hand in front of the man I didn't pull away.

Michael ordered an espresso and the man went to work, pressed the ground coffee into a cylinder, put the cylinder into the machine, flicked the switch. Water started to drip.

"It warms you up and gives you a jolt," Michael said. "You sure you don't want one?"

"No thanks."

"If I didn't drink it in the morning I'd never leave the house."

The man finished making the espresso, handed over the cup. Michael paid and the man smiled and we went back outside.

"You sure you don't want to try some?"

"I'm sure."

We walked south along Hudson Street.

"I saw a dead man yesterday," I said.

"Where?"

"On the subway. The One train. My father is seeing this woman who's a photographer. She takes pictures of dead people."

"Why does she do that?"

"She published a book of photographs about dead people and she might publish another one."

"Who was the dead guy? Someone famous?"

"No. Just some guy on the subway. It was so strange. It was like he had just fallen asleep only he was dead. It makes you think."

"What did it make you think?"

"How easy it is to die."

"It's like seeing a traffic accident," Michael said. "Everyone slows down. The first dead person I saw was in a car wreck. He was stretched out on the highway and the way his body was lying there I could tell he was dead. Everyone drove more slowly for miles after that. I was watching the speedometer and no one went over the speed limit."

"That's one way to react."

"What's the other way?" he said.

"You can speed up. Speed up and feel alive. I think that's how my father lives. He's always speeding."

"I like that."

"At least he used to."

"What changed?"

"I don't know if he changed. He met this woman. The photographer that takes pictures of dead people. He seems happy with her so I think he's slowed down a little."

"Wasn't he happy speeding?"

"I don't know now."

We got to the corner of Barrow Street. Michael downed the rest of the espresso like he was drinking a shot and threw the cup on the sidewalk. He didn't think twice about littering. I didn't know him.

"Speed," Michael said and he stopped and kissed me.

He kissed me harder than he had last time and I kissed him back harder and I could feel his hands in my hair, moving down my back, pulling me to him, pressing against me. I felt warm. It was a cold night with the wind going from uptown to downtown and my back was facing uptown so I was getting most of the wind, but I still felt warm.

The door to the bar across the street opened and closed. My father had once told me it was a cop bar. I had asked him what that meant. He said it was a place cops drank after their shifts. He said other people drank there too, but mostly a lot of cops from the Sixth Precinct. My father didn't like cops and for good reason. What he did was not exactly upstanding work. I heard laughter to my right. My back was facing uptown. My right arm was facing west, toward the bar. Michael held me tighter and kept kissing me. I opened my eyes. There was a card store on the corner. A display of Valentine's hearts in the window. I closed my eyes and heard the laughter.

I knew what a good stride sounded like. I had been running for years and I had passed many runners and some runners had passed me. You can hear the footsteps of poor runners. They are plodding and not graceful at all. You can hear the breathing of poor runners. They exhale too fast and struggle to inhale. Their breaths are choppy, inconsistent. Inconsistency is the sign of the amateur. The approaching footsteps against the pavement were heavy, the rhythm of work shoes and not running shoes, the breaths loud, uneven, out of shape. I felt Michael's hands leave my back.

There were three of them. Jeans and flannel shirts and jean jackets that seemed not enough for a cold night. They were thick men. Their eyes were drunk, the creases around their eyes deep. I could smell them, like the alcohol was coming through their pores. Their lips were thin. All three of them had thin lips. Not like Michael's lips at all.

My father had taught me about the advantages of keeping a poker face from an early age. I kept my eyes steady and kept the shivering, another kind of shiver, from being visible. This one was all in my stomach and I held down the puke and forced myself to look at one of them, the one that separated himself from the other two men and stepped a step closer. I looked at him eyes to eyes.

"What?" I said.

"I'm the one should be asking the fucking questions," he said.

"What do you want?"

"For starters I want you two faggots to stop kissing in public. It's fucking disgusting."

"It's a free country," I said.

"A little too fucking free," the man said.

He broke my stare then. His thin lips were tight. He was looking at his friends. The man dipped his left shoulder to get everything behind the punch. I tried to move, but Michael was next to me. My ear felt hot and I was on the sidewalk. My teeth sent a shock through my jaw and up into my head. It was cold and hot at the same time. Cold concrete. Warm blood coming from my nose. I heard feet, his feet on the sidewalk, digging in, kicking. I heard Michael coughing from far away. I smelled the man's breath through the blood. I felt myself being lifted. It was the man. He was lifting me up. He was telling me that he was the one asking the fucking questions. He was telling me that no faggot punk was going to talk back, no faggot punk was going to be fucking disrespectful. He pulled a lighter from his pocket. It was pink. A cheap pink plastic lighter. I couldn't move. I tried to lift my hands and to move my legs, but I wasn't able to. I felt drunk, but I'd never been drunk like this. My mouth moved. I was able to move my mouth. I asked the man what he was doing with a pink lighter. I couldn't help myself. Maybe that was the most drunken thing about me. That my mouth was moving. That I was talking. That I needed to talk. I said that pink looked good on him. I said that this faggot punk talked back to everybody, especially men with little pink lighters. Men were laughing far away and Michael was coughing far away. I felt a hand pulling down my sweatpants. That was the thing about sweatpants. They could be taken off so easily. No belt. No struggle. I felt a hand pulling down my underwear. I couldn't move. The man flicked his finger in front of me. Flame came out of his pink lighter. I couldn't move. I saw the flame move away from my face and down.

My pubic hair must have caught fire first. I felt the heat above my penis, a patch of heat, and then I felt the colder pain of fire against the underside of my balls. It felt like the flame was tighter there and more intense. I tried to cry out but the man was holding me by the throat and I couldn't move. I couldn't move and I knew his hand was under my balls, holding the lighter, the flame going up and up and in. It felt like it was going in. The last thing I remembered was the cold pain. Then I drifted off, numb and spiraling, like I was leaving me behind, running away, but I wasn't running.

Later, it might have been a minute or many minutes later or maybe more, time wasn't really moving like it usually moved, it could have been movie time for all I knew, but it was later, I saw myself being put on a stretcher, saw myself inside an ambulance, saw two men working on me, saw myself taken into a room, and then I started to go out again, running away, away from me but with me at the same time, running but not really running, speeding up instead of slowing down but not really.

# 12

MY FATHER WAS THERE.

Above me and in front of me.

I could feel his hand on my forehead.

I felt like shit. Groggy and nauseous and there was the pain in the places I'd felt pain before only it was more of a throbbing pain. Like waves in a storm, some bigger than others, but none small.

"You're fine," my father said. "You're fine. There's nothing to worry about. You're fine."

"I don't feel fine," I said and my voice sounded slow.

"Of course you don't, but you are. I checked. I spoke with the doctors and nothing was damaged. Nothing was really damaged. So you're fine."

"It hurts."

"I know it hurts."

"It hurts down there."

My voice was slow.

"I know," my father said. "But you're fine."

"My teeth hurt."

"As soon as you're out of here we'll go to a dentist and he'll cap them and they'll look brand new. Better than brand new. You'll have teeth as white as a movie star's."

"When am I getting out?"

"Soon."

"Why not now?"

"They have to make sure you're all okay."

"You said I was fine."

"You are fine."

"What is it? Tell me."

"They just have to do a small skin graft and then you'll be done."

The word graft made me sick. I coughed like I was going to puke, but I didn't puke. I hadn't puked when I was on the ground. I hadn't puked when he'd burned my balls. I hadn't puked when I'd walked out of the restaurant. I coughed again and the cold sweat went through me, made my forehead bead up and my father wiped the sweat away and said I'd be fine, I'd be fine, and I closed my eyes and listened to his voice and fell asleep.


When I woke he was sitting in a chair near my bed reading a paper. He didn't care about headline news. He said the same problems happened over and over again. He wasn't a real sports fan so the sports pages were out. The only part he read were the movie reviews and he only read the reviews after he'd seen the movie. He liked to see a movie fresh, but afterwards he liked to compare his thoughts to what the critics thought. The reviewers were usually more generous than my father. A wave came and then a bigger wave of pain and then a big wave.

"I'm awake," I said.

My father looked up, stood up and came over. He felt my forehead.

"I don't think you have a fever," he said.

"Did they do it yet?"

"Not yet."

"It hurts down there. It throbs and hurts."

"Of course it does."

I realized I was moving my tongue over the edge of my chipped
front teeth. My tongue was like a blind animal exploring and exploring, the new contours making it move and move. Even my
tongue felt slow. I tasted blood. I wanted my tongue to just be a
tongue again, just a tongue waiting for food or drink. Or a kiss. We
had kissed and then the men had come.

I looked down at myself. My legs were spread. There were dark
bruises on my shins and scabs. I took a breath and held down the
puke in my throat and forced myself to pull up the hospital gown.
There was a bandage over my crotch. Above the bandage the skin
looked like it had bubbled up. My ribs had purple bruises that
looked yellowish in the middle. I coughed and I remembered him
coughing.

"Where's Michael?" I said.

"Who's Michael?

"The kid I was with. The kid I was with when this happened."

"There wasn't anybody else there."

"They beat up somebody else. I was with somebody else."

"There was no one else there."

"No one?"

"Just you."

"I hope he wasn't hurt," I said.

"Who wasn't?"

"Just a friend."

"Where does he live? He'll remember who did this to you. Do you remember who did this to you?"

"Three guys. One guy. He was with two other guys. The one guy did it."

"Who was it?"

"I don't know."

"Would this Michael know?"

"I don't know. No."

"The police came by when you were sleeping. They have some questions for you."

"I got beat up," I said. "They beat me up. Case closed."

My father's jaw was clenched. He was nodding his head, but not for me. He was nodding his head for himself, the spring coiled tight inside him. He was nodding to let some of the tension out, forcing himself to appear calm for his son. I knew all of my father's expressions.

"The police think it was something else," he said.

"It wasn't anything else."

"They think it's something else because they burned you where they burned you."

"The guy was sick."

"Where can I find this Michael?"

"I don't know," I said.

"You don't know where he lives?"

"Not really. I don't really know him."

"Tell me what happened," my father said and in that question were all the questions.

The pain in my crotch throbbed. I coughed the nausea out. He had coughed. He had gotten away. I didn't know if I would ever see him again, but he would be a part of me, one of the big stories in my life. I knew from my father that there were only so many life stories. And I knew that first stories were big stories. Early stories were the ones you could distill all the other stories into. It was time to tell my father my story. It wouldn't be like the stories he often told, edited versions of movie plots. It was real and there was no other way to tell it except to just tell it. I forced myself to focus. I was out of it, me but not me, not like when it happened, but in a lighter way, a drip by drip way from the liquid bag hanging above me. Drip by drip. I let the first drip out.

"I was kissing a boy when the men attacked us."

My father nodded. His nod was for me. Different. But not different at all. My father understood. Maybe he had known. Maybe he hadn't. It didn't matter anymore. He understood. I knew he understood, just from his nod, just from his eyes on mine, making his eyes kind for me, and the wave of pain went away for a moment. I had known all along, but now I knew it, knew I was just his son, still his son, nothing different. I breathed out. I had been holding my breath.

I told him the rest, told him about the three men and then the one man, and he nodded and nodded and when I was done he kissed my forehead and said I felt fine and he smiled his best calm-eyed smile to let me know everything was okay and then he left the room.

I was drugged, but I think I heard him walking down the hall. I think I heard a door open and close, a bathroom door, I think, and I think I heard him scream, a primal scream, a scream that came from his gut-love for me. He had not judged me. He didn't judge others, not that way, and he hadn't judged me. The scream was out of helplessness. He wanted to get rid of what had happened to me and he didn't know how. He wanted to take my pain, but he couldn't. He was helpless and I had never seen my father helpless before and I think that is what I heard. That was the scream.

One of my father's favorite movie moments was from *The God-father*, when Sonny finds out that his sister's husband has beaten her.

She calls Sonny up and when he gets to her apartment she turns from him so he can't see her bruises. When Sonny finally does see her face, when he realizes what has happened, he takes his hand, his own hand, and bites into it. The rage from within is turned in on himself, on his hand. I didn't know if my father had bitten his own hand. He needed his hands. His hands were his work. The scream sounded like that bite. Inside. It came from inside and turned in on itself and then I think I heard the bathroom door open and close and then my father was next to me.

"Are you hungry? Are you thirsty? I can go down and get you something."

"Where am I?" I said.

"St. Vincent's. The same place you were born."

"Home sweet home," I said and smiled for my father to let him know I loved him and that the worst was over and that he didn't have to scream.

I had been born in this hospital. I wanted to ask more. I had told my father about me and I wanted my father to tell me about me, fill in the big blank in my life that was my mother. I didn't know if she was a one night stand, or a woman he'd seen for more than a single night like Anna, or if something else had happened, if she had died in childbirth or soon after, maybe even here at St. Vincent's.

"Do you remember the day when I was born?"

"Of course I remember it."

"What was it like?"

"I paced in the waiting room and when I heard I had a son, I bought cigars for all my friends."

"Very funny. What happened?"

"You were born. I took you home. You started growing up."

"Was she like Anna?"

"No."

"Did you love her?"

"I love you," he said. "And you're fine. You're going to be fine."

He wiped my forehead, but he was also trying to make my questions disappear. It was a strange and silent deal we had made. He had charmed me out of knowing my past. I had accepted his charm to please him. He was my father. I was his son. That was all.

My father went down. I watched the bag above me drip, drip. He brought back a slice of pizza from Two Boots and a root beer. The soda felt soothing. I only ate half the slice. It hurt my teeth.

A man knocked on the open door. He was a tall man, with red hair and pale blue eyes. His blunt nose was red from the cold. He introduced himself as a detective from the Sixth Precinct and asked if I was up to talking. My father reiterated the question for me, telling me I didn't have to talk if I wasn't ready. I said I could talk. It was strange seeing a detective standing next to my father. He had no idea what my father did.

The detective asked exactly where the attack had occurred. I said across the street from Barrow's Pub. The detective asked if it happened directly across and I said it had. My father said Barrow's Pub was a cop bar and looked straight at the detective until the detective looked away. The detective asked if I knew the perpetrators. I said I didn't. He asked what they looked like and I kept my eyes open to stay focused on the questions and not on the dripping bag and I described them as best I could. He asked if I could describe the men to a sketch artist. I said I would try. The detective asked if anybody had threatened me lately. I said not really. He asked what I meant by not really. I said I was sure that whatever threats had been made against me would not have been known by these men. He said he would rather be the judge of that. I told him how someone had written the word FAGGOT on my locker. Maybe I said that for myself. Maybe I said it so it would be easier to tell this stranger that I had been kissing a boy. The detective asked the next logical question the way I knew he would. He asked if I thought the attack had been a bias attack. It didn't take a detective to figure that out. My balls were in bandages. I said the man kept calling me a faggot, when he hit me and when he flicked on the lighter and when he burned me. The detective asked if there was anything else he should know. I said I didn't think so.

"He was with someone," my father said.

"Who were you with?" the detective said.

"A kid. Someone named Michael. I think he got beat up also."

"What's Michael's last name?"

"I don't know."

"Where does he live?"

"Near Gramercy Park. I don't really know him."

"And Michael didn't know these men?"

"We were together. The men came out of the bar. They called us faggots. That was how it started."

The detective closed his notebook. He said he'd send a sketch artist over. He said he hoped I felt better and that he would do everything he could to find the men who had done this.

"It was one man," I said.

"You said there were three of them."

"Only one hurt me. The other two were just along for the ride."

"If you go along for the ride, you're in the car," the detective said and left the room.

"That's a pretty good exit line," my father said and smiled at me.

"We'll have to put it in the movie version," I said.

"Yes, we will."

My father smoothed his thumb across his lips and I would have done the same except my arm was hooked up to the IV and every time I moved it hurt.

# 13

THEY TOOK SKIN FROM MY ASS. THEY UNROLLED A PIECE LIKE
the top of a sardine can and grafted the good skin over the dead skin
where my pubic hair had been. My balls had been burned, but they
weren't third-degree burns. A part of my scrotum had melted into
my thigh. That skin had already been separated with a scalpel.
Those were the gruesome details.

They kept me drugged most of the day. There were a lot of dead
spaces in my memory and then I would have some strange dream
and when I was with it, more with it than out of it during a specific
moment, I had the residuals of the dream with me, the bad feeling
or the anxious feeling, but I didn't remember what had happened.
There was no plot. Just feelings underneath.

In the evening I was less drugged. It hurt. Not just my crotch,
but all over. My neck. My arms. My ribs where I'd been kicked.
Even my legs, which I thought could take anything. I was getting
used to the pain, but it still took me over. I wasn't interested in eating and I didn't think I'd ever be able to get a hard-on again. I
didn't even care. I didn't puke. I would cough and feel the puke

coming up in my throat and then it went back down. When I could think, I thought about what had happened, and it wasn't like thinking at all. It was a picture that just kept coming in and out of focus. The whole thing was like a slow-motion scene, the pink lighter in close-up before it disappeared.

My father sat in a chair next to my hospital bed. He was there the whole time. The only time he left was to go down to get us something to eat. I imagined him paying for the food. I imagined him not wanting to get caught so he could be with me. He had never been caught, but now I imagined him taking no chances. He tried to make the time pass by telling me stories that I knew were based on movies he'd seen. He told me about some of the movies we would go to as soon as I healed, which would be soon, he reassured me. I couldn't concentrate on his stories. I was in pain and the pain made me fidgety, made me want to move my legs and arms, but when I moved it hurt worse. It was a claustrophobic feeling without being stuck in anything. I was stuck in myself. Stuck in my body. I started to understand a partial definition of mortality. The pain was mine and mine alone and it took over everything and made me feel how fragile I really was. All those miles I had run meant nothing.

My father had managed to get one of the police sketches. I wasn't sure how he'd done it, but I was sure the sketch artist didn't know. At some point my father's skilled fingers had touched the paper and pocketed it while the artist asked me about the thinness of the man's lips and if his eyebrows were straight or arched. The sketch my father had taken wasn't the final sketch, the one the artist would give to the Sixth Precinct, but it was close. My father kept looking at the sketch, memorizing it like it was a side for an audition, lines to be digested and then spit out.

Right before visiting hours were up, Anna came into the room. Her hair looked just-washed and even the fluorescent lights couldn't dull it, so deep and dark, and I remembered seeing her the first time, sitting on the steps in front of our building with my father, surrounded by cigarette and cold-air smoke, the open sound of her laughter in a city where real emotions were too often closed. She looked very young even though she had to be about my father's age. She took off her coat and placed it at the bottom of my bed. She was wearing a sweater that showed off her neck, graceful and flat in the back, like a fighter's, like my father's. There was a kid at Stuyvesant who had fought in the Golden Gloves and his neck was flat like that and sometimes I thought of him.

Anna had a present for me. She didn't bring flowers or chocolate or a book to read. She had blown up a photograph of the dead man on the subway. It wasn't even of the dead man. It was of the man's hand holding the bag with the box of Wheaties, the letters visible through the plastic bag. She knew I'd been looking at the Wheaties box. My father would have known. He probably did know, even if he wasn't the one taking the photographs. He was aware of almost everything. I hadn't been able to look too long at the man's face. Maybe that wasn't the important detail. Maybe the Wheaties box was the detail, the ironic Breakfast of Champions motto highlighting the now-you're-a-champion and now-you're-not quality of death, the fragility of it all, how quickly something could change, alive then dead, intact then burned, on the corner of Barrow, then on a hospital bed. I looked at the hand in the photograph. He had been the first dead man I'd ever seen.

"You noticed me looking at the Wheaties box," I said.

"That's why I brought you this photograph. It's the one I think you would have chosen."

"You're probably right. It was hard to look at the man's face."

"It looks like a different kind of sleep. Still yet disturbing. And fascinating as well."

In the subway station she had tried to put a spin on things, to make it seem not so bad for me, how a real mother would talk to a son, I imagined, but now she was telling me what she really felt. I had been through some hard truth and now she felt she could talk hard truth, completely, one person to another person.

"Will you do the second book?"

"I don't know yet. How are you feeling?"

"I don't feel like a champion."

"Stop," she said and laughed. "You'll feel like a champion soon. I know it's easy to say from this side of the bed, but you will. Your father said everything went well and you'll be out of here in no time."

"And I'll have something new to put on my wall."

"A change of scenery is always good, even in your room. I always change what's on my walls, switch the pictures around. I see things anew that way."

Anna took her hand, put it around my ankle and squeezed it gently to let me know she felt close to me.

The blown-up photograph was kind of a sick present, but unique. My father kept joking with Anna about it. She said that everything was relative and a few burns were nothing compared to dying on the subway. My father said the message in the photograph was clear, not subliminal at all, and Anna said that was why she liked it, that the plastic bag was that thin, that the line was that thin, but still we constantly blocked death out. My father looked me over and smiled. He said it would be a thin line before I started running again, as thin as a starting line, that I'd cross it with my first stride and run forward. I had no desire to run. Anna placed the photo on the bedside table so that it leaned upright against the wall. On the table were a box of tissues and a kidney-shaped puke basin.

"How are you?" Anna asked my father.

"I'm fine," he said, but that was for me. His anger was underneath and she heard it too.

"They'll find him," she said.

"They haven't found him yet."

My father gave Anna the artist's drawing. He said it wasn't the final one, said it was almost done, but not quite done, and that he wanted her to fix it so he could really see the man's face. I could see the man's face. If I closed my eyes his face was right there if I wanted it to be. The face the police artist had drawn was close, not exact, but close. I couldn't tell what was off, what made the drawing a cartoon of the man and not the man himself.

"I know you can draw," my father said.

"I can draw," she said.

"Ben will work you through it just like he did with the cop."

"Maybe Ben is tired of talking about it."

"It won't take long."

"Maybe you should let the police do their job. That's what they do. They look for the bad guys."

"They never found me."

"You're not a bad guy," she said and my father didn't say anything, but his eyes went sleepy and she said, "You're not."

"They still never found me."

"Give them some time to look for the man," she said.

"Fucker," my father said.

"Give them some time."

"Ben said something was missing, that it wasn't quite there. I want you to draw his face."

I remembered the scream I thought I'd heard coming from the hospital bathroom. I remembered Sonny Corleone putting his hand in his mouth and biting down. I remembered Belmondo. Movie memories my past memories. Movies my past, even in St. Vincent's where I'd been born. During one scene in *Breathless*, Belmondo steals a car from a Paris garage, but he sits in the passenger seat on the way out. Jean Seberg sits in the driver's seat. At that moment they are connected, and connected in crime. At that moment she knows him.

"Give them a few days," I said.

"Draw it," he said.

Anna sighed and nodded her head and it was like she had picked up his gesture, the nodding of the head, for herself, and for him and for what might happen.

"Oh boy," she said.

"I'll get a pencil," my father said and he left the room.

Anna was looking at her photograph propped against the wall. Her eyes were out of focus. She was fast-forwarding all that could happen and I started to do the same. It was like a straight line. Where I had been burned was a line. The flame had been an upward line against my flesh, and the skin graft, the color just a little off, was a perfect line up to my belly button, about the width of the chalked line that I stood behind before a race, the line that is painted across the track that separates not-yet racing and racing, the line that once passed says you're now in the race and when passed again says the race is over. Like the line of love, I thought. Once crossed you can't go back. Like the line between past and future. Or maybe really the line between past and now. The now my father spoke of. When I raced I would take a breath and wait for the starter's pistol to explode and then I would cross the line and there was no more thinking about what was going to be because it was. It happened that fast.

"Do you want to do this?" Anna said.

"He wants to do it."

"Do you?"

"My father has always taken care of me. If you don't draw it, someone else will. He gets his way."

"Perhaps he does."

"I'm sure you know this, but I've never seen him with a woman the way he is with you."

"Thank you for saying it."

"Sometimes I feel like I'm the older one with him, but not really. When he has to be the father he always is."

"He's a father first."

"He is. He's a great father. But he's also yours. I really don't know anything about that kind of love, I'm still too young, but I know he's also yours."

My father came back into the room. He'd found a pencil. He'd found a notebook. He got his way. One of the larger waves of pain went over me and I held my breath and waited for it to pass.

"You'll be fine," he said.

He knew me that well, knew when it hurt the most.

Anna stood next to me with the pencil in her hand and we looked at the police sketch together. I closed my eyes to see the man's face and opened my eyes. I described the man again. As if putting a transparency from my mind over the actual sketch so I could see where the lines were slightly different. The lines were most different around the eyes and the mouth. I told her the lips were off. She asked how they were off and we worked through it together. She drew much differently than the police artist. Her hand flowed, but the marks seemed darker, firmer, as if she already knew what he looked like and she wasn't afraid of making a mistake. I liked how bold she was. If my father was Belmondo, she was Jean Seberg after she met Belmondo. Belmondo had caught the American woman's attention. He was so different from her. She was more conservative, but she was bold for seeing someone like Belmondo, and she became bolder, bold enough to steal a car, bold enough to run after him when he was shot. Anna was bold, had been bold before she met my father I could tell, but I also knew my father had rubbed off on her, that when she nodded she had picked up more than a gesture. Her pencil strokes were bold, her photographs were bold, the way she talked to me, like an adult, was bold, and the way she kissed my father like he kissed her was bold. In *Breathless* Jean Seberg moved her thumb over her lips.

Anna moved her hand. The eyes became his eyes. The lips became his lips. I hardly had to say anything and then she was done.

"That's him," I said.

My father took the drawing and looked at it for a long time.

"I don't like this," Anna said.

My father kept looking at the drawing. The muscles in his jaw were clenched and didn't unclench.

"What are you going to do with that?" she said. "Let them look for him."

"There's big stealing and there's little stealing," my father said.

"What does that mean?"

"It was a cop bar," my father said.

"Were they cops?" she said.

"I don't know."

"Did you ask?"

"I don't have to ask. They protect their own. Cops. Guys who drink with cops. It was a cop bar. There's a reason they haven't found him yet."

"Oh boy," Anna said.

"So they came out of the bar and crossed the street," my father said to me.

"I heard laughing," I said. "Then I heard running and then they were in front of us."

"And the other two did nothing to stop him?"

"I don't know."

"You see? They protect their own."

"Everyone protects their own, Jared," Anna said.

"So do I. That fuck opened up a lighter and burned my son. Think of that. He took the time to open up his fucking lighter and hold it there and burn my son."

"Stop," she said, but no laughter followed.

I saw the tightness in my father's jaw. I saw the beginning of the scream.

"I don't care who he is," my father said. "I don't care how drunk he was. I don't care."

"Stop," she said.

He folded the drawing in half and then in half again and put it in his pocket.

The nurse knocked on the open door and said visiting hours were over. Anna got her coat and put it on. I told my father to go too. I said I needed some sleep. I thought maybe she could calm him. The waves were starting to come faster now, faster at night. The sea always looked roughest at night. I held my breath and waited and a big wave passed. My father said he wanted to stay and I told him not to. I told him I'd sleep better alone.

"Come with me," Anna said and then she smiled for me and walked out.

"Go on," I said and the way it came out I sounded like the father.

My father felt my forehead. He said I felt fine. He picked up his coat and kissed me good-bye. He told me he loved me. I listened to his springy footsteps on the hospital floor until they were gone.

I held my breath until the next wave passed and waited for the next. There were all kinds of men. Different men. Men like me and Michael. We were boys, but we would become men, become men soon. Different. But not different at all. I had been judged different. Men like the one who had called me a faggot. Men like Belmondo, a movie man, but still a man, the distillation of a certain kind of man in eighty-nine minutes of film time. Men like my father. The rolling shoulders of a fighter and the flat neck, the anger in the jaw, the tender kiss he'd given me, soft and still cool on skin that had not been grafted.

# 14

HOSPITAL REGULATIONS SAID THEY HAD TO TAKE ME TO THE exit in a wheelchair. My father persuaded the nurse to let him push me. When we were on the ground floor he zigzagged the chair back and forth, and when we hit a straightaway in the corridor he started running, sounds of speed and sharp turns coming from his lips, sound effects for me, making me feel like I was on a ride. He wanted me to hit the street smiling.

The cold air was a relief. It was real air and the sunlight was real and the people walking past were not aware that inside St. Vincent's people were sick and in pain. Outside, people worried about their little day-to-day problems, which was really the only way to live. Getting from moment to moment without too many big thoughts, thoughts that were on the other side of the thin line. Outside, after having been inside for so long, the now that was my father's philosophy seemed natural, right. I stood up. I breathed the air and squinted into the sunlight and knew it was a now-moment before the rest of life came in.

We walked slowly home. It hurt to walk, but not so badly. The pain of the first days was far away. My father cupped his hands and I watched the familiar smoke of his breath. We stopped in Two Boots for a slice of pizza. I was hungry again.

The apartment looked strange to me, as if I was revisiting it after a long time, as if I had grown, almost literally, since I'd been there, a little kid's perspective different from an older kid's, a few inches taller making the view change. I stayed at home instead of going right back to school and I was glad to stay away. I could already imagine the whispering when I passed through the corridors. I wondered how long it would be before someone filled my locker with more graffiti, printed FAGGOT in bold letters, and I also wondered if I would bother rubbing it off.

My father changed my bandages and took care of me and always made sure to tell me how well my skin was healing, how it looked as good as new. The dentist capped my front teeth. At first my tongue kept rolling over the caps, automatically, but then I got used to them until I hardly remembered how my real teeth had felt. Just like I could hardly remember what it was like before everything had happened. I better understood my father's now-philosophy. My now was all I really knew.

I watched a lot of movies on TV. I took a lot of walks around the block. I thought someone would call me, someone would check to see if I was okay. But nobody called. None of the students. None of the teachers. Nobody from the track team. Not even James Worthen. I was probably just part of another story he could tell with false authority like walking out of the diner. And Michael. He didn't call either. He didn't have my number, but I knew he could find me. He could have found me if he'd tried. But he didn't.

After a few weeks, I was almost ready to return to life. I'd read ahead in my textbooks so I wouldn't be behind in school and the doctor said I would be able to start running soon. If I could get back into shape, if I could run as fast as I'd run before, then I'd know I was truly better, my complete recovery symbolized by the time on a stopwatch.

I was almost ready to go on, but my father wasn't.

Maybe he was waiting for a change and my getting hurt was the catalyst. Maybe he needed something to make him cross his own new starting line.

I wasn't there when it happened, but I read the newspaper accounts afterwards. While reading I kept thinking about the goods and the bads, the phrase I'd written on that essay when I'd blanked out, the phrase that had become part of our repertoire. *The goods and the bads.* In many ways it was more accurate than advantages and disadvantages. On the most basic level it really was about goods and bads. Most of my memories were goods, but some of my memories were bads and it was to my father's credit that he allowed most of the bads to happen off-camera for me. He played those scenes when I wasn't there. But I read the papers afterwards and what happened became a vivid picture for me, as if I'd been there. It was very much like a movie experience. You sit in the audience and watch from the safe distance of your seat. You can always remove yourself from what's happening if you wish, if the movie gets too scary or too sad. You can move your eyes from the screen to break the moment, look around the theater, look at the outlines of heads in the dark, look along the aisle, at a stray kernel of popcorn or an empty soda cup. Or you can stay there and let yourself become part of the movie and so the scene becomes part of you. What my father did became part of me, as if I was a direct observer, as if I could have stopped it if I'd tried, almost like the two men that observed the one man as he took the pink lighter from his pocket, pink like the new skin that was still too new, pink and raw and tender.

I wasn't there, but I was so close to my father that I was.

The man had been caught, scheduled for a trial, let out on bail. It turned out the man wasn't a cop. He was an electrician on Staten Island who happened to have a lot of cop friends. A lot of cops lived in Staten Island, the only borough that felt like suburbia even if it was part of the city. He did work for cops, he hung out with cops, and one article described how he'd been pissed off at the whole Abner Louima case because some lowly immigrant was responsible for ruining the lives of at least three police officers. According to a neighbor, he was quoted as saying Louima probably started with the cops and probably deserved a plunger shoved up his ass and was probably a faggot. So this man who was an electrician, who hung out with cops, who hated everybody but people like himself, was out drinking in Barrow's Pub when he'd seen me and he'd seen Michael and he'd done what he'd done.

The man was out on bail. Charges had not even been filed against the other two men. The district attorney stopped returning my father's calls. My father wasn't surprised at all. To him, there was a clear line that divided most sides, and they were on the other side, all of them. He'd call the DA's office, leave a message with the secretary, hang up the phone, and his jaw would be clenched. One time he asked me about Michael. He told me that Michael would help the case, that he was the only witness to what had happened. I told him I didn't know Michael's last name. I told him I didn't know exactly where he lived. I told him I hardly knew Michael. It wasn't a lie. Not really. My father left it alone. He would take Anna's drawing from his pocket, unfold it, look at it, refold it, put it in his pocket. There was nothing smooth about how he put the drawing back in his pocket. The most oblivious victim would have felt my father's angry hand.

My father found the man's address in Staten Island. I could picture my father looking over a map to see the best route to get there.

The address wasn't far from the ferry so that worked out well. The newspaper didn't say whether my father took the ferry across the harbor and then walked the rest of the way to the man's house or if he took a bus. My guess was he walked. If he walked, fewer people would see him unless they happened to be looking out the window and saw this man, my father, walking with his overcoat on and his hat pulled low, his springy walk from another time, moving forward, a stranger in their streets.

Jared Chiziver took the ferry on Sunday evening. He stood at the front of the boat like we had done, me and Anna and my father just doing a New York City thing with no motive but to go somewhere and return. He faced the cold air and looked out, out at the water and the Statue of Liberty welcoming everyone, out at the shore of Staten Island getting closer and closer. He nodded his head for himself.

The man lived in a small house. My father waited across the street. There was a pickup truck in the driveway and next to the driveway was a sports car propped up on cinderblocks. The tires had been removed so it was the chassis and bare wheels.

My father reached into his pocket, took out the drawing Anna had done of the man, looked at it, folded it, put it back in his pocket. My father blew into his hands and waited.

He thought about me in the hospital bed, the pain that his son had gone through, the memory that was his memory even though he hadn't been there, connected to me as I was connected to him, his memories mine and my memories his, which was why he saw the man's finger flick the lighter, saw the flame, saw the fire hit flesh.

Jared Chiziver waited in the cold until the man came out. The man's face was the exact face on Anna's drawing. The man was going to pick up some food and bring it back to his house. My father walked across the street. He looked at the man and the man looked back, not seeing disrespect in my father's eyes but something far more disturbing. He saw nothing in my father's eyes. He was about to ask my father what he wanted when Jared Chiziver threw a punch to the man's jaw and knocked him down. If my father had been thinking, he would have used his left hand, the hand he didn't use for work, but my father had been clenching his jaw too long to think. He hit the man with his right hand.

The man fell to his knees. My father threw two more punches, a left and a right, and the man fell forward. My father lifted the man by his hair. He dragged him over to the steps of the house and dropped him to the ground. My father went over to the propped-up car and chose a cinderblock. He held the concrete in his left hand and walked back to the steps. A cinderblock was perfect. He always said he lived off the land and concrete was city land. My father's right hand was already starting to swell. He'd broken it when he threw the first punch. The man was waking up a little, but he was still out of it, too out of it to stand on his own, too out of it to scream for help. My father unbuckled the man's belt and pulled the man's pants down just as my pants had been pulled down. He pulled the man's under-wear down just as my underwear had been pulled down. My father forced the man down until the man was kneeling in front of the steps, almost like he was praying, only his hands hung limply at his sides and were not clasped in front of him. My father sat down on the steps next to the man. My father took the shaft of the man's pe-nis in his fingers and placed it flat on the first step.

With his left hand my father held the man firmly so the man couldn't move and with his right hand my father brought down the cinderblock. The shaft of the man's penis exploded, smashed flat against the step. Blood shot out the hole. Crushed flesh and carti-lage. No real bone to keep it intact. The man must have come out of it then. He must have screamed. He must have puked. He must have looked down at what had once been his penis, but was nothing but a pink pancake covered in blood. He must have gone out all the way after that.

The man's penis was cut off in the hospital. He remained in intensive care for days. He would spend the rest of his life pissing out a plastic hose. The papers didn't say if come came out of the hose, or if he could even come at all. By the time the man passed out from the pain and the sight of the useless flesh between his legs, my father was walking back to the ferry. He probably sat inside instead of hanging out on the bow. He probably nodded once to himself and then didn't nod at all. He probably moved his thumb across his lips as if he were cleaning the last distaste from his mouth. Eye for an eye. Cock for a cock. He was my father and that is what my father did.

And so my father was free in a way. He had always done what he wanted, but I had been his responsibility and in that one act, that complete act, in protecting me completely, he was also letting go. He was letting go of the restlessness that was in him. My father's restlessness was always there. Anna had taken some of the restlessness, but when I was hurt the restlessness returned, forcefully, and since he didn't seem interested in his usual outlet, anonymous women, good for a night, his restlessness had raged close to the surface. It was easy to see. In real life and on film. Sometimes Anna brought her photographs to our apartment and the difference was a clear line. Before what happened to me. After what happened to me. The creases around my father's eyes had become more defined and his eyes were far away. Her simple pictures showed everything. When my father came back from Staten Island another line was crossed and he was changed again. His eyes came back. Even his body seemed looser, as if he'd stretched some of the spring out of his muscles and he was more calm, less coiled. I knew part of his coil came from having me. I knew that. He went out when he was restless. He left the apartment and acted like he was alone and in the morning, when he came home, mixed with the leftover alcohol, was another hangover symptom. He felt guilt. He never felt guilt over stealing, but he felt guilt over me. To be hungover alone was one thing. To be hungover in front of his son was another. Maybe hurting that man had been a higher high than going out. He wasn't sick afterwards. And he had done it for me. In most ways he had done it for me. I sometimes questioned my father about his hangovers, but I didn't say a word about his new freedom when he returned from Staten Island.

The goods and the bads. It was a strange push and pull. He had protected me and yet he had uprooted me. We had to leave New York City. He had really done the all-or-nothing this time, all the way, and now he was free to continue living all-or-nothing. Once the race starts, you might as well run your hardest and if you relax into the race, the speed increases. With that irrevocable action, my father entered into a true state of living in the moment. He could do whatever he wanted because of what he'd done. What was there to lose? I don't think he thought too hard about losing me or losing Anna or even losing himself when he did what he did. Maybe he had already lost himself and there is also freedom in that. He had lost himself by loving her and he had lost himself by exacting revenge and most of all, he had lost himself by possibly leaving me. If he got caught, we would not be together. But on that day he looked like he only felt the high, the high of having done what he truly wanted. I'd felt a little of that when I'd walked out of the diner. That's why I walked. I felt the power that comes from having nothing to lose. That's why Belmondo smiles at the world. That's what makes *Breathless* breathless. My father had done something outside the rules, outside what is civilized. It was not the controlled hand inside a pocket. It was the uncontrolled hand smashing cement down on a man's penis. And for a moment his freedom was contagious.

That night when he returned, his laugh was more open than it had ever been. He had lived low to the ground, he had promoted little stealing, but now he was free to live high, to steal big, to be a movie character completely, in reality. When he came home that night, almost giddy, he had already decided to take us away. He spoke of going south like it was going west. He spoke of adventure on the road. He spoke about moving fast, just moving fast. He couldn't wait to feel the speed.

My father wanted to drive to Florida. He wanted to leave the winter behind. He didn't say what had happened in Staten Island. He said he was tired of the winter. He said he was tired of cold hands. And Miami was a great city, a warm winter place to get lost in for a while. And Anna had a car. And she worked on her own time so she could leave. And I had been out of school long enough where I could leave too, without anyone noticing. I didn't care. I would be with him. I would be with them. It would be an adventure. I heard it in my father's laugh, in his giddy voice, and at that moment I was feeling free too. I had kissed Michael and in that I had crossed a certain line, had let go of something I had held inside too long. And Anna had a subject to focus on, my father. He had committed a big crime and his eyes would light up for her photographs. And just as Jean Seberg had done in the movie, Anna would go along for the ride and look at the ride, she would be in it and watching it at the same time. The whole movie was in and out. Belmondo himself was playing Bogart, so he was in a movie and acting a movie. And my father could suddenly act anyway he wanted, completely. He could move his thumb across his lips exactly like Belmondo who had moved his thumb exactly like Bogart because they both had nothing to lose. And love was part of that, the now kind of love, the all-or-nothing kind of love, the breathless kind of love, a love that was a higher high than a father's love for his son.

Driving to Florida. Driving that on-the-road drive that was the man's activity in America. Like riding into the sunset. Our trip, in many ways, was all about men. All about men and their cocks. Smashed cocks and burnt cocks and jacked-off cocks and whose cock was bigger. Men against men. Men with men. A man's love for his son. A man's love for many women that changed to a man's love for one woman. A man's need to be free. What did I think of in that moment? When he told us to pack our bags? Nothing really. I was working from my gut like my father. It felt right at that moment. That was enough. It felt right. My father was laughing and I laughed too and he held me around and I held him and we moved in a circle, so perfect it looked choreographed.

He packed his old valise. I had to help him zip it closed because his right hand was too swollen. He was still giddy, anxious to drive, to speed on the highway, to feel the Florida sun. But his hand, now more purple than blue, now far too swollen to pick a pocket, stopped the first thrill I'd felt. Things had been changing all year for me, but not like this. This was different. This was big. This was the end of something, a crossed line, and I knew it beyond knowing it. My father put his good hand on my shoulder.

"Don't worry," he said.

"I think you broke your hand."

"It's nothing. It will heal in no time. I'm fine."

I packed my bag. He told me not to forget my bathing suit. He packed the money under the bathroom sink into a small duffel bag. He zipped the duffel bag closed so I wouldn't have to. When Anna honked the car horn downstairs my father looked at me and smiled his easy smile, the smile in his eyes but also in his mouth now, and he started to laugh.

"All right," my father said.

He locked the door and we went down.

Our breath turned to smoke. The exhaust was smoke. A man-hole cover on Bedford Street smoked. It was like our city was providing the proper cover to escape.

## PART TWO

# breathe in

# 15

WE DROVE OUT OF THE CITY AND THROUGH NEW JERSEY IN no time. My father always said New York to Miami was the easiest drive to take when people questioned him about why he didn't fly to Florida. It was Route 95 straight south.

I sat in the back like I really was a kid in a two-parent family with my father in the driver's seat and Anna in the passenger seat. We sang songs that were from another era, my father belting out army tunes like "Over There" about the enemy over there, which had been across the Atlantic and not along the Atlantic like we were going. Anna quickly picked up the words that I knew from years of repetition. She had a good voice and wasn't afraid to sing as loud as my father, and with them singing that loud I sang loud too. We'd pass cars and the passengers would look in at us, fascinated by the three people with their mouths wide open. When our throats were sore we listened to the radio.

Anna's car was a 1968 Plymouth Valiant, gold in color, sort of like a shield, and looking very much out of date. The seats were off-white vinyl and the dashboard had nothing digital about it. When we went to Florida on our own, which had been always, we rented cars. My father and I had become experts on the newest midsize, mid-price American vehicles. We'd decided that Chevys drove better than Fords, that Pontiacs made the most noise, or at least the Grand Am we'd rented did, that Dodges felt tinny, especially around the roof, but this was our first Plymouth that I could remember and certainly the oldest car we'd been in. It drove smoothly for an old car. The engine wasn't too noisy and the heat worked fine. My father said it handled well, especially in his hands. He glanced at Anna, smiled, yelled an exaggerated *ouch* when she punched his arm. His right hand looked bad. Anna said we should stop at a hospital so a doctor could check it out, but my father wanted to keep driving.

"Even with a broken hand, I'm handling your car better than it's ever been handled."

"Keep it up," she said. "You'll be in the backseat in no time."

My father hunched himself over the steering wheel, mock-protecting his place in the car.

The seats were comfortable, and I liked the way the front and back seats were flat and had no partition between one side and the other. I stretched my legs out, breathed into the pain that went across my crotch until it went away, leaned back, closed my eyes. I pretended that Michael was with us, next to me, that he was running away from the city too and that his hand was moving along my leg. I pretended that what had happened had never happened. I felt myself start to get hard. It was the first time I'd felt that pull since I'd been hard against him, on the corner of Hudson and Barrow, his mouth on mine, before the laughter came in and I had to open my eyes. I opened my eyes. They were laughing. Not the man. It was just my father and Anna and the road in front of us and the heat working, making everything feel warm and safe, making it appear that the cold outside was just a mirage, that the jagged ice in the breakdown lane was just part of a set, couldn't really cut me.

We drove under the Baltimore tunnel, so much lighter and cleaner than the Holland tunnel that had taken us from downtown to out of town. We drove past Washington, D.C., the Washington Monument lit up far in the distance.

"America the beautiful," my father said.

I watched the world from the side window, the buildings close to the road passing fast, the buildings far from the road passing slow, the horizon to the west hardly moving at all.

"When I was a kid my parents always took us to faraway places," Anna said. "We never took the car. We always flew somewhere thousands of miles away and exotic. Hong Kong and Kenya and halfway around the world to Australia and New Zealand. The farther the better. Paris and Rome and London and New York were just little jaunts to my folks. I used to think they took these long trips just to impress their friends. As soon as they got somewhere the first thing they did was buy dozens of postcards. They'd go to the post office and choose the most exotic-looking stamps and send out cards to everyone to let them know how far away we were. It gave them something to talk about to their friends."

"It's better than talking about business," my father said.

"They didn't really talk about the places we visited. It wasn't about the impressions they had, or something they'd learned about another culture. They listed what they did. They did the obvious thing to do in each place. They even ate the obvious food."

"Well, why go to Paris if you're not going to see the Eiffel Tower and eat crêpes?"

"It was more than that. It was more. Even the pictures they took were like checklists. They took pictures and then moved on without ever absorbing anything. They crammed everything onto that roll of film to prove they'd been there. I hated the sound of their camera clicking away. The Eiffel Tower. The Arc de Triomph. The Louvre. Click. Click. Click."

"*Bonjour,*" my father said.

"Stop," she said.

"So how are you going to prove you were with us?"

Anna took her camera from her bag and pointed it at my father.

"Like this," she said and took the picture. *Click.* It was a pleasing sound, fuller and slower than the *click* my cheap camera made.

"*Touché,*" my father said.

He pulled into the left lane and passed a line of cars.

"So do you usually drive to Florida?" Anna said.

"Always. I never stepped foot on a plane."

"How come?"

"Because I never do."

"My father doesn't do anything he hates," I said.

"How do you know you hate it if you've never done it?"

"I hate it so much I refuse to even try. Plus I'm scared shit of putting my life in someone else's hands. If I'm going down, I want to be the one in the pilot's seat and since I don't fly, that doesn't seem likely."

"I guess I won't be driving this trip," Anna said.

"I'll drive. You'll ride shotgun. Ben will be the navigator in back. Now relax and enjoy the ride. This is your captain speaking."

Anna turned around and leaned over the front seat to look at me.

"Do you know how to drive?"

"I'm a city kid. All I know are subways."

"Well, you should learn."

"Is that an offer for lessons?"

"I could teach you how to drive."

"I'm ready."

"So. So would you trust your own son to drive you?" Anna said to my father.

"I'll have to see what kind of driver he turns out to be. If he's a natural like me, then I'll think about it. Maybe I'll think about it."

"And what makes you a natural driver?"

"I'm a natural," my father said. "Some things can't be explained."

"You don't explain a lot of things," she said.

"A thousand flicks of the eye. You see that? Watch my eyes. Side view. Rear view. Straight ahead. A thousand flicks of the eye."

"He actually thinks he flicks his eyes a thousand times," I said.

"I don't *think* I do. I *do*. I'm a natural."

"I once counted how many times he moved his eyes in one minute," I said. "It was eleven. He moved them eleven times and most of them were blinks."

"Ben thought it was eleven times. It was a thousand. In fact, it was exactly a thousand flicks per minute."

"What else are you afraid of besides flying?" Anna said.

"That's all, folks."

"I don't believe you."

"Right now, I'm not afraid of anything. I'm thinking about Miami and palm trees and summer cocktails and beautiful beaches that are actually blue. It's all good ahead of us. I'm here with a woman I can't wait to see traipsing around the pool in her new bikini. My son is in the backseat counting the flicks of my eyes. It's all good. I feel mighty. Mighty. I feel mighty."

"I love that word in your mouth," Anna said.

My father made a muscle.

"Feel that," he said.

"Stop."

"Feel it."

"Stop," she said and laughed and then felt his muscle, appeasing him the way I often did.

"Ben?" he said, his smile in the rearview mirror.

"No thanks."

"Mighty and free. I love driving at night."

Anna looked back at me. Her hair fell over her face. I saw how my father could see her beauty like for the first time every time he saw her. She seemed to have so many looks, and in the dark, lit by the diminishing headlights of cars we passed, she was worthy of breathlessness. I had seen Michael at night. I wondered what he would look like in daylight. If his lips would look as full. As red. As if the blood had been sucked to their surface.

"What about you, Ben?" she said. "What are you afraid of?"

"I'm afraid of men with pink lighters." I laughed to let them know I was joking.

"That won't be a fear ever again," my father said. "That's all over. That's past history and we don't worry about past history. You have nothing to fear."

My father wasn't joking. I had already guessed something had happened that had caused us to take a midwinter, middle-of-the-night trip to Florida. My father's hand confirmed I had nothing else to fear from that man. When his hand healed, when the black and blue faded, I wondered where we'd be. My father passed another car.

"Nothing to fear. You hear me?"

"I hear you," I said and my words were meant to appease him, more than feeling his muscle. "I was just joking."

"You're fine," he said.

Anna was still turned around, looking at me as if through a lens.

"I'm afraid before a race. I get sick before I have to line up on the starting line. If I fail at the thing I do best then what do I have left? I think that's why I'm afraid."

"You're more than a runner," Anna said.

"I don't know."

"You're much more," my father said. "You're mighty in many ways."

"You are," Anna said.

"I guess I'm just confused about things."

"You're at a confusing age," she said.

"I know that, but I'm still confused. I know how screwed up teenagers are. You can practically see the insecurity buzzing around everyone's head in school. What happened to me was different from that. I'm not confused about what I did. I'm confused about what happened afterwards."

"Of course you are."

"It's New York City. It's the Village."

I felt the pain across my crotch and breathed into it. Like breathing into a cramp while running, imagining the cramp, imagining the oxygen going there, taking the pain away.

"Everything's allowed in the city. And what I did wasn't wrong. I'm not different from anyone else. Not really."

"You're not," Anna said.

"Who cares who you like if you're not hurting anyone? I know people latch on to differences. I'm not that naïve. But it's so stupid. It's such a stupid thing to hate someone for."

"He was a stupid man," Anna said. "He was a backward man. He wasn't a man at all."

She didn't have to say anything else. I thought of Michael walking toward me, bundled in his down jacket, how his voice sounded in the cold, how his mouth felt in the dark, how his smile looked genuine, seemed real. I felt I had learned the truth of him, or some of the truth of him, even if we had only met twice. And if I was wrong about Michael, if I was just a kid fooling myself, I could pretend it was more. I remembered that he'd thrown his empty coffee cup on the ground. I had forgotten about that. I could pretend to forget about that. I could pretend to forget he'd run away. I'd heard him coughing and he was gone. I could pretend to forget he hadn't found me afterwards. He could have found me. He could have tried. I could pretend to forget, but he could have tried. I was confused about that. More confused than by the hate. By the word *faggot*. By the laughing man. By the pink lighter.

It felt late. I watched as Anna moved her hand to the back of my father's neck to stroke it. I watched her look at him. She knew his different looks already. I could tell that even from the backseat.

"I think we should stop for the night," Anna said. Her voice was low.

My father turned his head to her.

*"Bonjour,"* he said and his voice was low too.

We passed a sign with all the hotels listed, pictures of the different logos. The next sign listed all the restaurants. The next listed all the gas stations. A real highway oasis. My father pulled off the exit, took a right, and drove up to the entrance of the Best Western. Anna got out and walked to the registration desk. She didn't have to be asked. If she put the room in her name, no one would know where we were. The name Chiziver was out there, somewhere. She knew it. I knew it. I didn't know it all the way, but I knew it.

Anna came back to the car and we drove around to the room. It was bitter outside. We hadn't traveled that far south. We took our bags into the room and I immediately put on the TV the way I always did when we checked into a hotel. Some stupid late-night movie was on.

I used the bathroom first. My father asked me if I needed help and I said I was fine. I took off the old bandage. The skin color was just a little off. It didn't look too ugly. I tried looking at it like it wasn't my burn, like it wasn't me looking at it. It still didn't look too ugly. I hoped it wouldn't look too ugly. I put on the disinfectant salve, put on a fresh bandage, carefully stepped into a pair of sweatpants. Anna used the bathroom next. She came out wearing boxer shorts and a loose tank top. She was very comfortable around me. My father came out of the bathroom wearing his usual sweats. He asked if anybody needed anything and shut the light. Driving always bent time in a strange way for me. I felt very tired and I think we all fell asleep right away.

We woke when the other guests started checking out of their rooms. Squeaky suitcase wheels, cars starting in the parking lot, kids running around the hallways screaming. The sounds of families on their way to Florida for winter vacation. We all washed up. I put on the TV. The weather channel showed it was eighty degrees and sunny in Miami.

"Perfect," my father said.

Anna went to check out and my father picked up his bag and hers. I saw his jaw clench from the pain in his hand, but if I asked him how he was he'd just say *Fine.* I picked up my bag. It wasn't too heavy.

Stripped sheets and used towels lined the hallway. The maids were already changing the rooms, their cleaning carts unattended, easy access to free soaps and shampoos. Whenever we stayed in a hotel, we loaded up. I always felt like I was helping my father when I took hotel supplies and my father considered this stealing to be so common, the kind of stealing everyone did as they traveled across America, that he had no problem when I raided the maids' carts. I unzipped the top of my bag.

"Forget it," my father said.

"Why?"

"We don't need anything."

"What about for when we get back to the city?"

"Okay. Go ahead."

That was when I heard we weren't going back. Right before it happened, he'd talked to me like I was more than a kid and after it happened he looked me straight in the eyes. But when he told me to go ahead, his voice was all adult, almost dismissive, a father's voice to a young son who doesn't know about consequences. For a moment, my father was thinking beyond the now. For a moment, his voice sounded weary, like on his hungover mornings, but he wasn't hungover. I wanted to pretend I hadn't heard his voice.

I took a few soaps and a few shampoos and put them in my bag so my father wouldn't think I'd heard anything. But I'm sure he knew I was just going through the motions, just doing it for him.

I zipped my bag closed. No one saw a thing. I followed my father out of the hotel and into the lot where two kids ran around in circles.

# 16

THE WINTER HAD HIT AS FAR SOUTH AS NORTH CAROLINA.
Some of the pine trees along the road had been felled by ice, trunks
and branches broken in hard, snapping angles, but once we hit the
border of South Carolina the snow was completely gone.

We passed a military caravan, green trucks with soldiers peering at
us from jeeps. It was easy to see that the guys were checking out Anna.
Fingers pointed. One guy let his tongue hang in exaggerated lechery.
My father was not a jealous man and he laughed in the soldier's face.

"You have some not-so-secret admirers," he said.

"I love a man in a uniform."

"I better find a costume shop somewhere. What a motley-
looking crew. If we have to depend on these guys to defend our
country we're in trouble."

"Stop," she said. "They're just kids."

"Too young to drink, but old enough to fight."

They were probably only two years older than me, at least some
of them, and I wondered how they'd chosen such a regimented life.
A sergeant yelling orders about when to wake, when to eat, when

to march, when to stand at attention. I'd grown up with relatively free reign and didn't think I could handle the discipline from above. I disciplined myself to do what I had to do and I'd always done it. In school. In track and cross-country. Long-distance running was perfect for me. The coach could go over some techniques, give some pointers, but while I ran I was far from anyone who could tell me what to do. I wouldn't have lasted in the army. And once they found out about me, the laughter would have come from many men, not just three men walking out of a bar. They would make jokes about not dropping soap in the shower when I was around. They would look at me as less than a man, as not a man at all. They would light me up if they could and there would be too many of them to go after. And the south was supposed to be less tolerant, maybe the least tolerant part of the country. The soldiers kept staring at Anna. Some of them, after the initial once-over, looked at my father. We stood out as northerners. The way my father and Anna were dressed and their manner, even as seen through a windshield, must have seemed foreign. They looked city. They looked big city. And I was city too. Even in generic sweatpants and running sneakers, I still didn't look like the soldiers in the truck.

The army caravan inspired my father to sing "Over There" again and "You're In The Army, Mr. Jones." Anna laughed at the words. She asked my father how he knew so many military songs and he said he'd picked them up watching old war movies.

"The new war movies don't have any songs," he said. "There's a soundtrack that might follow the soldiers around and capture the time period of the war, but in the old movies the soldiers actually broke into song."

Route 95 was so straight that at times it felt like we weren't moving at all. The miles were punctuated by stops at the rest areas, for gas or for a burger or to take a leak, which was an experience for me each time I unzipped my fly and saw the bandages, the new skin underneath, the piss taking a little longer to come out because I was concentrating on other things.

We pulled into a rest stop so my father could get a Coke to wake himself up. Anna said she'd be happy to drive, but my father said he was fine. When my father said he was fine people always believed him. He had that confidence, a steadiness that I felt was a key quality of manhood, real or movie. There were many parts to manhood, of course, and many kinds of men as I well knew, but a grown man, an adult man, could make others naturally rely upon him. When we traveled and my father said he was fine I was able to fall asleep without worrying. Maybe that was because I was his son, he had carried me around as a kid and driving was just an extension of that younger time, but he always was fine when he said so. He always was fine.

I watched my father and Anna walk into the rest station. They held hands easily and seemed oblivious to everyone who passed them. There was something about the movie star in both of them, that aloof quality that I'd seen in real stars walking around the city. Even the smallest stars had an aura about them, probably from being watched so long, probably from being pampered, from getting more sleep and eating better food and living in better apartments than most other people did. And part of the aura was just theirs, what had made them stars in the first place. My father held the door for Anna. She went inside and he followed. I stayed in the backseat, opened the car door so I could get some fresh air. It still hurt to walk around. The air smelled like spring, like the water was evaporating off the ground and spreading its fresh scent, strong enough to cut the exhaust and gasoline smells. People weren't wearing winter coats when they got out of their cars. The first row of palm trees would start soon enough.

It was strange that everyone I knew was in school. If I didn't get back soon I would miss the beginning of track season and with that could go all my potential scholarships. I assumed the coach would eventually try to track me down, what a good track coach should do, but he'd get no answer when he called. He'd join the long line of women on the answering machine asking to speak to Jared Chiziver. I doubted anyone would really miss me. No one had called after I'd been burned. A few absences in a row and a student was forgotten, as if he'd never existed. Social bonds loosened so quickly in school. I wondered if Michael had walked along the Hudson River since that night to see if I might be there stretching out after my run. He ran. He must have run. I heard him coughing and then he was gone. I wondered if he ran before the man finished burning me or if he ran when the ambulance arrived. I hoped he was scared. I could forgive him if he was scared.

I watched my father walking towards the car. He looked happy in the sunlight. He pushed his hat back on his head to get the light in his face, like he would start his tan here and be good-to-go once he got to Florida. He threw me a candy bar. I caught it. A Milky Way. Some habits were never broken. He took a sip from his soda and put the cup on the Valiant's roof. He blew into his hands. He put his finger in his mouth and I heard the brittle break of a nail. He inspected his finger and bit the tip of the nail off his next finger. Then he looked at his hand. He tried to make a fist, but it wouldn't close all the way.

"You need to get that looked at."

"Look," he said and held his hand out for me.

"Very funny."

"She'll be out in a minute. We'll make Miami by tonight without a problem."

"And then what?"

"Then we'll find a hotel and take a vacation. We need a vacation. The Florida sun will make us all better."

"Are we staying at the Holiday Inn?"

"No. We'll do it in style this time. I was thinking the Fontainebleau."

"We can't afford the Fontainebleau."

"We can afford it. Don't worry about money. Money's no object, as they used to say."

My father tipped his hat forward on his head and smiled. He still had his overcoat on. He really did look like a small-time gangster from another time against the backdrop of people in shirtsleeves.

"We need to keep some money for later," I said.

"We're going to live in Miami like we've never lived before. We've always loved the Fontainebleau."

It was true. We'd been going to Florida since I could remember. The first hotel we stayed at was called Attaché-by-the-Sea in Hollywood, Florida. It wasn't a bad hotel and they had a big pool and a high dive that I jumped off when I was five years old. My father had let me. He thought it was great that his kid was a fearless swimmer. I had fear, but seeing how proud my father was, I copied his poker face as I stood on the board and pretended I had none. My jumps weren't beautiful. I pinched my nose and squeezed my eyes shut, but I did jump. The Fontainebleau was an early memory too. As a kid, the hotel appeared gigantic to me. I remembered the downstairs lobby stretching forever, filled with plush chairs and shops that sold everything from beachwear to fountain ice-cream sodas, which my father bought me as a treat at the end of the day, the fizzle of seltzer tickling my throat. Everyone at the hotel looked relaxed and rich. I saw my father bump into a few people and excuse himself. As I got older I knew what the bumps meant. The Fontainebleau had once been the most famous hotel along the Miami beachfront. It was from another time, an art-deco crescent painted white.

"You think we can get a room there? Won't it be full?"

"We'll get a room. Maybe we'll even get a suite and stay for a while."

"I packed like we were going on a short vacation."

"Spartan existence. A pair of pants, a shirt, a bathing suit and you can live a full week in Florida without going to the laundromat once."

My father took the cup off the Valiant's roof and drank.

"Don't you want to walk around, stretch your legs?"

"I guess I should."

My father gave me his left hand and helped me out of the car. I walked to the gas pumps and back. Anna walked up to us, her lipstick fresh and red.

"Look at you two," she said.

"What?" my father said.

"It's hot out. Take off your coats. We're in the South."

"Tough guys keep their coats on as long as they can."

"Oh boy."

Anna reached into the car and took her camera from her bag. She looked at us through the lens. My father made a gun with his index finger and I did the same, pointed it straight ahead. Anna took the picture and another.

"Let me to take one of you," my father said.

"You drive, I take the pictures."

"So that's why you came along," I said.

"Maybe," she said.

"Is it really?"

Anna looked at me and then at my father.

"I came along for adventure. And other things."

"What other things?" my father said.

"I came along for you. To be with you."

"Good answer."

"Stop."

"No stopping now."

"Stop. It's more than an answer."

Anna kissed my father. His hands didn't push her away. I took the empty soda cup off the Valiant's roof and threw it away along with my candy wrapper. I took off my coat and walked back to the car. He was holding the door for her. She got in, we got in, and my father merged onto the straightaway of 95.

A few miles down the highway we caught up to the military caravan again. The guys started waving at the car before they could really see us. As we approached we saw their faces, all laughing and smiling, pointing at Anna.

"I'm well liked in the South," she said.

"Very well liked," my father said.

One of the soldiers was yelling something. My father told Anna to roll down her window. She made a face at my father, shook her head like he was a kid, like I sometimes shook my head at him.

"Go on," he said.

She rolled down her window and sat back in her seat, the wind pressing her hair against her face.

"New York City," the soldier yelled.

My father honked the horn.

"The Big Apple," the soldier yelled.

My father slowed the car, cut behind the truck, cut into the breakdown lane, sped up until he was parallel to the soldier. It was loud. Tires on gravel. Wind. Speed.

"Stop," Anna said. "You're crazy."

She was looking at my father, but I could see her smile, could see the beginning of a laugh, one of her open laughs, a laugh, I sometimes thought, that bordered the hysterical.

"Where you all headed?" the soldier yelled.

"South."

"How far south?"

"As far as we can go, soldier," my father said.

"U.S. infantry. Bravo Company," the soldier yelled and made a muscle, and then all the other guys in the truck made muscles.

My father lifted his arm and made a muscle too. They couldn't see it since he was still in his coat, but they all cheered anyway.

My father started singing "This Is the Army, Mr. Jones," screaming out the words so the soldiers could hear him above the speed and the highway noise. They were listening to the words like they'd never heard them before and they probably hadn't. This was an army that didn't sing the way the old army had, or at least the old army in my father's head.

The second time around some of the soldiers started catching on, sang the tune and as many words as they could remember. My father sang the words a third time. The soldiers joined him, singing and laughing. By the fourth time through everyone was belting out the lyrics. All the soldiers on the back of the truck. Anna. Me. My father leading us all, his good hand out the window, rising and falling like a conductor's. We went through the song over and over and then my father hit the horn, kept it there and the soldiers cheered and lifted their arms and shook their fists in victory. My father slowed the car, cut behind the truck, cut into the left lane and sped forward. He passed the truck and the next truck and the next, passed the whole army caravan, and for a moment it felt like we were the only civilian car on the highway. I could hear the cheers of the soldiers behind us, or at least it sounded that way. Maybe it was just the speed, the charge of gasoline through the old Valiant's engine.

We shot forward. My father knew how to make the big exit.

# 17

THE SMELL SAID WE WERE APPROACHING SAVANNAH. IT CAME through the closed windows, a foul chemical odor that we'd found out years ago was from the paper-making factories nearby. We pulled off the highway the way we always did to eat at Morrison's Cafeteria. It was a chain not found in the north, which was part of its charm. They had good catfish and great key lime pie, and like all on-the-road traditions it was something to look forward to, a marker for our trip. If we were driving south and eating at Morrison's, it meant there were many more miles behind us than ahead of us and Miami was within easy reach, a state away even if it was a long state, a thick finger pointing into the Atlantic. My father wanted Anna to experience our yearly drive the way we drove it, meaningful markers and all, so we stopped for a late lunch. It was nice walking into the familiar cafeteria and seeing all those plates of food lined up on the glass counters, the most striking colors the cherry and grape Jell-O offset by the whitest whipped cream.

Morrison's held no memory for Anna, but I could tell that she liked it right away. She always surveyed her surroundings, a new room or a different view, as if she were trying to figure out the composition of her next photograph. She surveyed people too. She would look at them as if she were far away and then, at least with my father and me, she would look at us like she was the closest person in the world, as if she would be happy to cup her face with her hands and stare straight at us forever. My father did that too. He looked closely. In *Breathless*, Belmondo rolls up a poster of a painted woman and looks at Jean Seberg through the hole like a director looking through a camera. My father had no rolled-up poster, but he watched Anna taking in the cafeteria, studied her studying it.

"The famous Morrison's Cafeteria," she said.

"Famous for us," my father said. "And it sure beats McDonald's."

We each took a tray and slid it along the counter's metal groove built specifically for sliding. I pictured some worker greasing the groove every morning so the trays would move smooth and fast. We all got the same thing, Anna following our Morrison's tradition. Catfish with tartar sauce. Greens. Mashed potatoes with gravy doled out by a man in a chef's hat. There were plenty of pre-cut pieces of key lime pie stacked on the dessert shelves and we each took a plate of pie. I put a plate of cherry Jell-O on my tray. The driving had made me hungry.

"Take all you can eat, but eat all that you take," my father said.

He was in military mode, he'd sung to the soldiers, so he was promoting the army's way of eating. I lifted my eyebrow in an exaggerated arch.

"At ease," my father said.

My father opened his wallet and paid for our meal. The cafeteria was a tough place to take from since the cashier was standing right there. I saw the thick wad of bills in my father's wallet and guessed that there was more money hidden in his pockets. So far, on this trip, I'd seen my father pay for everything. All the money that was under the sink could keep us going for months in New York, but there wasn't that much if we were really going to stay at the Fontainebleau.

We found a table at the far end of the cafeteria. My father liked to sit in corners or at the far end of dining rooms so he could survey the room. He said he'd learned that trick from Wild Bill Hickok in *The Plainsman,* who always sat with his back to the wall, afraid of being shot in the back. Belmondo was shot in the back. My father learned his moves from movies. And he liked a wide perspective before he zoomed in. Sometimes I pictured my father at the highest part of Fifth Avenue, looking over all the people breaking for lunch, a colorful sea of pedestrians with my father at the top of the wave. He would choose one person and move toward that person and take from that person and disappear into the crowd, underwater, only to resurface somewhere else.

The catfish was fried and crispy and tasted great with tartar sauce and squeezed lemon and the mashed potatoes were real and not from a mix. The best part of the meal was the key lime pie. Anna took a bite and said it was delicious, certainly worth the trip.

"Are limes the key to the pie or is it a key lime, named after the Florida Keys?" my father said, holding a piece of pie on a fork in front of his face, inspecting the layers of crust and green and cream with exaggerated intensity. "That is one of the great mysteries. One day I have to find the Morrison's pastry chef and ask him."

"Why not drive to the Keys and find out," Anna said.

"We've never gone there. Have you?"

"I always wanted to go to Cuba. I suppose Key West would be the next best thing."

"We can take a day trip there," my father said.

"Maybe we should go to Key West instead of Miami," I said.

"You love Miami."

"We could try something different. We don't need to go to the Fontainebleau. We could find a place in Key West. There must be plenty of hotels there."

"We're going to the Fontainebleau. I've got this trip all planned out."

"Do you?"

"I do," he said. "I've planned the trip of a lifetime. Now eat your key lime pie and let me worry about the details."

I did as I was told. I rarely argued with my father anyway and I knew, even though I didn't know the exact details preceding this trip of a lifetime, that I was somehow responsible for our drive south. The Jell-O was too cold. The whipped cream was too sweet. I asked Anna if she wanted to try some, but she said that anything that glowed neon bright was not going inside her stomach. My father walked up to the counter to get another piece of pie. Anna watched him walk.

"Have you ever been to Florida?" I said.

"I've been there before. Not for a few years."

"Have you ever driven to Florida?"

"No, this is the first time. The other times I've flown."

"Does anyone know you're with us?"

"Don't worry. No one's keeping tabs on me."

"Just checking," I said. "You can't be too careful."

"No, you can't," she said.

"I'm just making sure."

"Are you always this careful?"

"Obviously not."

"Stop. I didn't mean it like that."

"I'm this careful now. I have a feeling I have to be. I just wanted to make sure you were with us. With my father and me."

"I'm with you," she said.

She was looking hard at me. Her eyes didn't move.

"Here," she said and took the fork from her pie plate and put it through the red Jell-O. She took off a bite-size chunk, put it in her mouth and swallowed, her eyes on mine the whole time.

"A Jell-O pact," she said. "Cherry Jell-O redder than blood. Thicker than water. Okay?"

"Okay," I said.

My father returned with his pie.

"I love this stuff," he said. "How's your Jell-O?"

"It's very red," I said.

"Have another bite of key lime," he said to Anna, putting a fork full of pie in front of her mouth.

"I'm done," she said.

"One more bite. This bite will taste like Cuba."

"Stop," she said.

He put the piece in her mouth, a smudge of whipped cream on her upper lip.

"Havana," he said.

She wiped the cream from her lip, laughing.

My father finished his pie, left a few bucks on the table for the busboys and we walked back to the car. The sun was low in the sky. The Valiant stood out in the parking lot, its gold color and boxy shape.

We drove south.


When we passed the first palm trees, their open fronds always a signal of optimism for my father and me, he pointed them out, but I had already seen them. We were officially far from New York. Soon we drove past the Florida border and stopped in the Welcome Station for free orange juice, a routine left over from when I was much younger and needed as many breaks as I could get. As a kid, the concept of free juice, or free anything, was too good to pass up. I had been too young to see the irony that much of the orange juice I drank in New York was free, or at least not paid for. In the Welcome Station there were stacks of brochures for all the sights in the state, the Monkey Jungle and the Alligator Tours and Disney World and the glass-bottom boat rides in Silver Springs. When I'd been a kid I used to grab all the colorful brochures, which gave me something to look at in the car during the final push to Miami. I didn't take any brochures, drank just one cup of free orange juice.

Route 95 became crowded as we approached Miami and when we passed the signs for West Palm Beach the highway seemed to transform into a city avenue. It was still an interstate route, it was still 95, but the cars jockeyed for position as if they were on Fifth Avenue, rushing to get downtown. Horns went off. Lane lines weren't followed. A broken-down car plugged up the left lane. For stretches of the highway it was stop and go, stop and go, like a Manhattan traffic jam. The cars themselves also looked New York City. For most of the trip the roads had been full of Chevys and Fords, practical family cars, and annoying SUVs that blocked the view in front of us. This part of 95 had the rich cars that I was used to seeing at home. Mercedes. BMWs. Porsches. Jaguars. It felt like we were in the city even though we weren't in the city. There was speed in the air, the speed of possibility, of summer nights, and Florida had summer nights year round. I always loved coming into Miami. Maybe it was because it was our vacation spot every year. Maybe it was the new look of the landscape. Maybe it was the clean ocean and the Olympic-sized pools. Maybe it was me and my father and no one else, sharing a hotel room and having fun. When he was in Miami my father didn't go out, didn't come home drunk, didn't do anything but spend time with me and during those two weeks, every year, I never thought about the past because the two of us were constantly present together.

It was night, but still light from all the lights on the highway. In the summer there were always thunderstorms in the afternoon and one time, driving into Miami, a bolt of lightning had actually touched down on a light pole next to our car. The snap of thunder reached us immediately, no distance for the sound to travel.

We drove past the different towns. Delray Beach. Boca Raton. Pompano Beach. Fort Lauderdale. Past the sign for Hollywood where we'd stayed when we'd first come to Miami, where I learned to swim, where I felt my first memorable pain, and the memory made my new skin burn. I was on top of the high dive. My father sat on a lounge chair below. I waved. He waved back. He was always watching me. Around water. On the high dive. In the city. When I was very young he let me wander, but he was always there. I stood on the high dive and looked down at the water to feel the light feeling in my five-year-old stomach, part of the thrill, most of the thrill, which went from my stomach down to my crotch. I curled my toes over the board. I closed my eyes, held my nose, jumped, felt the lightness in my stomach increase. On the way down my body must have fallen forward. Instead of hitting the water feet first, I did a belly flop that knocked the air out of me. I couldn't breath when I came up. I opened my eyes and forced myself to swim to the edge of the pool, no air coming in, forcing myself to get to the edge, and I held on until I was able to pull myself out. I went to my father and that's when I started crying, finally able to breathe, losing my breath in sobs. My father said he'd seen my beautiful belly flop. He told me I was fine. He held me until I stopped crying. I sometimes wondered why he hadn't jumped into the water to save me. I think it was because he had seen me swim. I was hurt, but not so hurt that I couldn't make it out by myself. Maybe that was the lesson he was always teaching me. Like the motto *run within yourself*. Run as fast as you can, but not so fast that you can't complete the race. Like the military food motto. *Take all you can eat, but eat all that you take.* Like diving off the high dive. Take the risk as long as you can make it out. I hurt myself, but I made it out. That was the lesson. That was how my father lived. When he took. When he went out. But as we drove south it seemed different somehow. There were three of us instead of two of us, but it was more than that. I had a nervous feeling in my stomach, like I was falling, but I didn't know if I could take the drop or the pain at the end of the drop. I had taken the pain, but this was different. I didn't know where the end would be, where we'd hit water. I knew that if the drop lasted too long, getting out was impossible. Jumping off the Brooklyn Bridge killed people. With too much speed the water turned hard as city concrete.


The sign said Miami. My father wove through the traffic, as if he were on Fifth Avenue outcabbing the cabbies. We had driven down one whole side of America. A long drop from New York City.

We got onto Route 1, the beachfront avenue, and drove past all the hotels. The old people had eaten their dinners and were inside. Young men and women walked the sidewalks, some in bathing suits and sunglasses, beautiful bodies everywhere, bare feet in sandals, palm trees lining the way. I saw a kid about my age walking alone with a towel draped over his neck, his legs thin and smooth, his head bent like he was counting the cracks in the sidewalk. There was something in how he walked from his thin hips, aloof but aware that he was being watched by someone, somewhere, that made me wonder if he was like me.

"There it is," my father said.

And there it was. The Fontainebleau.

"It's beautiful," she said.

"I told you."

"You did tell me."

It was majestic, curved and white, poised to take in the sun. My father pulled in hard, stopped hard, parked right in front of the lobby. He got out of the car before Anna could and walked forward, his shoulders rolling.

Anna and I waited in the car.

"Remember," I said.

"I remember."

"You ate that Jell-O."

"Yes. Yes, I did."

She didn't turn around, but she nodded her head once, for me, for her, for my father, nodding just like he did. That's what happened when you were with someone for some time. If Michael and I had gotten to know each other, I might have done things like he did. And he might have done things like me.

My father came out smiling, walking tough, but looser now, loose from having done what he'd done and loose from the warm night. He'd walked in with his coat, but now he held it. The muscles in his arms filled his white T-shirt. His hat was pushed back on his head so that his face was all there, ready to take the sun full-force if the sun had been out and it would be, tomorrow. He tanned well. I guessed Anna tanned well. I was fairer than my father, not my hair, but my skin, and my skin always went red before it went brown. My father leaned into the window.

"We are officially checked into the Fontainebleau. I always wanted to say that."

"It's the Fontainebleau Hilton now," I said.

"It's still the Fontainebleau."

It wasn't as beautiful as it had been, but he pretended not to see that. I left it alone.

My father popped the trunk and we got out of the car. A bellhop placed our three bags and my father's duffel bag on his cart, a lighter load than what he was probably used to. We followed him and the cart through the lobby, into the elevator, up to the top floor, along the plush corridor and into the room, two king-sized beds and a big screen TV and beyond that a large sliding window that the bellhop opened so the night breeze could come in. My father walked out on the balcony and lifted his arms.

"This is the life," he said.

Anna and I went out on the balcony. The Atlantic Ocean was before us, the waves breaking evenly, white-topped, and beyond that the dark blue, black really, that touched the sky, a nighttime horizon that didn't seem so far away. If it had been a film, it would have been a good shot. It wasn't the kind of photograph Anna would take. There were no half-dead men or full-dead men that she could see. I looked at her and she was taking it all in. My father went into the room to tip the bellhop and came back out on the balcony.

He stood straight. He looked straight at the ocean. He made his left hand into a fist and beat his chest on the balcony of the Fontainebleau, where he'd always wanted to stay.

"Mighty," he said.

# 18

I WOKE BEFORE THEY DID. I GOT OUT OF BED, QUIETLY PUT on my bathing suit and went down to the pool, partly because I wanted to stretch my muscles and partly to give my father and Anna some time alone.

I walked through the plush lobby of the Fontainebleau. I understood why my father wanted to stay here. It was different from any hotel we'd been in, wide and airy and rich. It was the comfort that came with money. It was the comfort of safety, or at least a good illusion. In Manhattan protection came from doormen and taxi rides. In Miami it was the large lobbies with the sea air coming in and the dimpled white stucco that seemed to keep the world and all its hardness out there, far away. I walked out the safe side of the lobby, beachfront, not streetfront. The sun was already bright. I'd forgotten to pack sunglasses and would have to get a cheap pair at one of the sidewalk stands.

I had kept my burn out of the water for the time the doctors told me. I was nervous about every new thing I did with my burn, but I was back in Florida, the place where I'd first jumped in, and it was time to start living again. It would be time to start running soon. I took off my shirt and walked to the pool. It was shaped like a lagoon, an elongated clover shape with palms all around and a waterfall. It had that aqua-blue, shimmering quality that comes just after the water has been freshly cleaned and chlorinated. I dipped my foot in. It was cold. I waded in on the steps. My father said how once you got your crotch under water it was easy to adjust to the temperature. He never waded in, he just dove, but that was his theory anyway. I got up to my crotch and shivered once. It was a strong shiver. I had been burned and the burn was still fresh in my memory. I felt the puke in my throat and forced it down. I breathed in, held it, lowered myself into the water, to my chest, to my neck and then dipped my head. I started to swim. I did the breaststroke, slowly, methodically, aware of every part of my body, moving my legs until I felt the pain and then moving them just a little more, just past it. I thought it might be good to push the pain just a little. That was my theory.

I swam back and forth, the cool water going over me, and I relaxed into the laps. The sun warmed me and the palm trees were still, coconuts bursting just under the fronds. People started coming down from their rooms.

I swam until I felt more tired than hurt. I missed that fatigue. I swam to the steps and climbed out of the pool and wiped the water off me. The pool boy was walking around with towels. I walked to the beach chair where I'd left my things, put on some lotion, pointed the chair to the sun. I imagined my father and Anna waking up, his hand moving to her, between her legs, touching her, her hand touching him and then he would be inside her and move and move the way he did, the grace from his springy walk in his movements inside her, the energy focused on her and maybe then he would see the way I had seen with Michael, after I came, when the world seemed to slow down and the night became clear, like I could see further, like I could see the brightness of every light, the sharpness of every line and maybe he would see what he had to do, how we really couldn't stay here too long. Maybe Anna would see too and help him with his decision. Or they would both come down and ask me what I thought and together we would figure out the details, beyond the details that my father had figured out. He had a plan, but it wasn't a plan I should hear and that worried me.

The sun dried me quickly. I almost fell asleep, that stage where the sounds start to get far away. I heard her laugh far away, her repetition of *Stop, stop* before she laughed some more. He was entertaining her, joking for her. I heard beach chairs being pulled along pool tiles. I opened my eyes and there they were, my father in a new bathing suit he must have found in the gift shop and Anna in a bikini. Her toes were painted red. My father was tipping the pool boy.

"How was it?" Anna said.

I squinted my eyes so I could look up at her.

"It's a strange pool to swim in. You can't exactly do laps."

"I meant how did you feel?"

"It hurt a little, not much."

"Good," my father said. "Great. You'll be fine in no time. Is it cold?"

"Once I got to that all-important level it wasn't so bad."

"Put a towel over your bathing suit in case the sun gets through. Scars shouldn't be in the sun."

"And you put some lotion on."

"I will."

My father believed that if you combined different lotions with different SPFs they would equal a good number. A sun protection of 3 and a sun protection of 8 would add up to a safer 11. He knew it was ridiculous, but insisted it was true.

"Put on fifteen," I said.

"I'll put on whatever adds up to fifteen."

"My father thinks you can add up SPFs," I said.

"You can," he said.

"Maybe in your world, but not in the real world."

"Top of the world, baby."

"The ozone is ripped at the top of the world."

My father put his arm against mine.

"Look at that," he said. "Not a mark on me and that's from my special lotion combinations. I have it down to a science."

"Well, put some fifteen on anyway." I threw him the bottle.

My father did Anna's back left-handed, then walked to the pool's edge. He dove in and started doing laps as best he could in the lapless pool.

"So how do you like the Fontainebleau?" Anna said.

"I can't believe we're actually here. We used to walk through the lobby, but that was as far as we got. Our hotel always looked tiny compared to this place."

"It's all relative. I've stayed in some Manhattan hotel rooms that were bigger than most people's apartments. The bathrooms had more money put into them than some people make in a year."

"Why did you stay in hotel rooms if you live in Manhattan?"

"Friends come in sometimes."

"Do you have a lot of friends?"

"No. Not really."

"Do you have a lot of acquaintances?"

She knew I was testing her.

"I don't stay in hotel rooms with acquaintances."

"Good. I think that's good. I wonder how many Manhattan hotel rooms my father has stayed in."

"Does he have a lot of friends?"

"He has no friends."

If my father had friends, real friends, real connections, I think he would have been calmer year round. Whenever he returned from

176

our summers in Miami, the pattern started. He'd say he was restless and he'd go out and I knew exactly how he'd be the next morning. Sometimes he seemed to hate his life. Sometimes he stopped going out for a few weeks, didn't meet women, didn't drink, but it never lasted. I was happy he'd met Anna. More than happy. The man that my father could be was clearer now that I'd seen him with her. But he was with Anna in Miami and we had left New York and it was all relative. Eventually he might see his days away from New York from the long shot, distill them into one day, and then he'd need a new high, a movie-high, even if it were reality. I hoped he wouldn't. I hoped that wasn't part of his plan.

"I've seen bathrooms like that," I said. "There's another world out there. And here. This is another world."

Anna sighed. Maybe she knew I was thinking about worlds with a different scale. Worlds less restless.

"Were you close to your parents?" I said.

"Not like you and your father. You rely on each other. My world had big bathrooms."

"And big kitchens. Your father was a chef."

"Yes," she said. "Yes, he was. You remembered. It's a world you can get used to very quickly. I think it affected my work."

"It did?"

"I think if things are too easy then they're too easy. I grew up with money so I always forced myself to live low after I moved out, to not get too comfortable."

"But then it's just an act."

"Perhaps. Perhaps not. If I don't live extravagantly, then I'm not living extravagantly."

"We've always lived like Spartans. That's why I don't know what we're doing here."

"Your father needed a vacation. You needed a vacation."

"This isn't a real vacation. He's on the run."

"Stop," she said.

"It's true. You know that."

"I don't know anything."

"Sure you do. In *Breathless* the American woman pretends not to know anything at first. But she knows."

"Your father had to leave New York. And you're his son."

"And what are you?"

She didn't say anything.

"Do you love him or is this just a ride for you?"

She didn't say anything.

"I'm asking you a question."

"I've seen *Breathless*."

"Good. So do you love him or is it a ride?"

"In *Breathless*, did the American woman love him?"

"You tell me."

Anna pulled her hair behind her ear, like after she laughed especially hard, but she wasn't laughing.

"Yes," Anna said. "I think she did."

In the movie it's hard to tell. In the movie they're watching each other so much they rarely talk, really talk. In the movie she says to Belmondo, *I want you to love me, and at the same time, I don't want you to. I want my freedom.* In the movie she says, *Between grief and nothing, I will take nothing* and Belmondo responds, *Grief is only a compromise, and you've got to have all or nothing.* That's it. The line. The big line. All or nothing. That's why we were at the Fontainebleau and why he was with Anna and why, I knew, he was running.

"Look how happy he looks," she said and I thought I saw all or nothing in the way she gazed at my father moving through the water.

"He loves to swim," I said.

Anna put on a pair of movie-star sunglasses and leaned back in her chair. Her hands were at her sides, fingers open and easy. I realized my own hands were clenched. I loosened them.

"My dad liked to swim also," she said. "We had a house right on the ocean in St. Martin and he swam every day. That was the purest thing he did. He'd go out even when there were jellyfish washed up on the beach and no one else dared set foot in the water."

"I hate jellyfish."

"Have you ever been stung?"

"Once when I was a kid. By one of those little man-o'-wars. It happened right up the beach from here. In Hollywood. So does your dad still swim?"

"He's dead."

"I'm sorry."

"He was old. He had me when he was old. I'm the youngest of three by many years."

"My father and I are both only children."

And I thought how we were alike in that, only children and only children, just kids in a way, staying at the Fontainebleau, the first ones in the pool. Everyone else seemed more adult, more settled. I looked at the people on their beach chairs. There wasn't a restless body in sight.

"The city seems far away," I said.

"We'll go into Miami proper and get our fix later."

"Do you have your camera on you?"

"I always have a camera. I have my point-and-shoot in my bag."

"Take one of my father swimming. He gets lost when he's swimming. That's pure happiness in his face."

"You really are like the father sometimes," she said.

"Just sometimes."

Anna sat up and took off her glasses. She looked at my father and took the camera from her bag.

"You're right," she said. "Unadulterated joy. Capturing joy on film is the hardest thing to capture. Here."

She held the camera out to me.

"No," I said. "You take it."

"He's your father. You've known him your whole life. Take the photograph at the exact moment when you see his joy the most."

"You know him too."

"Not like you. You have a history with him that I don't have."

"My father doesn't believe in history. You take it."

"Go on. All you have to do is point the camera at him and press this button on top. Get him right at the moment you think is best."

"What about the composition? What about all that stuff our art teacher told us about?"

"Forget that. Forget all of that. Focus on your father. See what comes out."

My father was swimming towards us, doing the breaststroke, his body lit by the sun, the palm tress behind him, the beach behind the trees, then the ocean.

"Go on," she said.

I took the camera and pointed it at my father. I waited until he was completely on the up part of the stroke, when it looked like his whole body might lift out of the water and I pressed the button.

"Go on," she said. "I have plenty of film."

I took another and another, focusing on him coming up and up, waiting for his eyes to be completely open, the smile in them not for anyone else but himself, the smile in his eyes from enjoying the heat and the water and just being, in the moment. When he came too close, when I knew he would shift his focus to us, I stopped taking pictures and handed her the camera.

"You have steady hands," she said.

She put the camera in her bag and took my hands in hers. She pressed my fingers together.

"No holes," she said.

"Where?"

"Between your fingers there aren't any spaces. You'd survive in the desert. You'd come to an oasis and you could drink water without spilling. Jared has holes."

"Maybe my mother had no holes."

"Maybe she didn't."

"He never talks about her. But maybe she had no spaces between her fingers. I had to get that from someone."

"Your father has perfect hands for what he does. The holes probably make his hands feel lighter. And they're steady. Steadier than yours even. They're the steadiest hands I've ever seen."

"When did he tell you about what he does?"

"He didn't. That's how we met."

"He was taking from you?"

"I love how you two say that. No, he wasn't taking from me. Although I'm sure he could have."

"He could have," I said and I heard the pride in my voice, proud that my father was best at some things.

"I have no doubt he could have taken from me," Anna said and smiled.

"So how did you meet him?"

"I was walking down Fifth Avenue during lunch hour and this man rubbed his hand against my ass. He did it once and then again. The third time there was no mistake about it. There was no mistake about the first time, but the third time made it official. I turned around and told the lecherous bastard to go fuck himself. He called me every degrading name in the book, but when I took out my cell phone and told him I was calling the cops he shut up. Your father was standing a few feet away, smiling. I didn't know what he was smiling about so I started to stare him down, but when I looked closely I saw that he was simply amused. The man that had touched me started walking away and bumped right into your father. Your father moved him out of the way and the man kept walking. Then your father came over to me. He was still smiling. He said he had a gift."

"I bet I know what the gift was."

"He took me out to lunch on the man's money."

"You didn't care?"

"The man was a shit."

"The people he takes from aren't all shits," I said.

"I'm sure they're not. But everyone steals from everyone in some way. Little stealing. Like your father says."

"What do you steal?"

Anna lifted her sunglasses so she could look at me, eyes to eyes.

"I'm stealing some time with your father. I'm taking some photographs of a man on the run."

"That's honest."

"It is," she said.

She was looking closely at me.

"So what do you steal, Ben?"

"I don't know."

"That's a safe answer."

"I let him do the stealing."

"You let him take."

"I let him steal my past. It's part of the deal we've made as father and son."

Anna didn't say anything.

"Big stealing," I said. "That's what I'm afraid of."

My father was walking towards us, dripping. He pulled his hand through his hair.

"That was great," he said. "It's not exactly a lap pool, but I did ten grotto-lengths. Ten Olympic-length grottos. That's the distance we use here at the Fontainebleau. I can feel it in my arms."

He made a fist with his right hand, but it didn't close all the way. It was still purple.

"I'm ready for a drink," he said. "I did my exercise and I'm ready to start this vacation. What will it be?"

"I haven't exercised yet," Anna said.

"Get in the pool. Do some grotto lengths. Do some Olympic-length grottos."

"I'll have vodka," she said.

"Vodka for the lady. And what will the young man have?"

"The young man is underage."

"Not today. What will you have? We're on vacation."

"I'll have what you're having."

"I was thinking margaritas. A little sweet. A little sour. A lot of tequila."

"I'm switching my order," Anna said.

"Margaritas all around. Come with me, Ben. Let's go rustle up some ingredients and get this party started."

I sat up and squinted at the sun.

"I need sunglasses," I said.

"We can rustle those up too."


We drove down Collins Avenue and stopped at a little strip mall. First we went into a tacky gift shop that sold everything for the incoming tourist. My father looked over magazines and sundries while I stayed in the background trying on sunglasses from the rack. I found a pair I liked, round lenses that stayed close to my eyes. I nodded my head, just a little, and put the sunglasses back on the rack. Someone else came into the store and the cashier's focus went there. We walked out of the shop, the sunglasses snug in the waistband of my father's trunks. He was fast. Sometimes he would joke about how fast he was. He would raise his hand over a rack of shirts in a department store, or a display of sneakers in a sports store, wave his hand once with a quick flourish, like a magician, pretending he'd made everything disappear.

We went into a liquor store and my father bought two bottles of tequila, a bottle of Cointreau, a bottle of sour mix and three heavy glasses. He paid cash. We went into a supermarket and got two dozen limes, a box of kosher salt and a pitcher. He paid cash for these as well. If he'd worn a coat he could have filled his pockets with the limes, but it was Florida and it was hot. If he'd worn a coat it would have been one of those telling details like in a B movie where the bad guy walks by and something seems off and it's because he has a coat on to conceal something. That's the mistake that leads to the arrest. A coat in the summer. No one wore coats in Miami.

We drove back to the Fontainebleau. The sunlight was already so strong that the vinyl seats burned the bare skin under our legs. My father had to handle the steering wheel gingerly. The Valiant's gold exterior turned almost white under the glare.

We went up to the room. He cut the limes in half and told me to squeeze them into the pitcher. I knew his hand was hurting. I squeezed the limes while he got ice. The green pulp looked tart. He poured in the alcohol, three parts tequila to one part Cointreau, added the sour mix and tasted the margarita.

"You can always add, but you can't take away."

He added a little more Cointreau, took a sip, said it was perfect.

We took the elevator down and my father set up shop on a small beverage table next to our chairs. He asked the pool boy to get him a plate from the kitchen and the pool boy came back a minute later with a plate. My father put the kosher salt on the plate, bit a hole into a lime, rubbed the top of each glass, pressed the glasses into the plate until the rims were perfectly salted. He put ice in each glass and poured the margaritas. It made the sound of summer refreshment.

"To a great vacation," my father said, lifting his glass.

"To a great vacation," Anna repeated.

"To now," my father said.

I didn't say anything.

We touched glasses. The margarita was sweet and strong, cold and hot at the same time. The tequila burned the back of my throat.

We stayed in the sun and drank. I closed my eyes behind my new sunglasses and let the warmth take me over. When I drank with my friends it was always a rush to get drunk, a quick buzz, and then there was all that talk about how wasted everyone was. It was boring. Drinking margaritas poolside, the elegant Fontainebleau behind us, the lagoon-shaped pool before us, the sun high in the sky easing everything out, felt like a vacation. I pretended it was complete joy. I closed my eyes and I could feel my cock getting hard under my bathing suit.

I was in and out of sleep. My father's voice and Anna's voice were in the background at times, at times I heard glasses refilled, at times I thought I heard the Atlantic's waves breaking onto the sand. When I got up I was wet from the heat. I went into the pool. The alcohol took the edge off my burn so it was easy to swim. When I was done I put on some more lotion and told my father to put some on. He poured me another margarita.

A calypso band started playing at the other end of the pool. Drums and a bass guitar and one of those cone-shaped metal drums, which were often played in the subway stations and sounded like the Caribbean. The lead singer had a Jamaican accent. I was drunk enough to think everyone else was probably drunk. The tequila was in my father's eyes. He was looking at the band and smiling, his feet moving to the rhythm automatically. I couldn't see Anna's eyes behind her movie-star sunglasses, but she was smiling too. The singer went from one song to another and then he announced it was time for the famous Orange Dance contest with some very excellent prizes. He announced the rules of the game. Couples had to place an orange between their foreheads and dance. If the music was slow they had to dance slow. If the music was fast they had to dance fast. The couple that danced longest without dropping the orange would be champions of the Orange Dance.

Some couples got up from their chairs and started walking to the band.

"Can you dance?" my father said to Anna.

"What kind of question is that?"

"I've never seen you dance. I'm guessing you're a wonderful dancer, but I might be wrong."

"Can you dance?" she said, stretching out the you, a mock-challenge in the line of her mouth.

"Of course I can dance. I make Baryshnikov look stiff. Can you dance?"

"I can dance."

"Can you dance with an orange?"

"I've never danced with an orange."

"I don't like to lose," my father said.

"I like to win," Anna said.

"*Bonjour,*" my father said.

He stood up from his chair, took a breath as the alcohol settled into his upright position, reached out his hand, lifted Anna up and held her so she wouldn't have to balance herself the way he had.

"What are the prizes?" I said.

"I dance for more than the prize," my father said and spun himself away from Anna, then stood there, one hand on his stomach, one hand in the air.

His eyes were lit and he knew it. He smiled. He didn't need to pretend he wasn't drunk. He didn't need to hide, not in the safety of the pool area at the Fontainebleau.

I followed them to the band and stood with the other spectators. There were nine couples, and each couple was given an orange. I watched my father hold the orange in his left hand, as if he was just holding it, but I saw the muscles working as he squeezed the fruit. He was always looking for the angle. A flattened orange was easier to dance with than a hard, round one. I watched him place the orange on his forehead, just above his nose, and he brought Anna to him and she pressed her forehead against the orange. My father took her around the waist. They moved in a circle. Then he took the orange from between their heads and worked it in his hand some more while the bandleader repeated the rules in his exaggerated Jamaican accent. When the music was slow the brave contestants had to dance slow. When the music was fast the brave contestants had to dance fast. If the brave contestants didn't dance fast enough, they would be disqualified. If they touched the orange with their hands they would be disqualified. If the orange fell they would be disqualified. If they drank frozen orange juice they would be disqualified. Everyone laughed at that. The bandleader wished everyone luck. He told the couples to place the oranges between their heads. He walked around to make sure everyone was set. Then he pointed at the musicians and they started to play.

At first the music was slow. The couples had no problem moving in easy circles, the oranges between their heads. Some of the couples were laughing. Some were taking it very seriously. My father was the only one talking. He was telling Anna how to move, telling her how easy it was, smiling for her, his hips moving in rhythm to hers. The bandleader pointed at the musicians and the musicians picked up the musical pace. The couples had to move in faster circles and the oranges started to drop. Two couples were sent to the sidelines, then a third and a fourth. There were five couples left and the bandleader signaled the musicians to play faster. The bandleader was telling the couples to dance, to shake their butts, to sway their hips, to feel the music, to hold those oranges in place. The crowd was growing, people coming to see all the excitement. I looked at their eyes to see if they were drunk. Another orange fell and the couple was sent to the sideline.

"Dance, dance, dance, shake it like you mean it and dance," the bandleader shouted into the mike.

One couple started laughing as their orange rolled all the way over to one side of their foreheads and then all the way to the other side and then the orange fell and they were out. My father was talking to Anna and she was talking back. They were saying how easy it was to each other. Their bodies were moving together. I could see them in bed, talking, working each other to where they wanted each other to be. It didn't bother me. Not at all. I thought of how I would move with a man. I ran gracefully. I would move gracefully. I had touched him gracefully. I would touch others gracefully when I was ready. It seemed pure under the Florida sun, and with the tequila in my veins. It was pure. Barrow's Pub was far away.

The bandleader was next to my father and Anna. He was telling the crowd it looked like we had a couple of ringers. The music got faster. Another orange dropped and the couple walked away.

It was down to two couples. My father and Anna and a young couple with dark tans. They looked alike, more brother and sister than lovers and maybe they were. The two oranges looked steady. The bandleader pointed to the musicians.

My father and Anna moved round and round, fast and fast. The other couple moved as fast. The bandleader pointed at the musicians again and the metal drum sounds echoed off the pool, loud, the two couples moving, the oranges holding them together, bound by the symbol of Florida, foreheads pressing in, eyes close, hips moving, feet moving, round and round and round. The crowd was getting into it, screaming for the couples to keep going. The bandleader was circling the couples with his microphone, telling them to dance, dance, dance. The orange between my father and Anna started to roll sideways. They steadied it and moved it back to the center of their foreheads. The orange of the other couple started to roll. First to the side and then down. The guy crouched to even it up. They were still dancing round and round. The bandleader was yelling *Dance, dance, dance.* People were clapping. People were shouting. The orange started to roll, and roll some more and the guy lurched to steady it but he couldn't and it fell and my father and Anna kept dancing, their orange in place, moving in fast circles, not yet knowing they had won, still trying to win, but they had won already and the bandleader tapped my father on the shoulder and announced that this brave couple was the winner.

My father took the orange from between their foreheads and kissed Anna just for her. The crowd started whistling. My father and Anna came over to me and took me in their circle. I was too drunk to be embarrassed. I was drunk enough to be happy.

The bandleader handed my father a bottle of champagne and a gift certificate for dinner at a local seafood restaurant. My father un corked the champagne, took a swig, Anna took a swig, I took a swig and then he passed the bottle to the couple who had come in second place and they drank too. The sun was past the midway point in the sky. I shielded my eyes in my taken sunglasses to look at it.

The band started playing a new song and the crowd returned to their pool chairs. My father tossed me the orange they'd won with. It had been squeezed soft. I lifted the orange to my nose to breathe in the sweet scent. The grove from where it had been picked was still inside. That connection remained.

# 19

WE DRANK EVERY DAY. I WOULD DRINK ENOUGH TO TAKE THE pain away and then drink a little more, like the way I was swimming, pushing harder each day. They drank more than I did. The three of us were turning darker. The alcohol lit up my father's eyes and he was more handsome than ever, his hair made blonder by the sun, his eyes clear and green, lit.

It felt like a vacation. It was an art to keep the buzz steady, to drink just enough so that it wasn't too much. I knew theirs was steadier, but they never went too far or got sick. If this went against my father's all-or-nothing philosophy, it was fine with me. In New York I sometimes heard him puke, the end product of his night out flushed down the toilet or caught in a plastic bag, but here his drinking was without regret. My father seemed to know just how many drinks he needed and Anna needed and how much I needed. I let him decide when to make me a fresh margarita. When I felt the buzz I would drink a little more and then stop. They were also smoking cigarettes, a lot of cigarettes. They never offered me any and I wouldn't have taken.

I lost track of what day was what day, or if it was late morning or early afternoon. Sometimes I would close my eyes and then when I opened them it would be evening. Time seemed to be happening far away, flowing smoothly on its own, the sun moving across the sky inevitably, but the inevitability wasn't sad since everything seemed to blend with the alcohol as easily as the gentle swaying of the palm fronds. In school the clock was in constant focus. When would the period end? When would the day end? When would track practice end? When would the alarm go off to start it all over again? But at the Fontainebleau we woke when we woke, we slept when we slept, we swam when we swam, we ate when we were hungry, we drank just enough from morning to night. Some could judge my father completely derelict for handing drinks to his son, a minor. He wanted me to be happy.

Some days my father would take the car into Miami and come back a few hours later with something to eat, Indian River grapefruits or cheesecake from The Cheesecake Factory, like he'd made the excursion just to get food.

Some days Anna would leave the hotel and go to a darkroom she'd found at a local college. She'd return with her photographs, the paper still smelling of chemicals, and bring the ones she liked best down to the pool for us to see. There were a few of me taken when I wasn't looking. I looked tan and healthy, but in most of the shots my eyes were distracted. Through her lens, she saw me clearly, saw how the Miami vacation was just pretend for me. My father's eyes had none of that concern. He was just drunk enough, just far away from the world enough, just now enough where the pretending had disappeared. In the now of each photograph, swimming in the pool, sitting in a lounge chair, drinking a drink, smoking a cigarette, moving his thumb across his lips, my father looked like he could stay in Miami forever, like time wasn't even a factor.

The pool was crowded. Coconut and fruit-scented suntan lotions mixed with the chlorine smell from the pool and the smell of the sun against the pool deck. There was salt in the air too. It felt like the middle of summer.

My father said they were putting on a fight card downtown. He'd taken me to the fights once, but I hadn't liked them. He was good about that. If I didn't like something, he didn't press it on me. I much preferred going to baseball games, hanging out, talking, listening to the sounds, ball against bat, Yankees fans yelling, watching the players run, how they touched the corners of the bases to minimize the distance, how their uniforms fell on their bodies. My father always made great sandwiches for the games with cold cuts from Faicco's Pork Store. Soprassetta with provolone. Pepper turkey with Swiss. Roast beef with American. He put oil and balsamic vinegar and mustard on the bread and added roasted peppers and sliced tomatoes and wrapped them in wax paper like a professional sandwich man. He would take a bag of peanuts or popcorn from D'Agostino's and sometimes, on the crowded subway ride back from the Bronx, he'd take a few bucks for dinner out afterwards.

"I've never been to the fights," Anna said.

"A Cuban guy's fighting the main event. Now's your chance to see Cuba."

"Now's my chance to see a Cuban guy fighting."

"He's probably an American citizen by now. I hope so for his sake."

"Why is that?"

"Things are easier here."

"If you're rich."

"I have no problem with spreading the wealth a little. That's why the Cuban guy is fighting here. I bet he caught the first good raft he could get to Florida."

"They support the arts a hell of a lot more in Cuba."

"So what? They're not free to express themselves, so what's the point?"

"Are we?" Anna said.

"Have you ever been censored?"

"Not in so many words."

"Me neither. Not in any words. I'm free."

"Your freedom is an illusion," Anna said.

My father moved his thumb across his lips.

"Is it all a movie to you?" she said.

"It's not just a movie. It's *Breathless.* Is it all reality to you?"

"I'm here with you. You tell me."

"I don't have to tell you," he said. "I just showed you. Go on. Do it."

"I don't want to."

"Do it for me."

"No."

He moved his thumb across his lips. He stayed on Anna's eyes.

"Go on. Just once."

It was the first time I'd seen them fight. They were going round and round, but not like the orange dance. This was their first slip, a slip from drinking, from sitting too long in the sun. I saw the restlessness in my father. He wanted to stop it, but he wanted to make his point at the same time. His eyes were on her eyes. Lit eyes on lit eyes.

"Just once," he said.

She lifted her thumb and moved it across her lips.

"Thank you," my father said. "Real thumb. Real lips. Breathless."

He poured her another margarita.

"Should we go to the fights?" he said.

"Would you like to go to the fights?" she said.

"I would. And the fights in Miami are better than the ones in New York."

My father said that for my benefit, so I asked him why they were better.

"They just are," he said and smiled.

"Thanks."

"You're very welcome. We'll get a steak dinner and go to the fights."

"Sounds like a boys' night out," Anna said.

"Not at all. It's all about equal opportunity in this country."

Anna left it alone. My father refilled his glass from the pitcher. The margarita was not so yellow, watered down from the melted ice. I closed my eyes to the sun.

"It's not like the movies," my father said. "Especially the bad boxing movies. When a guy gets cut, he bleeds real blood. If Rocky took that many shots in real life he'd be dead."

"I saw a bullfight in Pamplona," Anna said. "The bulls didn't have a chance. By the time the matador entered the picture, the bulls had been run ragged, speared and stabbed. And when the matador made the kill, some of the bulls started coughing blood and staggering all over the ring. It seemed senseless. But I suppose it's like everything. You have to know it to fully appreciate it."

"Did you run with the bulls?" he said.

"No. I just saw the runners coming into the arena after they'd run. They looked exhausted and alive at the same time. They looked like they'd cheated death."

"You might appreciate the fights tonight. The really skilled fighters are graceful and poised and you can tell right away whether a fighter is a professional or just some kid making his way up the ranks."

"At least it's man on man."

"I promise you won't see one slaughtered animal anywhere near the place."

"I'll take my Leica along. See if there's something to photograph."

"They're at the Miami Arena. I'll find out where it is and we'll drive over."

"I can drive," she said.

"I'll drive. I'm fine."

I kept my eyes closed. I heard him lift his margarita, ice against glass, and take a long swallow.

"What a day," my father said. "What a string of beautiful days."

"I never taught Ben how to drive," Anna said.

I opened my eyes. It took a moment before they adjusted to the light. It was like I was blind for a few seconds, then the spots disappeared and I could see.

"You can still teach me."

"It's too crowded in Miami," Anna said.

"Not as crowded as New York."

"You need wide-open roads. I learned how to drive when we took a trip to Australia. My father told me to get into the driver's seat. He sat in the passenger seat and didn't say a word. When I asked him what to do, he said I'd been watching him drive my whole life so I should know what to do. So I did what I remembered seeing. It worked. There was nothing to hit for miles, not even a kangaroo."

"I could probably conduct a subway," I said.

"You probably could."

My father tapped out a cigarette and offered one to Anna. He lit hers and then his, his fingers smooth on the lighter, practiced moves made perfect. In *Breathless* Belmondo chain-smoked. One cigarette lit the next. I wondered how many cigarettes my father had lit, for how many women, in how many bars and maybe it was all meant for now, for him to be perfect here, in this city, with this woman, on this day, and if that was so, then maybe it was all justified.

They finished their cigarettes and we left the pool. I carried the empty pitcher and glasses the way I always did. That was my big Florida responsibility. We walked through the lobby and my father bumped into a man. It was not a drunken mistake. The wallet was on the floor and my father bent down to pick it up before the man could think anything. He gave it to the man and the man thanked him. My father's hand had not healed right. He'd failed his own test.

We went up to the room, showered, changed. On TV the local news anchor seemed less professional than the New York newscasters. He tripped over his words. The first item was about a resurgence of carjackings near the airport. That was big stealing. The chief of police said he'd deployed undercover patrol cars to put an end to the problem once and for all.

"That's what he thinks," my father said.

My father wore a jacket over his white T-shirt. He put on his hat.

"B Movies, cigarette moves," my father said and tilted the brim.

I laced my high-tops. I wore new running shoes to run, old running shoes to school and Chuck Taylors when I was getting dressed up. I wore the one button shirt I'd packed, sky blue that went with the warm night.

"Carjacking never caught on in New York," my father said. "I guess there are only so many crimes a man can commit in the South."

"I think they're tougher on crime here," I said.

"Southern justice."

"They execute people in Florida."

"Watch out. You better not bring those sunglasses I took for you. If the authorities find out they'll put you in the gas chamber and close the door."

"They don't use gas chambers anymore."

"I meant the guillotine."

"Very funny."

"When they gave Gary Gilmore a choice of how to die, he wanted to be shot. That's the way to do it. It's loud. It's dramatic. It doesn't mess with your face. Looking good."

The newscaster tripped over a word, then finished the sentence about a bad day on Wall Street.

Anna came out of the bathroom. Her lips were bright red and her dark hair was up in a bun so she looked like a fifties moll. She wore tight pants and heels and a sleeveless shirt that showed off her shoulders.

"You two look handsome. I like my men to clean up well."

"Hello," my father said, stretching out the *lo*, a one syllable wolf-whistle.

"So. So do I look the part? Like the kind of woman who goes to the fights?"

"If the boxing commissioner knows what he's doing, he'll hand you the round cards and make you the ring girl."

Anna lit up a cigarette. My father checked himself a final time in the mirror. He lifted his eyebrow for my amusement.

We went down, walked through the lobby, my father and Anna looking perfect in the art-deco hotel that was a trip back to another time. We got into the car, the seats hot from the sun, and pulled onto Collins Avenue. My father didn't drive like he was drunk. He just drove a little slower and stayed in the right lane. His hands were steady on the wheel.

We stopped at a steakhouse. The parking lot was full, a good sign in many ways. The more crowded, the better the food. The more crowded, the easier to walk. My father had been restless. The three of us didn't exactly look inconspicuous, especially with so many of the tables taken up by old people, most of them wearing white, the men with their pants hiked up and the women with arms that dripped skin. It was early to be eating and old people ate early. I doubted these people were going to the fights. We were seated at a booth and handed oversized menus that described oversized steaks. My father's face was unreadable. Would he pay? Would he walk? His money had to be running out. I didn't know what he was doing about the bill at the Fontainebleau. The man's wallet had fallen to the floor.

We all got New York sirloin steaks and baked potatoes and lettuce wedges with Roquefort dressing. My father ordered a glass of red wine for Anna and a beer for himself. I told the waiter that water would be fine.

"Steaks and a fight," my father said. "I feel mighty."

The salads were big and I couldn't finish my steak. My father ate the rest of my steak and some of the rest of Anna's. He had a big appetite, but never seemed to gain any weight. No one wanted dessert so he asked for the check. He told Anna to have a cigarette outside and told me to join her. He slid Anna the car keys.

Anna stood and walked out and I walked behind her. She moved gracefully in heels, her head held high. The old men watched her. We walked through the parking lot to the car.

"Would you like to drive?" she said.

"Now?"

"If you can drive in this situation, Manhattan's streets will feel like a breeze."

"He'll be out in a minute."

"You only need a minute to drive up to the front of the restaurant."

She handed me the keys and waited. I opened the door for her. She slipped into the seat and smiled.

"Well done," she said.

"I watch my father."

I walked around the front of the car and got into the driver's seat.

"Now what?"

"You put the key in the ignition and take it from there."

"Now you sound like your father," I said.

I turned the key and the car started. I put the car into Drive and pressed my foot on the gas. It went forward too fast and I took my foot off the pedal and put it back on more softly. This time the car didn't lurch. We were out of the space and moving forward. I turned the wheel to the left and the car went to the left. I straightened the wheel and the car went straight. I kept my foot gentle on the gas and drove to the front of the restaurant and took my foot off the gas.

"He'll be out in ten seconds," I said.

"You think?"

"When I was a kid and we went out to eat, my father used to predict when the food would come out of the kitchen. He made it into a game so I wouldn't get so impatient. He always got it right. Every single time. He would count down from ten. He was very dramatic about the whole thing, counting down the numbers real slowly, and before he got to zero the waiter was at our table with the food. He called it magic-ing the meal."

Anna counted down from ten and at two the restaurant door opened and at one Jared Chiziver appeared, like magic, walking easily forward. I opened the door, slid over, my father sat down in the driver's seat, closed the door, moved the car forward, his foot gentle on the gas, and pulled onto the avenue.

We were lined up three in a row on the Valiant's front seat.

"So my son is now in charge of the getaway car. You've come of age, kid. We're running a regular family business here."

"I only drove a few feet."

"It doesn't matter how far you were driving. You were driving."

"He was driving like a pro," Anna said.

"Of course he was. He's my son. We've got style."

"Belmondo style," Anna said.

"I like that," my father said. "Belmondo style."

His hands were steady on the wheel.

"Belmondo style," he said again and laughed like it was the beginning of a movie.

We drove to downtown Miami. This part of the city looked like the city. Buildings crowded together. Cars against curbs. Fire hydrants. The smell of dog piss. Our windows were down and my father pulled up to some guys sitting around a small table playing dominoes. He asked them for directions to the arena. They looked my father over. They looked the car over. When Anna leaned across the front seat to speak, they looked her over and their hands stopped fumbling with the dominoes. She said something in Spanish. The guys responded. I could tell by their gestures where we had to go. I understood Anna's *gracias*, and I understood their *senorita bella*, and Anna told my father where to go.

"*Mantequilla*," he said.

"What about *mantequilla*?"

"Nothing. I like the way it sounds."

"It means butter."

"I know. *Mira* means look. *Mantequilla* means butter. That's the extent of my Spanish. *Mira. Mira. Mantequilla.*"

We drove until we saw people parking their cars and walking in one direction. My father backed into a space and we got out of the car and followed the people. We passed a liquor store. My father went in and came out with a small bottle of tequila.

"Now we can toast the victors," he said.

"What about the losers?" I said.

"We can drink to them too. As long as they're brave. If they're brave we'll toast the losers."

A man was waving tickets, asking people if they were selling tickets, the most famous scalper line. My father went over to him. He often bought scalped tickets at Yankees games. He always got a few bucks off the price and he liked supporting private entrepreneurs instead of big corporations. If a man was playing an angle, if he was creative enough to turn a profit outside the rules, my father respected him. That was his favorite part of the American way, beyond the dream of hard work leading to success, beyond a kid surpassing his father. Playing the angle had a touch of the revolution to it, the oppressed seizing opportunity that led to equality, the poor guys making a couple extra bucks. My father asked for three tickets. The scalper said he had three great seats for one hundred bucks. My father asked to see the tickets. They were forty-dollar seats.

"A little steep for so close to fight time," my father said.

"Welcome to Miami. One hundred bucks," the scalper said.

"I don't know these tickets."

"What's there to know, my man? They're paper. They've got the fights printed on them. They're great seats."

"Ninety bucks and you can walk me to the door."

"The door's right there."

"In New York City they print counterfeit tickets everywhere. I know the crime of choice around here is carjacking, but I want to make sure these are real."

"They're real, man."

"And there are plenty of other scalpers. When I get ripped off it eats away at me. It ruins my day. I'm having a good day so why not keep my run going and walk me to the door?"

"One hundred bucks."

"Ninety bucks and a stroll to the door."

"That's less than what I paid for them."

"No it isn't."

"Damn," the scalper said. "Come on."

He started walking with us. He gave Anna a sideways glance, then looked at me, and then he just looked ahead, putting on his best jaded-face.

"I used to know a guy from New York City," the scalper said. "I knew a lot of guys from New York City, but this one guy in particular lived in my neighborhood. He was an old guy came down here for the warm weather like everyone comes down here. Every time you saw him he'd shake his head and say *Same old New York.* He was a crazy old man. He must have lived in Miami twenty years before he died, but every time you passed him he said the same damn thing. *Same old New York.*"

"Maybe he was homesick," my father said.

"I don't know about that, but he was definitely crazy."

The scalper stopped in front of the entrance. He stood there while my father had his tickets ripped and we were allowed in the door. My father nodded to the scalper.

"Same old New York," my father said.

The scalper shook his head, then smiled, then started walking back to make some more money, who's selling tickets, his routine.

The arena was crowded. The ring was lit, a bright red canvas with a Budweiser logo on each ring post. Boxing crowds were different from baseball crowds. They congregated to feel, not just watch. These were tough men. I looked at my father. He fit. He was a tough man like they were. He wasn't the only one with a springy walk or lit eyes or clothes that made him almost a character. What separated him was that he had the smile in his eyes as he walked. If the world was the same old, same old, he still came off fresh. If he was jaded, it only showed the morning after a night out. When he took people's wallets he had to feel the adrenaline rush, no matter how many times he did it. Maybe all that adrenaline was what kept him young. When he went out with women, all those women, good for one distilled story, it had to be a little different each time and maybe that kept him young too. And here in Miami, doing whatever he was doing, he was cutting into life's monotony, keeping it at bay, feeling *mighty*, the word he loved to use. And the smile in his eyes could break into unbridled happiness when it spread to his mouth, when the happiness became a part of him, when he played around to make me laugh, to make Anna laugh, to make himself laugh, and that was a way to separate himself too. Joy was rare. Joy was hard to capture, Anna said. It was also hard to feel. But it was part of my father. At least sometimes.

We found our seats and sat down. Me first and then Anna and then my father, on the aisle. The seats were close to the ring and I could see that Anna was taken with the atmosphere. Her eyes were lit beyond the alcohol. It made sense. She was with my father. He was on the run. She was attracted to the danger, to the adventure of it all, and she would steal some photographs. Anna had grown up rich. Maybe that was some of it, some of why she had pulled up in her Valiant and left New York with us. I wondered if James Worthen and his Park Avenue crowd would choose to take this trip, or if walking out of a diner, skipping out on a check, was as far as they'd go. Anna had gone farther. She'd made a choice to go farther. I'd gone farther, but the choice hadn't been mine.

Anna started taking photographs of the ring and of the crowd and when the first fighters walked down the aisle, bouncing up and down, shaking out their arms, their colorful robes catching the light, she photographed them. There was nothing half-dead about any of this. Anna talked of wanting to find a new subject and the fights were close to death sometimes, close to criminals sometimes, close to my father sometimes, a part of him I was sure Anna recognized in his walk, his ropy muscles, his eyes when they went hard.

The two fighters went all four rounds and when the decision was announced the victorious fighter raised his arms. My father unscrewed the bottle cap and had a quick shot for the winner and a quick shot for the loser and passed the bottle to Anna.

"That was something," Anna said.

"They're just kids. Wait until the main event. Then you'll see the skill."

"I don't understand how they stand up to those punches."

"If you can't take a punch, you don't last long in this business."

During the third preliminary I went to get a soda. They were enjoying the fights, but I didn't feel what they seemed to be feeling. The line at the concession stand was long and slow. It didn't matter. I was in no rush. Time was outside, like it was when I sat by the pool. There were no women on line, just men. The ones speaking were speaking Spanish. In the arena a shout went up and then a louder shout. One of the fighters must have been hurt.

I got a soda, walked back to our seats. I passed a kid with his hair brushed back wet and a welt under his eye. I recognized him as the winner of the first fight. He was smaller than I was, and probably close to my age, but his demeanor was so confident that he seemed like a man already. He looked at me, as if he expected me to congratulate him. He was very good-looking. This was his night to be recognized. Someone came over to him and shook his hand and our eyes broke and I walked on.

In the main event the Cuban fighter fought with total control. I didn't know the fights, but it was easy to see what my father had explained to Anna. I saw the movement and the grace and the constant awareness of the ring. He had a beautiful body, more dancer than brawler. I watched his leg muscles flex and relax as he moved around the canvas and when his back was to me I looked at the flatness of his neck. In the eighth round the Cuban fighter hit his opponent with two hard body shots, two dull thuds that made me wince. The crowd stood as the fighter fell. The referee counted him out and the Cuban fighter was lifted to cheers. He made a muscle for his fans. Anna walked toward the ring and into the area where the press sat. No one stopped her. She stood right under the winner and photographed him.

"Do you think she liked the fights?" my father said.

My father unscrewed the cap. He didn't care about concealing the bottle anymore. The main event was over and if they threw him out that was fine. He took a swig.

"Was that for the winner or the loser?" I said.

"That was for me," he said and smiled.

We waited for Anna to finish. The ring was cleared. Two more fighters came in, started to fight. I looked around the crowd. The fighter from the first preliminary was sitting with some men and laughing the easy laugh of someone who had won completely. I wanted him to catch my eye, but he didn't. I stretched out my legs. It didn't hurt much. I would have to start running soon.

When the final decision was announced we left the arena with everyone else, slow walking, the men not as springy in their steps going out as coming in, as if the fights had also sapped their adrenaline. My father's eyes were still lit and so were Anna's. They'd finished off the bottle. It was still warm outside and my father went back into the liquor store. I could see the new bottle in his jacket pocket. We walked to the car and started to drive around the city blocks. His hands were steady on the wheel, but he had to be drunk. I noticed the spaces between his fingers and I pressed my own fingers together to see the difference.

"Are you lost or just trying to get lost?" Anna said.

"You can't get too lost in Miami," my father said. "It's like New York. If you get lost, you just look for the Empire State Building and you can situate yourself. In Miami, you just need to find where the ocean is. A1A. Straight back to the Fontainebleau."

"Let's find the ocean," I said.

"First things first," my father said and took the bottle from his pocket, unscrewed the cap, took a drink, passed it to Anna.

"If the cops stop you, you'll be in trouble," I said.

"Do you see any cops around here?"

"There could be. They said on the news there were more cops out looking for carjackers."

"I can walk a straight line. I can drive a straight line."

"You have an opened bottle in the car."

"Look, Ma, no hands."

My father let go of the steering wheel, but the car didn't swerve.

"I was never able to use that line," I said.

My father put his hands back on the wheel.

"I look at everything you do," he said.

"Did you ever bring her to Florida?"

"What makes you ask that?"

"Just curious. Did you?"

"Florida is my escape. It always has been."

"I'll remember that."

"It's your escape too now."

"I'll remember that too."

"Are you trying to cut into my high?"

"I'm just asking you a question."

"No questions allowed. We're taking a drive. A thousand flicks of the eye."

My father started laughing, but it was a mean laugh. I wasn't supposed to talk about how he'd stolen my past. I wasn't supposed to ask questions.

"How's your hand?" I said.

"It's fine."

"That's a lie. It's not fine."

"We're in Florida. It doesn't have to be fine."

I could see the clench in his jaw so I knew I'd gotten to him. Maybe in Florida he didn't have to keep a poker face. Maybe that was part of his escape too. Maybe he didn't care if I got to him or not, not really. He drove through the streets. He was looking for something. He took a left and another left and stopped at the stop sign.

There were three young guys hanging out on the corner. The fashion trends that started in New York had traveled south. Their baggy pants and oversized shirts spoke of concealed things even if nothing was concealed. I'd heard that all fashion trends started in prison. Violence or threats of violence influenced style. I wondered if a handy pink lighter would go mainstream. Very chic. Very hot. The guys looked over the Valiant, looked at us, the white people inside. My father pulled to the curb.

"You have any gum?" my father said.

"I have a cigarette," Anna said.

"That should cover it."

She tapped out two cigarettes and handed one to my father. He took the lighter from her hand and lit hers first, then his.

The way they inhaled and let the smoke out looked good, but it was stupid. He was in shape and it was stupid. And just because he had escaped to Florida didn't give him the right to be stupid, not when he was all I had. My father leaned over and kissed Anna.

"You taste good," she said.

"Not a trace of liquor?"

"Just a trace."

"Let's see if these kids do more than extra work," he said.

"They look serious," she said.

"Oh boy," he said. "Serious business. Hold on."

He got out of the car and started talking to the three guys on the corner. He turned to us, winked, and then walked down the street with one of the guys. Anna and I waited. The two other guys looked us over and then went back to talking.

"You want to hear some music?"

"I don't care," I said.

"Which way is the ocean?" she said, but she sounded like she was talking to herself. "Which way?"

"Whatever he's doing, you can stop him," I said.

"I don't know what he's doing."

"He's doing something stupid."

"All's fair in love and war."

"Are you drunk?"

"Why?"

"*All's fair in love and war.* That's a cliché."

"I know. *Breathless.* Is that better?"

I didn't say anything.

We waited in the car. No music. Just Anna smoking down her cigarette and me looking out the window. It was a lousy neighborhood, but there was nothing I could do. I couldn't drive away. I couldn't run away. I could walk, but I didn't know which way and I wouldn't just leave my father.

He came back. He got in the car, started it up, drove. He got on a highway that wasn't A1A. I looked out the side window and saw the lights of Miami, far enough away to be defined away from us. There was a billboard advertising Alligator Boat Rides at the next exit. My father got off. The road was not a highway, and my father turned onto another road that was full of potholes. There were no lights. There were few cars. He drove until he found an even smaller road branching off into what looked like swamp. He turned onto that road. We were all alone, in the middle of cattails and brush. He stopped the car.

"I have to see how it feels," he said.

My father got out of the car. The headlights were on, and he walked to the end of the beam. I watched him take the gun out of his jacket. He held his arms straight and pointed the gun into the brush. A quick burst of flame and an explosion. I couldn't believe how loud it was. His arms jerked. I could feel the adrenaline shoot through my body, as much a reaction to the sound as to what he was doing. My father held his arms straight again, his left hand taking the pressure off his right hand. He pointed the gun into the brush and fired. The explosion was loud, but I was already a little used to it. My father's arms didn't jerk. He fired one more shot. Then he tucked the gun into his pants and walked to the car. He leaned into the window and smiled.

"I always wanted to shoot a gun," he said.

"How did it feel?" Anna said.

"Mighty. It felt mighty."

# 20

I WOKE EARLY. THEY WERE ASLEEP. THEY'D GONE OUT TO A bar after we'd come back to the Fontainebleau, but I stayed in the room. There had been an old Hitchcock movie on, *Notorious.* Cary Grant plays the spy and Ingrid Bergman plays the woman he has indoctrinated for a secret mission. My father's favorite moment was when the two lovers walk across the living room so Grant can make a call. They are kissing and holding each other and the call, an important call to the head of the secret service, becomes secondary to their kiss. Ingrid Bergman says, *This is a strange love affair.* It was a perfect line for the moment and one that she supposedly adlibbed. It had become the most famous scene in the film. I'd watched the film and then I'd fallen asleep. I heard my father and Anna come in, heard them go into the bathroom together and turn on the shower so that I wouldn't hear them and later I heard them get into bed.

My father's arm was draped over Anna. His back was to me. I could only see Anna's hand, resting on my father's leg, her fingers relaxed, feeling protected. Behind the curtains I saw some light so I knew it was morning. I got out of bed, put on my bathing suit, put on my sunglasses. They didn't even move when I opened the door.

I swam in the pool, looking at the shape of the pool as I swam, at the palm trees, at the sun. I kept seeing my father standing there at the end of the light and then the burst of brighter light and the sound had gone through me. On the drive back they were drunk and laughing and louder than I had ever heard them and my father kept asking her if he looked good shooting a gun and she kept telling him he looked like a natural and I just sat there and listened to their stupid shit.

It was like he'd gone crazy. That was the scariest crazy of all, seeing someone you knew, you loved, go crazy. A kid on the Stuyvesant track team had a mother who was manic-depressive. Right before a race, just as we were setting ourselves at the starting line, a naked woman started running in circles in front of us, her arms outstretched, a child's version of an airplane. She was laughing hysterically. The kid ran over to his mother, put her arms down, put his arms around her. It was a brutal moment, embarrassing and painful and a memory that would be his forever, a memory he wouldn't be able to separate out whenever he looked at his mother. He knew her, he knew her when she was just his mother, but every now and then she went crazy and that day she went crazy in public. I ran over to one of the bigger guys on the team, one of the shot-putters, took his sweatshirt and handed it to the kid. The kid put the sweatshirt on his mother, helped her fit her arms into the sleeves and then he walked his mother to the school where they called an ambulance. I felt like that kid when we drove back to the Fontaine-bleau. I knew I would always have that memory of my father. Getting out of the car, lifting the gun, firing. There was nothing I could do to cover it up, no easy sweatshirt-solution. The kid's mother was laughing as he walked her away. My father had laughed in the car. Mighty. Mighty. Stupid joy.

I finished the swim. The new skin didn't feel as tight. I walked over to the beach and down to the harder sand, just above where the breaking waves reached. I took a breath. That nervous breath. The breath that goes in and in some more and when it stops the decision is set for good. The breath I'd taken as a kid in Florida when I jumped off the high dive. The breath I took before the race began. The breath my father must have taken before he'd shot that first shot.

I started to run.

It was slow running, self consciously marking my steps, keeping my feet even, my body centered, holding my weight in my shoulders to take away the strain from my crotch and stomach.

It hurt and then it hurt less. My legs opened up. The miles and miles were in me and they moved me forward. My heart fell into a natural rhythm and my lungs expanded. I ran along the beach, past empty lifeguard chairs, past hotels and condominiums, and then I turned and ran back.

I was tired when I finished. I had lost something in the weeks away.

They probably weren't up yet and I didn't want to see them hungover. I walked through the lobby to Collins Avenue. It was still early and there weren't many cars on the road and none of them were expensive. My legs were heavy. If I walked far enough I could go back to the room and sleep while they lay out in the sun.

I raised my arms straight in front of me, pointed my finger like a gun, and pretended to shoot. I made my arms jerk. Then I did it again and kept my arms steady. I said it out loud. *Bang*. It was a kid thing to do.

There was a *click* in the distance. And then another and another. It wasn't a gunshot at all, but a flat sound that echoed. I walked to where the noise was. Two old men were playing shuffleboard. The red and black disks slid along the smooth stone court. The man with the red stick shot his disk into the tip of the triangle, the highest point value. That was the hardest shot, the one that needed the softest touch, that went against the instinct to push as hard as possible. The man with the black stick had one disk left and he pushed it hard, slapping the red disk off the court. The flat sound echoed behind me.

I walked back to the Fontainebleau. They weren't at the pool so I found a free chair and stayed in the sun. My calves were already starting to hurt, but it wasn't bad. The skin around my crotch hurt, but it wasn't bad either. I closed my eyes behind my sunglasses and fell in and out of sleep to the sounds of kids splashing, parents yelling, the pool boy moving chairs across the pool tiles and then the sounds faded.

I woke when my father put his hand on my shoulder. I opened my eyes. He was alone. No Anna. No pitcher of margaritas. He sat down on the lounge chair next to mine, hunched forward, his arms on his knees. His eyes were red and his nose had a shine to it from cigarettes and tequila. His hat was pushed down on his head. The smile he gave me was tight.

"How are you doing?" he said.

"I'm fine. Like you always say, I'm fine."

He looked at me, challenging me to go on, but maybe he just wanted me to vent, to get it all out of me. I thought about staying quiet, but I couldn't.

"Was she impressed?" I said.

"With what?"

"With your little gun demonstration."

"I wasn't trying to impress her."

"You bought a fucking gun. You were shooting a fucking gun."

"Watch your mouth."

"What are you going to do? Shoot me? You went crazy."

"I didn't go crazy."

"I thought you were done drinking like that. I thought you were done waking up and feeling like shit. I thought she took away the restlessness."

"It was just a night out."

"It wasn't just a night out. You bought a gun. You were drunk and you were shooting a gun. You didn't even care that I was there."

"Of course I cared."

"No you didn't. I just happened to be there. You went crazy. You were crazy."

"That's not true, Ben."

My father leaned back. He looked into the sun and turned his eyes to slits, the creases defined.

"Another hot one," he said.

"It's always hot here. We should get back to New York and get back to our life. I need to get in shape. I need to get back to school one of these days."

"You will."

"When?"

"Soon."

"I ran this morning. I'm ready to get back."

"Beautiful. Were you fast?"

"No."

"It's your first day running. We'll race later. Maybe I'll finally be able to beat you."

"You've been drinking too much. You've been smoking too much."

"We're on vacation," he said.

"I think we should go back to the city."

"I can't go back," he said and kept his eyes on mine. "You know that. I've been running too. I'm on the run."

I knew it, but hearing his words made me know it. He had taken us along for the run. As a runner I ran in a circle. My long-distance races always finished right at the place they started. I wasn't a sprinter who went from one place to another, fast and forward. My father was the sprinter type. His stride became natural when he was really moving.

"Where are we running to?" I said.

"I'm not sure yet. For now, we're staying put at the Fontainebleau."

"For how long?"

"For as long as I can afford it."

"Your hand is bad."

"It's fine."

"Did you ever drop a wallet before?"

"Not until last night."

"Then your hand isn't fine."

"It's nothing compared to what you went through," my father said. "You went through the worst. You had your balls burned. Think of it. You had your balls burned and you came out of it and you're running."

He hadn't seen what I had gone through, just what I had gone through afterwards, but I knew he thought about it all the time, pictured it, made it vivid.

"You're the one running," I said.

"Running in luxury," he said and smiled.

"It's not funny. You scared me last night."

"I'm sorry about that," my father said. "There's no need to be scared. You're a brave kid. After what you've been through, nothing should scare you. Life can only get easier."

"Life wasn't so hard before."

"It wasn't. But now you know you can get through anything, no matter how hard."

"Like the belly flop."

"What belly flop?"

"When I was a kid. When we stayed at the Attaché. I jumped off the high dive and did a belly flop and swam to the side of the pool even though it hurt. I couldn't have been more than five."

"I forgot about that."

"So it's not such a life lesson. I already learned it."

"What you went through was more than a belly flop. There was no reason for that. Anyway, it's over."

"We can go somewhere else," I said.

My father adjusted his hat. He looked up and squinted at the sun again. A hard squint. A resolved squint. He knew how he looked at all times and maybe he was just doing that for me, directing the scene to evoke an emotion, show me that he had thought long and hard about what he was going to say.

"I've always told you about big stealing and little stealing," he said. "I've always told you it was smarter to steal small than to steal big and I've done that my whole life and I've never been caught. Thanks to little stealing we've lived a pretty good life."

"We're still living it."

"It is nice here, isn't it? The thing is, little stealing won't keep us at the Fontainebleau for very long."

"We don't have to stay here."

"Listen," he said. "You're old enough to hear this. I came down here to tell you what I'm doing. I knew you were upset last night. I knew you thought your old man was losing it shooting a gun into the swamps of Florida."

"You were crazy."

"I wasn't crazy. I can't go back to New York right now. And one job, one big job could keep us going for a while."

"What happens if you get caught?"

My father smiled his smile that was all in his eyes.

"I've got to take that chance," he said. "My hand is a little banged up so I've got to do something else."

"Something else with a gun."

"If I get caught you can handle it. You can handle anything."

"No, I can't."

"You can handle anything. You hear me? I'm not even fully gray yet and my son can handle life even when it's hard. That's enough to make a father proud."

"You're not going gray."

"My blond hair hides it."

"You're not gray. Look at you."

"Look at me. Look closely and you'll find a bunch of grays. Look closely and you'll start calling me your old man."

He said this for me, hoping I would laugh, but I wasn't laughing.

"Look at me. I like to think I've taken care of you pretty well. You're easy to take care of and you've taken care of me in your own way. I know that. And when that fucker did what he did to you, I took care of it as best as I knew how."

"That's why you broke your hand."

"Whatever. Don't think that way. Don't. Understand?"

"I understand."

"Good."

He lifted the sunglasses from my face, the sunglasses he'd taken for me, and put them on.

"Much better. That sun is killing me."

"She has money," I said.

"She has some money."

"She loves you."

"I never believe these things are going to last."

"What if it does?"

"We'll see. Anyway, I have to do something soon. I wanted to tell you. You're old enough to hear."

"You said this was just going to be a vacation. You said we were just going to take a break. You said big stealing was for suckers."

I wanted to scream, but I couldn't. There were people around. Like in a breakup scene where the man takes the woman to a restaurant, a public place, a reasonable place, to keep emotions in check. I had to keep my voice down, but my eyes were tearing up.

"You said it was for suckers."

"I'm in full control," my father said. "I'm fine."

"You weren't fine yesterday. You weren't fine shooting a gun in the middle of nowhere and laughing about it afterwards. It's crazy. I thought you were crazy. And I feel like there's nothing I can do to stop you. If you think I'm old enough to hear what you're telling me, then I'm old enough for you to listen to me. It's crazy. Whatever you're thinking is crazy. We can find a place to live and start over."

"That's the kid in you talking."

"You're the kid."

"I'm a kid in some ways," my father said. "I admit it. But I'm old enough to know you can't start over. You can't."

"Why are you doing this?"

"I'm doing it. That's all."

"That's all?"

"Yes. That's all."

My eyes were tearing up. I breathed in. He wasn't listening. He wasn't going to listen. His jaw wasn't even clenched.

"So you just want my approval? You tell me you're going to do something big, you act like you're crazy, and you just want me to say it's okay?"

"I always want your approval," my father said. "But now I have to do something whether I have your approval or not."

"Why are you doing this?"

My father didn't say anything.

"Why?" I said, but it sounded like I was talking to myself.

I breathed in.

I looked past my father, I had to squint my eyes to keep out the glare.

"Looking good," he said.

"Because I'm squinting?"

"Because you're fighting the sun."

"Very funny."

"Because you want to scream at me and you're holding it in."

"You're right."

"Of course I'm right. I know you. You're my son."

My father moved his thumb across his lips.

"He was an actor," I said.

"He was real in the movie. He was right there."

"It was a movie. It was just a movie."

"No," my father said. "It wasn't just a movie. It was *Breathless*. It is *Breathless*."

I wanted to scream. But I didn't.

# 21

THE IMAGINED IS OFTEN MORE VIVID THAN THE REAL. IN many ways that's the appeal of movies. My father imagined what I had gone through. While he loved black-and-white films, I believe his imagination worked in color for that memory, which wasn't his memory, but was. In his eyes the pink lighter must have looked pinker, the flame hotter, the agony greater. I was his son, after all, and he took it hard. And I believe the image I have of my father crushing the man's penis with a piece of concrete is more horrible than it was in reality, if that's possible. What happened on my father's day of big stealing happened off-screen for me and since it has become a scene, the scene I've imagined, I have probably used too many movie conventions to make it all make sense. Still, my father liked simple movies the best, movies based on character and not plot. He hated easy shoot-'em-ups or special effects. The picture I have of that day, the picture I have imagined so many times since then and that has become my memory, as vivid as a real memory, as vivid as a movie scene seen over and over again, is all about character, with my father, as he always was and always will be in my life, the leading man.

So this is how I imagine it. I don't think it's that far off.

Jared Chiziver stood up from his beach chair. He leaned over and kissed Anna good-bye. He didn't care that people were watching. He never did. A camera could have been there, a foot away, and he wouldn't have cared. He took her head with the back of his hand and brought her to him and I saw their mouths hold on until he moved himself away, just past the reach of her lips. He looked at her. Eyes to eyes. Right there. Then he turned to me and kissed my cheek the way he did when I was a kid and he walked me to school, which hadn't been that long ago but seemed long ago, and that's when I knew. The day had been chosen.

I watched him walk into the hotel. The door opened. The door closed. I was no longer in his scene.

My father went up to the room to change. He put on a pair of pants and a T-shirt and a jacket, the same outfit he'd worn to the fights. He brushed his teeth and looked at himself in the mirror like before a night out. He put a few dollars in his pocket, fastened with a paper clip. He tucked the gun into his pants. He kept his shirt loose. He picked up his valise and went down.

The spring was in his step as he walked across the lobby. The smile was in his eyes, but it was a smile for himself. He was dressed like he was going to the fights, but he wasn't. He was dressed for himself. He was smiling for himself. The fighters we'd seen had been working toward a championship fight. That's what professional fighters hoped for. But before that championship fight, before they were lucky enough to get one, they had to work. That was why my father liked fighters. Because they worked alone and if they didn't perfect their skills most of them would fall quickly. They had to spend hours at the gym before their first amateur fight, they had to fight dozens of amateur fights before their first professional fight, they had to fight hard professional fights before their championship fight and when that happened, if that happened, the day of that big fight, the fight they'd been working for their whole lives, all those hours inside of them, all those fights inside of them, how could they not smile a little? My father had gone from Milky Way candy bars to being the best pickpocket around, never caught. He had put in the hours and he had learned how not to make mistakes. Now he was moving to the next level. So he was smiling when he walked through that lobby, his hat pushed back, his stride like a fighter going to the ring. He got the Valiant, opened the door, got into the car, savoring the moment before it actually began, enjoying the breathlessness of it all. He rolled down the window to get the Miami sun on his face. He put one arm out the window, his hand flat against the Valiant's gold metal. He held his other arm straight in front of him. He looked at his hand. His hand was still not right, but it was steady. He took a breath and popped the car into Drive.

He drove to the airport. The highway was crowded, but he didn't have to rush. He didn't have to use the horn or weave between cars. He'd given himself plenty of time. He found a radio station that was playing hits from the fifties and sixties and he sang the words out loud to the songs he knew, hummed the sounds to the ones he didn't, *la la la*s just like Belmondo.

He could hear the jets overhead. The red and blue insignia of an American Airline came into view, its landing gear out, and my father slowed so he could watch it descend. The plane tipped to the left, tipped to the right, a silver-winged wave. My father lifted his hand that had been pressed against the Valiant's door and waved back.

He parked the car in airport parking, took off his hat, placed it on the passenger seat, put on a pair of surgical gloves, took his valise and walked along the airport's peripheral road until he came to the National Car Rental lot. The logo had wavy green lines under the

N, more appropriate to boat rentals than cars. In Miami everything was close to the ocean. My father lit up a cigarette, just a guy flying in from somewhere having a smoke, but he was watching carefully. He saw a man with a piece of roll-on luggage and a briefcase strapped over his shoulder. The man wore a suit. He had a medium build. A bland face. No glasses. A conservative haircut. My father watched the man put the roll-on and the briefcase into the trunk. My father watched the man get into the rental car. The man took the time to test the windshield wipers and the brights even though it was daytime. He was a careful man. A responsible man. He was perfect. My father walked on, past the National Car Rental exit and along the road. He heard the man start the car. There weren't that many cars on the road and my father walked easily forward, holding his valise, taking a hit off his cigarette.

He heard the car stop and then pull out of the National lot and onto the road. My father walked into the middle of the road, a distracted-looking man smoking his cigarette. He heard the car slow. He turned to the car and smiled in fake surprise. He walked to the passenger side of the rental car like he had a question to ask. The man pressed the button and the window went down.

"Did you happen to see the American Airlines terminal?" my father said.

"I didn't. I flew in on Continental."

"I need to find American. Maybe you could do me a favor."

"What is it?"

My father squinted his eyes at the sun and looked up and down the road. He reached into his pants. He pulled out his gun. He pointed it at the man.

"How's about giving me a ride?" my father said.

The man took an accelerated breath. My father reached into the car and opened the door, threw his valise onto the backseat and sat down next to the man.

"There's nothing to worry about. I'm sure you've heard all about the carjackings in Florida. They're standard procedure around here. Orange juice and carjackings. The two big draws."

"Don't kill me," the man said.

"No one's killing anybody unless you get stupid. Then you'll have killed yourself."

My father looked at the man and nodded for him, but he was also nodding for himself, nodding that the first step had been taken and now there was no going back. There was comfort in that. It took the butterflies away.

"Stay on this road," my father said. "I'll show you where to go. And stay right at the speed limit. We don't want to get any tickets on the way. No need to jack up your insurance on top of everything else. They make enough money."

My father leaned back in the seat. He held the gun in his lap. He had already relaxed himself into the situation, like making the room his own.

The man drove cautiously. My father showed him where to turn, giving him plenty of warning so no mistakes would be made.

"First time in Miami?" my father said.

"No. I've been here before."

"Then you're familiar with the city."

"A little bit."

"Any restaurants you can recommend?" my father said.

"I don't know."

"I'm just kidding."

The man smiled. My father was glad to see he had a sense of humor.

"So you're here for business, I take it."

"Yes. I'm here for business."

"Me too."

The man was not bad looking. Not good looking. His voice was

Midwestern, nothing really discernible. He would have made a good extra, but he'd received his unlucky lucky break, he'd been given a small part with room to improvise. My father was letting him improvise. My father was putting the man at ease.

"So what do you do for fun?" my father said. "What do you do when your day is over and you have to unwind?"

"I go home. I spend time with my wife and kids."

"It's not easy raising a family these days."

"I love my family."

My father smiled. Like all good movie lines, the line had subtext. And maybe he really did love his family.

"But does your family love you?" my father said.

"I hope so," the man said.

"I hope so too," my father said. "That would be pretty depressing if they didn't."

"We're very close."

"Too many fathers don't spend enough time with their kids. Then the kids grow up and they're left with a few vague memories of their home life. That always struck me as sad. Most kids don't even know what their parents do for a living. Do your kids know what you do for work?"

"Sort of."

"You should let them know. I bet they'd be interested. I think it's nice when a kid knows what his father does for a living, beyond just saying, *Oh, he's an electrician* or *He works on Wall Street* or *He travels to Florida on business* or *He's a carjacker.*"

"Do you have a family?"

"Good question. But since you're not my kid I'll keep it vague."

They were out of the airport grounds and on the highway. The man stayed in the middle lane. Not too fast. Not too slow. He was good at taking directions. He was probably good at what he did. Competence was a rare quality and the man seemed to possess it.

My father told the man to get off at the next exit, giving him plenty of time to make the lane change. The man checked his mirrors, put on the blinker, moved responsibly into the right lane.

"The Camry rides nice and smooth," my father said. "No wonder it's the car most stolen in America."

My father was staying in character. The man pulled off the exit.

"Go straight," my father said. "So tell me. Did you ever steal anything?"

"No. Not really."

"Not really. Not really, but sort of. I knew it. Every man steals something at least once in his life. What did you take? I'm always up for a good story."

"I took candy bars when I was in college."

"The proverbial candy bar. I sometimes wonder how the candy companies stay in business. That's how I started too. I was telling somebody recently how all the great criminals must have started by stealing candy bars. So what was your story? They weren't feeding you right in the college cafeteria?"

"It wasn't even that. I just started doing it."

"Go on."

"I was a freshman and there was a university store right outside the dining hall where they sold notebooks and beer mugs with the school's insignia on them and college sweatshirts."

"And candy bars."

"Yes. And candy bars."

My father was just leading him on, making him a partner, needing a partner for what was ahead, and the man, now that he was talking, seemed to forget what he was doing, driving at gunpoint through Miami's streets, and he just relaxed into the moment the way my father already had. He seemed happy to reminisce about this private moment in college, a moment he probably hadn't even thought about for years. My father kept him going.

"So why did you do it? Just to get back at the school for charging you all that tuition money? You thought you'd cut in on the profits?"

"I don't know. I think I took those candy bars because I hated my freshman year. I was sort of lost and I was bored a lot of the time and I was disappointed. College was supposed to be this important time, but it wasn't at all. I used to go into the store every night after dinner and take a candy bar. Then I'd go over to the magazine section and while I was reading I'd put the candy bar up my sleeve. It was a rush."

"It's a high, isn't it?"

"It was."

"It's an even higher high when the stakes are higher."

"Right now I'm more scared than high."

"Trust me," my father said and smiled. "Trust me, baby. It's a high."

"Taking that candy bar was the most exciting time of the day. The pitiful part is that when my kids get to be college age I'll impart how important college is and what a great four years they'll have. I'll never tell them how bored I was. I'll certainly never tell them I stole candy from the university store."

"You'll put a fatherly spin on things," my father said.

"Exactly."

"The things we do for love," my father said. "Or something like that. Pull in here."

The man pulled the car over.

"Turn off the ignition."

The man did as he was told.

My father checked his watch and leaned back in his seat.

"This is the high we're going to have," my father said. "There's an armored car that's going to come by in twenty-five minutes. If you look closely at an armored car, or at this particular armored car,

228

you'll notice that there are three guards. One stays in the truck the whole time, in the passenger seat. On the passenger door there's a little hole you can put a gun through and start shooting if there's trouble. That's his job. We don't want to deal with him. What we want to do is deal with the two guards that get out of the truck. And we want to deal with them just after they've picked up some money from this bank and are about to put it in the back of the truck. That way it's just the two of us and just the two of them. There's no better fight than a fair fight, and two on two is fair."

"I'm not an armed robber," the man said.

"Today you're going to pretend you're one."

"How do I do that?"

"You sit in the car and look dangerous. You take off your jacket and put it over your arm and you keep your arm straight, like you've got a sawed-off shotgun in there, and you pretend you're the most ruthless, cold-blooded motherfucker in the country."

"And what if they don't buy it?"

"If you're good they'll buy it. Talk about motivation. A good actor never goes into a scene without knowing his motivation, and your motivation is so clear you'll do a great job. If you don't look like a killer, you'll get killed."

"This isn't acting. This is real."

"I keep hearing that. I don't know. I think the best acting is real. When you're watching a great movie you forget you're watching a movie. Believe me, when this is taking place it will be real and surreal at the same time. Actually it will be super real. And you're going to be a super-real killer with your arm pointing straight ahead."

The man was no longer relaxed, but that was okay. He had to understand this was serious, that my father could joke around and they could talk about stealing candy bars, but soon the stakes were going to change.

"I'll be outside the car dealing with one guard and you'll be in here dealing with the other guard. They know a shotgun blast can go clean through a windshield so you don't have to leave the car. You just have to look like you'll blow the guy's head off if he so much as thinks about being a hero. And at the rate these guys get paid, he'd have to be a moron to actually risk his life for someone else's money."

"Aren't you risking your life for someone else's money?"

"It's going to be my money soon. It would never be theirs. They'd never take that chance."

"It's a risky chance."

"Are you questioning me?"

"No."

"But are you questioning me?"

"I'm not."

"But are you questioning me?"

"No. I'm sorry. I'm not."

My father started laughing.

"Those repetitions are terrifying," he said and laughed some more.

The man kept his eyes on the road.

"You've got balls, don't you?" my father said. "I like that. You don't look like a guy with balls, but I bet you use that to advantage. I bet you're very good at what you do. Whatever you do."

"Thank you."

"And you're wrong. There's a difference between taking and protecting. You should protect what you love. I think that's the only thing worth protecting."

My father looked at the man, hard, and nodded once to impress upon him that the heroic choice would be to listen to my father, to protect what he loved. Words with meaning. Gestures with meaning.

"Big stealing," my father said for himself.

My father looked down the street. Cars. Pedestrians. Not a cop car in sight. The Miami sun bounced blinding light off the Camry's hood.

"So that's the setup. You'll act like a killer. I'll take the money. And when I get back in the car you'll pull out very quietly, not a burnt-rubber exit like they have in stupid movies, and I'll show you where to drive. Got it?"

"Got it," the man said.

"A quick study."

"Are you going to kill me?"

"Not unless I have to," my father said.

He was done talking. My father leaned back in the seat even more, adjusted the rearview mirror so that he could see what was going on behind if he had to, and watched the scene in front of him with half-closed eyes. He was in it and soon he would be in it even more. It was like one big improvisation. Like my father was an experienced actor, so experienced that the director would allow him to move within the parameters of the plot. He would have to get from point A to point B, but how he got there was his decision. He could be cold hearted. He could be funny. He could be nervous. He could be calm. He could be violent. He could check his violence. My father thought of Belmondo. Belmondo walks through the film acting like he doesn't have a care in the world except for the American woman he loves. There are things to worry about, Belmondo is in trouble, but with the woman he smiles and jokes and smokes and walks around Paris like it's a set, just background to their bond. And Jean Seberg loves his strut, his confidence, his cigarette moves. When my father saw Anna, he pickpocketed the lecherous man's wallet and took her out to lunch, but by the time he told her he took things on a more permanent basis, the bond was already there. It was too late. The same was true of kids. By the time kids learned about their parents, saw their parents as more than par-

ents, as people in their own right with definitions that extended beyond taking care of kids, the bond was set and usually, no matter
how hard the rebellion went, there could be no complete separa-
tion, no matter what.

My father checked his watch, looked into the rearview mirror
and there was the armored car, painted red, moving slowly down
the street. It appeared heavy, as if the bulletproof glass and rein-
forced steel were a burden on the wheels. The armored car passed
the rental car, pulled right in front of it and stopped. My father's
hands were sweaty in the surgical gloves. He took a breath and held
it for a moment, quietly, so the man next to him wouldn't hear.

"Don't look at them," my father said.

"I won't," the man said.

"We're just a couple of guys waiting for our friend to come out
of the bank. We're all going out to lunch. A bourbon and a steak.
Boys will be boys. Not a care in the world."

"Not a care in the world," the man repeated.

The back of the armored vehicle opened and the first guard
stepped down to the street. His gun was already drawn. He held it at
his side, barrel down. He wore a blue uniform. The bulletproof vest
underneath made his body look even stockier. The second guard
stepped down from the passenger seat. He was taller and thinner and
he held his gun the same way. It was easy to see from their body
language that the taller man was the one in charge. He walked
slightly ahead of the other guard and seemed to take his job more
seriously, his bearing upright, his eyes narrowed in a mask of tough-
ness that said he would use his gun if he had to and wouldn't feel
guilty about it. Maybe his job was all he had.

"You can look now," my father said. "The smaller guard is the
one I'm going to deal with first. He's the one that carries the money
so he needs to holster his gun. Then I'll deal with the taller guy. He's
the one you'll be pointing your arm at. My guess is that he has the

balls to go one-on-one, but not two-on-one. Of course he could crumble immediately and we could be in and out in no time. We'll see how it goes. There's also the one other guard in the truck. He might be able to see some of what's going on in his mirror, but he might not even be watching. They seem pretty comfortable with their routine. Any questions?"

"I just point my arm at the taller guy."

"That's all you need to do. As soon as you see me take my gun out, put your arm under your jacket and point it at the taller guard like you've got a shotgun you're ready to use. Make your eyes sleepy. It will relax your face. That's the scariest look of all. And when I get back in the car, pull out nice and smooth and drive."

The two guards walked into the bank. The armored truck idled. Jared Chiziver reached into the backseat and got his valise. He zipped it open and took out two pairs of tinted sunglasses and two fishing caps with *Miami* stitched across the front in cursive. He handed a hat and a pair of sunglasses to the man and told him to put them on. Hair covered, eyes hidden, they could have been anyone.

"Big stealing," my father said.

He sat there low in his seat and waited. He looked at his watch.

"Start the car," he said and the official quality of his voice surprised even him, not that his tone sounded emotionless, but it was so cold coming out that he didn't fully recognize his own voice. When he took wallets, he didn't have to give orders. He worked alone and he worked when he was ready. Big stealing. At least he appeared to know what he was doing. Making the room his own. Making the moment his own. Improvising. Acting and directing at the same time. Grace under pressure, but under the grace his heart was beating fast and hard and he took a long breath and held it and took a long breath and held it, but quiet, so the man next to him wouldn't hear.

"If you even think about taking off while this is going on I'll shoot you. I know you better than I know the guards and if you try leaving I'll consider it an act of betrayal and go for you first."

"I don't want to die," the man said.

"Then keep your arm straight and your jaw set and your eyes sleepy."

"I was supposed to be at a meeting right now."

"Think of it. You could be at a meeting, but instead you're doing something far more memorable. You're really living now."

My father tucked the gun in his belt. He looked toward the bank. The door opened and the two guards came out. The stocky guard held two canvas bags, one in each hand, his gun holstered at his side. The taller man held his gun pointed down, walking like nobody better fuck with him.

"Lights, camera, action," my father said and breathed in like before a jump.

He got out of the car. He put his valise on the ground, just another tourist with sunglasses and a goofy hat. He passed close to the stocky guard holding the bags, close enough to touch him, and put the guard's gun in his own belt. It was easy for my father to take the gun even with his bad hand. A holster was not a pocket. My father stopped like he'd forgotten something, a furrowed brow visible above the tinted lenses. He turned from the stocky guard, walked toward the truck, pulled his gun from his belt and put it against the tall guard's throat. The tall guard raised his gun and my father pressed his own gun harder into the guard's neck.

"There's a man in that car with a shotgun who will finish the job if I don't," my father said. "Don't be a tough guy."

The tall guard glanced at the car. The stocky guard was still holding the two canvas bags. Jared Chiziver told the tall guard to drop his gun. My father counted to three in his head, like magic-ing food for an impatient kid in a restaurant, and on three he heard the sound of metal hitting concrete.

"Let's make this quick," my father said to the guard holding the bags. "Grab that valise over there, put the canvas bags in the valise and then fill it up with as much as you can from the truck. I want bags with money, not checks. Now start filling that valise."

The guard moved. My father kept his gun pressed against the tall guard's throat.

"When they catch you I'll personally visit you in prison," the tall guard said.

"Conjugal visit?" my father said.

"What are you, a faggot?"

My father pressed the gun hard into the guard's throat.

"I don't like that word," he said. "I never want to hear that word again. Now shut the fuck up."

The valise was almost full. My father told the guard to hurry up. The armored car door opened. It was a different sound from a regular car door opening. It was heavy. Heavy hinges to hold heavy steel in place. My father pressed his gun into the tall guard's throat and inched him forward toward the sidewalk so that the third guard, standing near the front of the truck, would see his coworker with a gun at his neck.

"Now look him in the eyes," my father said to the tall guard. "Tell him to drop his gun and kick it over here so I can see it. I'll count to three."

The tall guard did as he was told. My father counted to three, but the magic didn't work.

"Tell him to kick the gun over or he'll have blood on his hands."

The tall guard took my father's directions, repeated my father's words. My father counted to three. The magic didn't work.

"Not smart," my father said.

My father grabbed the tall guard's throat, pointed the gun at the guard's knee, pushed past the pain of his broken hand, finger against trigger, and shot the tall guard's kneecap. The scream was all animal. It was the deepest kind of pain. A pain like his son had felt. The scream made it real, not just the picture of a neck with a gun against it and some hidden body holding the gun, but a man screaming from smashed flesh, cartilage, bone. My father counted to three and this time the gun slid across the pavement into view.

The valise was full. He told the stocky guard to zip it closed. The guard did as he was told. My father let go of the tall guard. The guard dropped, his blown knee unable to support his weight. He was screaming and his good leg started kicking against the pavement.

My father picked up the valise, walked to the rental car, got in. The man still had his arm extended under his jacket.

"You can put your arm down now," my father said.

The man put his arm down.

"You can put your hands on the steering wheel."

The man did as he was told.

"Nice and smooth," my father said. "Let's go."

The man pulled out slowly. My father held his real gun straight and looked at the guards. He nodded his head. An armored car was good for protecting money, sometimes, but it wasn't a chase car.

My father took off his hat and glasses and took off the driver's hat and glasses and shoved everything into the valise that was at his feet, heavy with canvas bags.

"You did well," my father said. "I wouldn't have fucked with you. You looked like the real thing."

The man didn't say anything.

"So how did I look?" my father said and started laughing.

My father directed the man to the highway and they drove back to the airport. They drove past the National Car Rental lot and past airport parking. My father had the man drive to the end of the loop, close to the edge of the runway, and stop the car. A plane lifted off. My father waited until the wheels were tucked in.

"You can get out," my father said.

"Can I have my luggage?"

"You'll get it eventually. The longer they don't trust you, the better. If you're just walking around without bags it looks worse for you. They'll figure out soon enough you weren't involved, but soon enough is better for me than right away."

"Why did you choose me?"

"Why does anyone choose anyone? Timing. You were here when I was here."

My father looked at the man, smiled with his eyes. The man opened the door and stepped out of the car. My father did the same and walked around the front of the car to the driver's seat. He stood looking at the man.

"Remember," my father said.

"Remember what?

"Today. You'll never forget today. When you think back on your memorable days, on the days that made you feel alive, this day will be up there. Right now, you're alive. As you're walking along this airport road back to your regular life, the life you left for a little while, you'll feel good. I guarantee that. You're alive right now. You're alive. Right now. Now."

And with the word still in the air, air that was quiet, one plane off, the next plane still waiting for clearance, a slight breeze coming off the ocean, the palm fronds moving with a hushed rustle, my father got into the car, tucked the gun into his belt and drove off.

He drove to airport parking. Parked the rental. Put the guard's gun under the seat. Took his valise. Walked to the Valiant. Got in. Took off the surgical gloves. Tipped his hat back, his face to the sun, smiling, the big stealing done. He drove up to the booth to pay for parking. A woman took his ticket.

"Dropping off a friend?"

"All done with that. I'm a free man."

"Are you really?"

"I'm feeling free," my father said.

"And where does a free man go on a weekday afternoon?"

"A free man goes wherever he wants. A free man does whatever he wants."

"I see," the woman said and smiled.

My father smiled back and held her eyes. He couldn't help it. If the flirting started, my father closed the deal. There was no deal to close, Anna was the woman he wanted, but the woman in the ticket booth was interested in this handsome man with his hat pushed back and his eyes lit with what he'd just done and his voice smooth and his body language that was all sex, an aura like a movie star. She lingered on his eyes. He lingered back. She looked him over and on his T-shirt were some spots of blood. Her expression changed, just a slight shift in her eyes, a slight tightening of her mouth, and my father caught the change. He paid for two hours worth of parking and drove off. He looked down at his T-shirt and saw the blood spots and he already knew the woman had written down his license plate, made some calls. My father slammed his bad hand down on the wheel. Big stealing. Little stealing. Big mistake. Little mistake. One mistake.

"Fuck it," my father said.

"Fuck it," my father screamed.

"Fuck it. I'm alive."

High. Another high. An all-or-nothing, big-stealing high. Like an all-or-nothing, one-night-stand high. The morning-after feeling had not yet set in and at that moment, like every moment that was all feeling and no thinking for my father, I believe he really was high.

He drove back to the hotel, weaving the Valiant along the highway, fast. He needed to get us. He needed to move.

That is how my imagined scene ended and the real scene began.

I saw my father pull into the Fontainebleau. I had been pacing on the sidewalk of Collins Avenue and there he was, the gold-painted hood holding the sun. His hat was tilted back on his head, his hands were steady, he was smiling, a real smile, a joyful smile, the kind of joy I remembered Anna had described when she'd spoken about the running of the bulls in Pamplona. The runners had escaped death in a way and so the moment was precious, life was precious, to be alive was the joy, the joy that comes after the adrenaline rush leaves you satisfied. My father looked satisfied. He looked at me. He honked the horn. He stopped the car. He rolled down the window. He said it was time to pack our bags.

# 22

ANNA WAS AT THE POOL. HER SUNGLASSES WERE ON, BUT BE-
hind them I knew her eyes were far away with her own vision of
what had transpired. When I told her he was upstairs packing, she
stood up as if she'd been expecting the news, touched my shoulder
once, and we walked through the lobby and went up to the room.

We all packed our things. My father's valise was full so he put his
clothes into my bag and Anna's bag. The TV was on and when the
news anchor described the details of the armored truck heist in Miami, I knew my father was the man they were looking for. They
mentioned something about roadblocks north of Miami and around
the airport. In the hallway the maids were cleaning, but I already
knew a few soaps, a few shampoos, were nothing. Little stealing was
over.

We went down. My father told us to meet him two blocks
south. We walked out of the lobby, the bags heavy, my crotch hurting from lifting my father's full valise. We walked along the sidewalk and waited.

We saw the Valiant drive by and we waited some more.

My father walked towards us, his shirt untucked, his new look, and I knew what was under the shirt, but he was smiling anyway. He held a newspaper folded in half to cover the Valiant's New York plates. He picked up his valise and we followed him across the avenue. There was no breeze and even the palm fronds looked heavy, but I don't think he noticed the palms. He threw the plates into a Dumpster.

"I'll never see my car again, will I?" Anna said.

"Hopefully not," he said.

"I've had that car for a long time. I suppose it was time for a new car."

"It was starting to deteriorate anyway. There was rust under the frame and once the body starts to rust, it's all over."

My father called a cab from a payphone and told the driver where to meet us. Anna took out her camera. She focused the lens on my father.

"You're glowing," she said. "Look up at the sun."

My father lifted his hat, wiped his arm across his forehead, put his hat back on, tipped it back, his face lit by the sun. He nodded his head once and then stopped the nod short, his eyes looking up, pupils practically touching lids, and the smile was in his eyes and it was more than that, his eyes were completely clear, like he could see everything, and I heard Anna press the shutter once and again and again.

"Joy," she said.

"All or nothing," my father said.

She ran out of film and started to load another roll. I went close to my father and spoke low.

"Are you rich?" I said.

"I'm not sure yet."

"Are you crazy?"

"Do you really want to know how I feel?"

"Tell me."

"It was crazy at first. Then I just relaxed into it and here I am."

"Here we are."

"That's right. Here we are."

"Another high."

"There's nothing wrong with highs," my father said.

"A few more," Anna said. "Look back at the sun."

My father looked up and Anna pressed the shutter.

The cab came. It was white, not New York City yellow. My father told the driver to take us to the bus station. The driver hit the meter and the first number turned. My father purposely made fake small-talk. We were from Chicago. We weren't looking forward to getting back to the cold, but duty called. Taking a bus wasn't so bad, especially since O'Hare Airport was snowed-in half the winter. It actually made sense to take the bus in the long run. The cabdriver didn't seem interested. He kept banging the top of the meter to keep the numbers moving, the dollars piling up.

My father paid and we went into the bus terminal. He told Anna to get us three tickets for Key West.

"Key West?" she said.

"I have my reasons."

"And what reasons would those be?"

"The pie. The famous key lime pie."

She laughed and he kissed her on the mouth. There was joy in her eyes too. She was with a man she loved, she was in the middle of an adventure, she had photographed joy. And for her there would be no repercussions. My father hadn't told her anything specific. She was just taking a trip to Key West with a man she'd met in New York City and his son. Anna walked gracefully across the station. My father rearranged the gun inside his belt. The metal was probably uncomfortable in the heat.

"Key West will be fun," he said. "U.S. 1 all the way down. You

243

can't go any farther than Key West and I've always wanted to see what the end of the States looks like."

"That's not why we're going there."

He looked at me with steady eyes to show me everything was fine, but it wasn't.

"Key West is the smart move," he said. "It's such a stupid move that it's the smart move. It's a dead end. It's the stupid move if you're looking to escape. They think I'm a planner. They think I'm going to make a long-term move. So let them blockade every northern route out of here. I'm going to Key West."

"We're all going to Key West."

"Yes, we are. The more the merrier. Listen to me, Ben. There's nothing to be worried about. You hear me? Nothing. Enjoy this. We're taking a trip. We're going somewhere we've never been before."

"You always said big stealing was bullshit romance. You said big stealing got you caught."

"I'm glad you listen to me."

"You're my father. I'm supposed to listen to you."

"Good. Then listen to me when I tell you to enjoy this. Go west, young man. Go Key West."

"It's south."

"Same thing. We're going to the end of something. We're going to the end of the States. It's an American adventure."

"No, it's not."

"Sure it is."

"Do you know what you did? Do you? This isn't a fucking movie. This is our life. I'm your son. You can't just put this life on me. You can't just take me to Key West and pretend it's some fucking game. You're making me crazy. Your going crazy is making me crazy. You're making me crazy."

"I'm not crazy," my father said. "And you're fine."

"I'm not fine."

My father put his hands on my shoulders and pressed his hands into my shoulders until it hurt. I wanted to cry out but I didn't. I didn't want to give him the satisfaction. I wanted to keep my poker face. It was stupid because my father could read me. He didn't want me to cry out either. He wanted me to prove to myself that I could take it, that I wasn't crazy at all. I should have cried out. I should have screamed. I should have broken down and fallen to my knees and held his legs and screamed. But I was too old to do that and I had gone through what I had gone through and he knew it. He pressed his hands into me harder. Then harder. Then he let go.

"See," he said. "You're fine."

Anna came back with the tickets. We were just a family, on vacation, taking a trip to the Keys to check out the destinations on the colored pamphlets. A tour of a submarine. A visit to Hemingway's house. A walk along the honky-tonk streets. We'd have to get a bigger cabinet in whatever bathroom in whatever apartment to fit all the stolen bills. If we got that far.

We boarded the bus. They sat next to each other and I sat across the aisle. No one sat next to me. I stretched out my legs and looked out the window. We drove to the end of Miami and past Miami and went over the first long bridge. The ocean looked calm. The sky was blue. It was a perfect day for sightseeing.

The horizon stretched far out, broken only by some sailboats and a cruise ship in the distance. I wondered if there were people standing on deck, doing parade-waves the way they did on the ocean liners going down the Hudson. Sometimes running along the river early in the morning I would see one of the Cunard ships pulling out to the Atlantic and I could see the people, lined up, looking at Manhattan, their arms raised, maybe to me. I ran faster than the ship, but the smoke coming from the blue stack, a gray plume against the early sky, was a sign of potential power. In New

York everything was on top of everything, people on people, apartments upon apartments, even the boats were close to the land, the Hudson River not that wide until it opened past the Statue of Liberty. Here everything was wide open. The ocean. The sweep of the bridge. The day that my father had made his own. Wide open and full of possibility and I looked at him sitting with her and he was happy, happier than I had ever seen him. He had been with this woman for a longer time than he had been with anyone in my memory. People had their little life philosophies, but my father was romantic enough to break his, at least with her, at least for a while. There are people who say they will never get married or they will never work a full-time job or they will never do this or do that, never, and after a while, the repeated statement becomes a decree. They won't break their word for fear of being seen as fakes, but the truth is the decree keeps them from living and so it's the decree that's fake. My father wasn't like that. He did what he did. He was doing what he was doing. He leaned closely into her and looked at the view on his side of the bus, the open space, and I knew the horizon my father saw went farther than I could ever see.

Key Largo. Like the movie. Tavernier. Platation. Islamorada. A pretty name for the fourth key in line. Layton. Marathon Key. An island that touched my legs. Big Pine. May Island. Cudjoe. Sugarloaf. Then the sign said Key West. The last bridge south.

We touched down on the small island, picked up our bags, got off the bus, walked through the station to the street. My father. Anna lighting up a cigarette. Me.

The people here were different from Miami people. It was closer to Manhattan, more of a melting pot of immigrants and artist types and there were gay people here too, many of them. Key West. Manhattan. Provincetown. San Francisco. In Middle America not all people were accepted and so they wandered until they got to some kind of end. An island. A hooked tip. A coast. And in Middle

America my father would not have survived. In New York City a player could be a player, anonymous forever. And now he had wandered to the end of something, from the metropolitan island to the southern tip of the states. But in Key West, there weren't the numbers. In Key West the anonymity would be hard to maintain. It wasn't the smart move at all. He could be found in Key West, a single bridge could be blocked, and my breath went short.

We found a cab and my father told the driver to take us to The Grand. I'd also seen the hotel's sign from the bus. Anna checked in while we waited outside.

"Are you hungry?" my father said.

"I'm fine."

The room was no Fontainebleau. It was small. The two double beds looked lumpy. The floor was bright orange. Next to the mirror was a painting of the ocean, waves breaking too dramatically.

My father unzipped his valise, took the moneybags out, looked into them, put the bags back in the valise. He took a run at the bed, jumped as high as he could, and dove onto the mattress, turning his body in the air so that he landed on his back. His shirt lifted and I saw the gun and then the shirt covered it.

"It's grand," he said and sat up. "It's fucking grand."

"Well done," Anna said.

"It's all grand at The Grand," my father said and his eyes were lit. "Now, we can either sit around this less-than-grand hotel room, or we can go out, see the scenery and celebrate. I say we get the hell out of here. Let's take a look at this island. Let's rustle up some key lime pie. What do you say, Ben?"

"What do you want me to say?" I said.

"I want you to say you'll join us."

"You know I will. This may be the last time I see you."

"Are you going somewhere?"

"Very funny," I said.

My father put his valise in the closet. He took some of his dirty underwear from my bag and put it on the valise. We left the room. The sun was starting to set. The sky was lined in pinks and purples. Red sky at night. We weren't sailors.

We walked around Key West. The gray painted boats docked in the shipyards were so different from the clean white of New York's ocean liners. These were utilitarian boats built to get to destinations. Their lines were not sleek. A submarine was open for public viewing, and we went inside and squeezed through the narrow corridors. My father turned to me and saluted.

The streets became crowded. Sailors. Cubans. Tourists. Men holding men's hands. Women holding women's hands. Chameleons skittered along the sidewalks and into the bushes. By day they changed colors, perfect actors, gray to green. At night they probably didn't bother changing. At night, when color went closer to black and white, it was easier to hide.

We ended up on Duval Street, slow-walking, so packed there was a name for the walk, the Duval Crawl. The drinkers seemed especially weighted down. We passed a newsstand. The headline read *Miami Truck Heist*. My father told me to pick up a paper and I did, feeling suspicious as I handed over a buck, took the change, looked at the headline and away. I gave the paper to my father.

"*The Miami Herald*," my father said. "Here's a quiz question for you. What paper did Jean Seberg sell in *Breathless*?"

"I give up," Anna said.

"Ben?"

"Whatever."

"*The Whatever Herald*? Nope. Guess again."

"*The New York Herald Tribune*. It's right on the poster."

"Give this man a prize," my father said.

"I'm not a man yet."

My father tipped his hat forward, read the article, nodded his head.

"Are you safe?" Anna said.

"Unless you call the cops like she did in the movie."

"I hated her for that," Anna said. "Even when she explained why she made the call, it seemed like a shitty excuse."

"Maybe she called because she loved him."

"She called because she was a coward. He was right to call her a coward. She called so she didn't have to fall in love completely."

"Are you a coward?" my father said.

"I'm still here."

"Why are you here?"

"You know," she said.

She had her eyes on his eyes, and stayed looking even as she lit a cigarette.

"I know," he said.

My father crumpled up the newspaper, bent down and started shining his shoes like Belmondo in the movie. He started laughing. I wanted to scream at him, but I didn't. I wanted to scream at her. The way she was playing along seemed so fucking irresponsible.

"Did they mention your name?" I said.

"No name. No picture. They just got the story."

"Let me see."

"There's nothing to see," he said looking up at me. "I'm fine. We're fine. We're all fine. And now my shoes are spit and polish."

"I guess you have to look especially good now," I said. "You're famous."

"Only to you."

"No. You'll be famous. You'll have your fifteen minutes. That's what you wanted all along."

"Fifteen minutes is fifteen minutes."

"How does it feel? Mighty? Does this make you feel mighty?"

My father stood up. I was almost as tall as him, but not quite.

He made a muscle.

"*Bonjour,*" he said.

He took a cigarette from Anna and lit up.

"Enjoy," he said.

He was looking at me like I was the stupid one. Like I was being unreasonable, bringing them down from their high.

"Fine," I said. "Fine. Get me drunk. You want me to enjoy this? Get me fucked up. I want to get fucked up. I want to feel all or nothing just like you."

"That's my boy. I knew you had it in you."

"Let's go crazy. Let's go fucking crazy. I want to go as crazy as you."

"I told you. I'm not crazy. And you're not crazy. But I will get you drunk. We should get drunk. We have something to celebrate. We're rich."

My father pretended to stagger forward, a mock Duval Crawl. He went into the first bar he saw and we followed him in. He ordered three rum and colas and then three more. The bartender had precut the center of each lime wedge so that it fit perfectly on the lip of the glass. I drank up. The light was in their eyes and I felt the light in mine. I drank until I didn't care. A young man was watching me and I watched him and he knew. He looked a little like Michael. His mouth wasn't as beautiful, but he had the same build, the same calm eyes. My father ordered another round and then we crawled on to the next bar and the next. Time skipped and I didn't care. I let myself fall into what my father had done the way Anna was letting herself fall, the way my father had fallen.

We went to a restaurant and ordered three big lobsters, drank more drinks, our eyes getting lighter. We cracked claws, dipped sweet meat into butter, started laughing because we were sitting around wearing bibs like three fucking kids. My father ordered another round and I told him I was going to the bathroom. They didn't care. They were laughing and eating and drinking.

I walked back to the first bar. The young man was still there. I knew he'd still be there and I walked over to him.

"I need a drink," I said.

"What are you drinking?"

"Whatever you're having. You were watching me, right? You were watching me."

"I was."

"Did you see the man I was with?"

"I was watching you," he said.

"Good answer. I like that answer. Do you live around here?"

"I live pretty close."

"Let's go," I said.

"You want your drink?"

"Let's just go."

We walked out of the bar, down one street, down another, space skipping, into a door, up some stairs, into a room. He poured drinks and I drank mine down. I took the bottle and drank and I felt the light in my eyes, strong and dizzy. Michael had kissed me first and I kissed the young man first. I kissed him and moved my hand down his back, pressing one vertebra at a time like Michael had done to me and I took his shirt off and took his pants off. I was being the player. I was being the leading man. He asked if I wanted to hear some music. I took off my shirt. I took off my pants. I saw a pack of cigarettes on the table next to his bed and next to that a pink lighter.

"Where did you get that?"

These were my words, the words in my head, but they weren't. He was talking. He was looking at the new skin around my cock.

"I was burned."

"Are you all right?"

"I'm fine," I said and I almost started laughing. Like father. Like son.

He was looking down at my cock.

"Does it disgust you?"

"No."

"Tell me if it does. I can take it."

"No," he said.

He put his hand on my cock to let me know. He put his mouth around my cock to let me know. I was looking at the pink lighter on the table. Time skipped. Space skipped. Three men came out of Barrow's Pub laughing. A pink lighter. Fire. Burn. And Michael ran away.

"Why did you do it?"

"Why did I do what?"

"Why?" I said.

I opened him up from behind. I opened him up and I forced my cock inside him. I fucked him and fucked him, my eyes closed, seeing the man with the pink lighter, and I fucked him and fucked him, the heat on my balls hot and then cold, and I fucked him and fucked him, and the man's face turned to Michael's face and Michael had run away, and I fucked him and fucked him, and my father said I had it in me, I was his boy, I could take it, I was fine, and I fucked him and fucked him, all or nothing, all or nothing, all or nothing, all or nothing.

# 23

I WAS AWAKE MOST OF THE NIGHT. THE OUTSIDE SOUNDS were tropical, lizards calling, insects scratching, broken by drunken shouts, and then I must have fallen asleep because I woke with a start. It was just them. They were laughing. My father sat down on the bed next to me, put his hand on my shoulder, and said they were going out for a walk and I should come along. His breath smelled of liquor.

"I'm tired," I said.

"You had a late night last night," he said. "Did you have fun?"

"I was drunk."

"We were all drunk. Come on, we'll walk off our hangovers."

He sang me the army song, about not having breakfast in bed anymore, and told me to come along. He rarely told me things. When he told me something twice, I listened. I sat up, rubbed my eyes, stretched my legs, aware of my crotch, the old pain and the new pain. I dressed and the three of us went out.

It was just past dawn. It was even a little cool outside, a relief from the string of hot days. Anna took off her sunglasses and tilted her head to the sky.

"Look at the light," Anna said. "It's so clean."

"That's why they shoot movies in the morning," my father said.

"Let me have the key," she said.

She went back to the room and came out with her Leica camera. My father watched to make sure she locked the door. Anna lit up a cigarette, the smoke defined in the early light.

"Key West," my father said to me, but he was watching her walking toward us. "What do you think?"

"I've tried to stop thinking," I said. "Just like you."

"We won't be here that long."

"Where are we going next?"

"I'm not sure yet. We'll play it by ear. We'll improvise."

We walked through the streets. There was almost no one out. Far from Duval Street, many of the houses looked beat up. A boy kicked a ball around a small front yard, the grass brown and burnt. My father stopped to watch him. The boy kicked the ball as hard as he could, glad to have an audience, and it went over the hedges and bounced on the sidewalk. My father picked up the ball and threw it to the boy. He caught the ball on his foot and dribbled it in the air three times before he lost control.

"Bravo," my father said, clapping his hands.

*"Mira,"* the boy said.

"I'm looking," my father said.

The boy lifted the ball with his foot and dribbled it three times and then it bounced away. He ran after the ball.

*"Mira,"* the boy said.

He dribbled it once and twice and three times and my father counted to four before the boy lost control of the ball. He ran after the ball again. He wanted to impress my father.

*"Mira, mira,"* the boy said.

*"Mira, mira. Manetquilla,"* my father said.

*"Manetquilla,"* the boy repeated and started laughing.

My father waved good-bye and we started walking. The uneven rhythm of the bouncing ball faded.

We wandered around. Chameleons skittered across the sidewalks, fast in daylight.

Anna focused her camera on me.

"I don't need to be photographed," I said.

"Just one."

"Why?"

"Because you look so damn happy," she said and took the picture.

Anna asked my father to keep walking. She took some pictures of him walking away and then he turned with his gun out and she took that photograph. He looked like a killer, but then broke into a smile, in his eyes, in his mouth, and she took the photograph right in the middle of his word *Mighty,* the *click* cutting the word in perfect halves.

Maybe he was mighty. He went out all those nights, night after night after night, and at the end of the night, in the morning, when I saw him, his hands went gentle as he pushed them away. It was a different kind of stamina. The playing. The drinking. The little stealing. Now his hand was broken and he wasn't pushing her away. He was playing for her camera, but he was with her, had been with her since they'd first met and he hadn't come home for two days. If he was restless it wasn't because of Anna. I knew that. I was tired. I was hungover. My restless night. When I came, I felt it all go out of me. I cried into his back, into his shoulders and I kept repeating the word, the question. Why. Why. Why. He had run. He had run away. I cried into the stranger's back. His hands were gentle on me, but I couldn't look at him. I cried in the street, stumbled back to the hotel. I wasn't a player. I didn't have that stamina and I didn't have that restlessness. I wasn't my father. I was closer to my new father, the one with Anna. I'd known that all along, but I knew it as the drink left my body, the steady pounding of my hangover headache strangely comforting in its rhythm, pushing the night before into the background. The sun pressed into my headache.

My father tucked the gun back into his pants. Anna took a fresh roll of film from her pocket, loaded the camera, put the used roll in her pocket. In the distance I could see the shipyard, gray boats in a still line.

"I once took a wallet from a very beautiful woman," my father said.

"Only one?" Anna said.

"Not as beautiful as you. She was very vain. Some women can look at you and then past you as soon as you look back at them. Only women can do that with their eyes. They see you, but pretend not to see you, as if they could never be accused of looking at you first."

My father walked straight at Anna, looked at her and past her with his eyes.

"Stop," she said and laughed.

"I'm learning, but I'll never get it exactly right."

"Well, it's a skill we're born with," Anna said.

"I think you're right. Anyway, this woman had perfected the technique. She was a pro. She was walking toward me and the first thing I noticed was that her bag was open. Then I looked up and saw her eyes on me, but not on me at the same time. Her bag was an expensive Prada, and it was more open than her eyes. Maybe she'd put some powder on before hitting the street and had forgotten to close her bag. I turned around and started following her open bag. It was amazing how many men not only looked at this woman, but also turned their heads and said something to her. They used the worst lines. They didn't have a chance, but some of them didn't even care. It was a cliché of what they were supposed to do, but they did it anyway. They were on the hunt even if it was futile."

"That's a skill men are born with," Anna said.

"I followed her for blocks. It was fascinating how badly the men tried and how bad they were at trying. And the men I felt most sorry for were the ones who looked back longingly and said nothing. When she had passed them, when their moment of possibility was over, I could see the frustration in their faces. I could see them resolving to take a chance next time, but I could also see they never would."

"How did you know that?" I said.

"I saw it."

"You can't see that."

"Yes I can," my father said. "Don't worry. I see more in you. I see much more."

"You're my father. You're supposed to say that."

"It's not a line," my father said.

I wasn't sure. Ever since we'd packed fast, jumped into the Valiant, driven south, Manhattan to Miami and then Miami to Key West, it had seemed like all the lines had been lines. But maybe that's what real words were. Good enough to be remembered, so good enough to be lines. When we recited lines to each other, my father and me, we were connected. The lines were our history. The lines were our past and it didn't matter that the lines were stolen from films. When we said them they were ours.

My father reached into Anna's shirt pocket and took her pack of cigarettes, tapped two out, lit them both in his mouth, handed her one.

"I followed this woman. I followed her all the way up Fifth Avenue and right in front of Tiffany's I reached into her Prada bag and took her purse. It seemed like the perfect place, all those diamonds on display a perfect background."

My father stopped for a moment. I saw him close his broken hand and open it.

"I wasn't done with her. I followed her some more. I was right behind her and every time a man gave her a line I would repeat the line in monotone. I must have recited ten lines, without enthusiasm, and the lines sounded ridiculous without any expression in them. *How you doing, baby? What's your name, sweetheart? I know I've seen you in magazines. Let me walk you to the altar.* Finally the woman turned around. She was smiling so I knew she had a sense of humor and she wasn't looking past my eyes anymore. She asked if I could come up with my own line. I told her I was one of the lucky ones, that I didn't need to use bad lines to meet a woman."

"You slept with her, didn't you?" Anna said.

"Just once. Before I left her place, I asked her how she did it. Of course she didn't know what I was referring to. I asked her how she could look at a man and then past a man at the same time. At first she looked like I'd caught her stealing, but then her face relaxed. You know what she told me? She told me it was easy. She told me that while she was looking in a man's eyes she had no interest in, she shut everything out of her head until there was nothing. If there was nothing behind her eyes then that's what the man saw. Nothing. She said men became discouraged very easily and an easily discouraged man was not the kind of man she was interested in."

"So you won her on persistence," Anna said.

"I didn't need to win her. I'd already taken her money."

"But you slept with her."

"I guess her confession appealed to my ego."

"Do I appeal to your ego?"

"You appeal to every part of me."

"That sounds like a line."

"It's the truth," my father said.

"Here," she said.

Anna walked toward my father, her eyes on his eyes, but past his eyes at the same time. My father nodded his head.

"Very good," he said. "Did you shut everything out?"

"I did. Until there was nothing."

Anna took a final pull off her cigarette, dropped it, pressed it cold with her heel. My father flicked his cigarette into the street.

"Is that easier?" my father said.

"I was just playing. I'm not a coward."

The sun had moved up in the sky and the day was starting. People walked. Cars moved. Life seemed to lead us to Duval Street, where we'd been the night before. It was too early for the Duval Crawl, but evening would come and the bars would fill and the madness would last until four in the morning, a routine that was probably as regular as the tide.

My father sent me into a store for the newspaper. The headline had changed, but my father found himself on page two. I saw it in his eyes before I even saw the paper. He burst out laughing. Anna and I looked at the drawing. It wasn't him, but it was close. The article described the crime, the executive that had been forced to come along for the ride, the cashier's attraction and suspicion at airport parking, the impounded Valiant near the Fontainebleau. My father was always looked at, but as people passed him on Duval Street the looks seemed full of something else, not nothing, and we couldn't be sure if they had read the paper, seen the face, made the connection.

My father tilted his hat over his eyes and we got off Duval Street.

"It's not a very good drawing," Anna said.

"It's a good thing I wasn't a movie star. There'd be an eight-by-ten available and then there'd be no pretending I'm not me."

"Big stealing," I said. "It wasn't you."

"It's me now. We better get back to the hotel. We better get the money out of there and figure something out."

My father looked at me. He knew all of my expressions.

"There's nothing to worry about," he said.

"Of course not."

He put his hand on my shoulder the way he did when he introduced me. *This is my son, Ben.* Then he let go.

"These are the best moments," he said. "It's a high. It's the high of life."

"Do you really believe what you're saying?" Anna said.

"Right now I do. That's all that matters."

"You're not pretending at all?" she said.

"If you pretend hard enough it's real."

"I don't know."

"When *Breathless* came out, the critics said Belmondo wasn't a real character. They said he was pretending to be Michel who was pretending to be Bogie, so he had no real identity. They were wrong. He pretends so hard he becomes real."

"Maybe he's just pretending that he's in love," Anna said.

"No," my father said. "He's in love."

My father took a cigarette off Anna and lit up.

"Go on," he said.

"What?" she said.

"Pretend."

"Pretend what?"

"Pretend this is the high. Force the high to go through you."

"I know how to do that," she said. "I know how to create that rush."

"Go on, then."

"I know how."

"Breathless," my father said. "Breathless. Breathless. Breathless. Breathless."

He was revving himself up, forcing the high through him, more and more, faster and faster until the now felt like the best now ever, the highest now ever.

"Breathless," he yelled. "All or nothing. Breathless."

"Breathless," she said.

"All," my father yelled. "Or nothing."

"All or nothing," Anna yelled and laughed. "We can go to Cuba." She was revving herself up too.

"We can be the first Americans to escape from the States," my father said loud.

"We can build a raft out of tires just like they do," she said.

"We can play baseball for the Cuban team."

"We can smoke Cuban cigars."

"We can drink Cuba Libres and take afternoon siestas on Castro convertibles."

"We can."

*"Mira,"* he said.

*"Mira, mira,"* she said.

*"Mira, mira. Mantequilla."*

They were cracking up. Like they didn't have a care in the world. Like the drawing of my father was just some cartoon for easy amusement.

"Find us some tires, Ben," my father said.

"Get us some baseball uniforms, Ben," Anna said.

"Buy us some Coca Cola for those Cuba Libres, Ben."

"Don't forget the limes."

"Don't forget the Castro convertible."

"We're not going to Cuba," I yelled.

"Of course we're not," my father said.

"It's not a game. It's not a fucking game."

"It's all a game. That fucker that burned your balls. Even he was playing a game."

"He was a sick man."

"He was playing. If I hadn't found him he would have bragged about what he'd done to you. In jail or out of jail. Wherever he was. He would have laughed about it for the rest of his life."

"The way you're laughing at what you did?"

"I'm not laughing at what I did. I'm just laughing. It's all a game. Women looking at you and looking past you. That's a game. Men talking shit, wishing it wasn't shit. That's a game. Little stealing. Big stealing. All games. Revenge. Violence. On-the-road adventures down one side of America. We're the biggest players of all. We've all got Hollywood in our blood. We went west and we found Hollywood. Even Belmondo. He was moving his thumb across his lips because of a movie he saw. He was playing. He was a small-time crook, but he was playing a small-time crook at the same time."

"He wasn't real."

"He is real. He plays so well he's real. That's reality. We're all playing parts. All these people walking around, all these people on the street right now, they're just extras."

"So that's what I am," I said.

"You're more than an extra."

"But I'm still in your little movie."

"And I'm in your little movie."

"And what about her?"

"Anna has her own movie. You and I are in it. She's in ours."

"But it's your movie right now," I said.

"Right now?" my father said like it was a dare he was proud of. "Right now? Yes it is. Right now it's my movie. And when you're in my movie it's all or nothing. All or nothing. That's the beauty of it. All or nothing and that leaves you breathless. That leaves you alive. Really alive. And that's real."

My father rolled up the newspaper and looked through the hole.

"Exterior. Key West. The camera cuts to a shot of a man with his son. The man is on the run, but the man and his son are standing still on a side street, talking. A beautiful woman looks on. The sun is hot in the sky. A police siren is heard in the distance."

The siren really was in the distance. I hadn't heard it. I trusted my father to know the difference between a police siren and a fire truck or an ambulance. There had to be other trouble besides ours in Key West, but this was my father's movie and I already knew the siren was for him.

"Places," my father said.

"We have to run," I said.

"Are you up to running?"

"I can run if I have to."

"If you have to, you can do anything," my father said.

He looked at me and nodded once and in that nod, in that moment, I felt I really could do anything.

"And *action*," he said.

My father started toward the hotel. Anna and I followed him. She lifted her camera and took one shot and then another.

We moved through the streets. Chameleons skittered across the pavement.

Yellow police tape cordoned off the front of The Grand. A half dozen police cars filled the parking lot and a half dozen more lined the street. One officer held my father's valise. It was wrapped in a plastic bag. The officer lifted it into the trunk of his car, slammed the trunk closed. The big stealing had officially been found.

With all the lights, with all the noise of the gathering crowd, we didn't hear the car behind us until the brakes were slammed. My father was always aware of everything around him. Before big stealing. Before I was burned. Before her. My father turned. A policeman was getting out of the car, staring at my father, everything in his eyes.

A shiver went through me.

My father started to run. The policeman started to run. Another officer got out of the car and started to run. I didn't have time to breathe in. I just started running. I ran after them, hoping I could keep up. My father was fast, his stride opened up when he sprinted, but the officers were fast too. I followed them, through the streets, weaving back toward Duval Street. I had to catch him. I had to put my body between them and him. They wouldn't shoot me. I was still a kid. I ran. It hurt down there and I ran. The skin graft burned. The new skin felt like it was unrolling. I ran harder. I passed one cop. He tried to knock me down with his arm but I kept running. It hurt but I kept running. I kept my eyes looking straight. Me. The cop in front of me. My father in front of the cop. My father cut through a space, the cop followed, I followed. My father was running faster than I'd ever seen him run, his strides completely open, his head high. My legs were heavy. My father's legs didn't look heavy at all. I forced myself to run harder and harder. It hurt but I ran harder. I was running but not away. I was running to my father. I ran past the hurt. I caught the second cop, ran past him. It was me and my father. My body between the cop and my father.

I called to him to stop. I needed him to stop. I needed him.

We were running. Stride for stride, father and son, me just behind him. Duval Street. A two-man race, straight to the ocean.

I could hear him breathing. I could hear myself breathing. I reached out my hand and touched his shoulder to let him know I was with him, to let him know it would all be fine and we moved stride for stride and my father turned and in turning the gun fell out of his pants and skidded along the street and for a moment his eyes were on my eyes and the smile was there and he was letting me know it would all be fine, that he was the father and I was the son, that he was my father and I was his son, and then he cut away from me to get the gun. My body was no longer in front of his body.

My scream was background noise.

The shot was loud.

My father put his hand to his back.

He stumbled forward, stumbled some more, started a slow run, slow and slower, and then he fell, just like the movie. His hat was off, he was on his back and I was looking down at him. The cops were near me, they had their guns out, but it was just for show. The sun lit up his face. Morning sun, on its arc up and not its arc down, like my father wanted, on the way up.

My father was looking up at me.

"Stay mighty," I said.

I was kneeling. I was holding his right hand. His hand was cold.

"Just stay mighty," I said. "Just stay mighty. Just stay mighty. Just stay mighty. Just stay mighty."

I couldn't stop. The same line over and over. There was snot and spit and tears coming out of me and I couldn't stop, couldn't catch my breath, I had always caught my breath, I was a fucking runner, but I couldn't run, not with him lying in front of me, I couldn't walk, not with him in front of me, I couldn't breathe, sucking for more air, a child's sucking for more air, all the edges going soft, the edges of his face, the water in my eyes.

"Just stay mighty."

He smiled.

"Just stay," I said, my words cut off by me, sucking for air.

The smile was in his eyes.

"I'm fine," he said.

"It's finished," he said. "Fin."

Fin. He said it like a fish fin. French for The End. I'd asked him why they'd written *Fin* the first time I'd seen *Breathless*. He remembered. He was smiling. His face was tan, but there was no color. I was just kneeling there. I was just looking down. The air came in and I just felt myself breathing.

"You're fine," he said.

He was breathing fast, short breaths, short and fast.

"Just stay mighty," I said, but it was just something to say, comfort in the repetition. I breathed. He breathed. When we ran together he breathed louder. He was on his back.

"Go on, Ben. One last time."

I knew what he meant.

"Go on," he said.

I moved my thumb across my lips.

He was in a puddle of blood, his blood, and the puddle was spreading, picking up gravel and sand and the red was so dark it could have been black and white.

"Now you're the star," my father said.

"No," I screamed.

"You," he said.

The sirens were filling up the background. My father was still smiling. He was breathing short and fast. His eyes moved to Anna.

"You get the shot?" he said.

"I got the shot," she said.

My father's smile was in his eyes, his eyes on Anna, but his eyes were going away.

"You are really," he said just like Belmondo said at the end of the movie.

He didn't finish the line. He knew to leave it alone, like a good player, like a good director, the line between his life and the movie he loved not a line at all. My father closed his eyes and he was young forever.

PART THREE

*breathe*

# 24

WE TOOK THE BUS FROM KEY WEST TO MIAMI. ANNA SAT ON
the aisle so I could be by the window and look out. I tried to look
at the horizon the way my father saw it and then I looked at the
horizon the way I always looked at it, but I couldn't remember that,
not fully. Like the new skin. Like the new caps on my teeth. Like
life before I was burned. I couldn't fully remember the before. And
I couldn't fully remember the before of living in New York with
my father.

Our winter vacations in Miami had always broken time in a nice
way, slowed it down, and when the vacation was over we were
ready to drive back to the city. My father would drive north in one
shift, pulling over for a few hours' sleep when he was exhausted,
putting his hat over his head. This time, we were in Miami so long,
and then Key West, that time had broken differently. The days
changed into other days like I was drinking, but I wasn't drinking. I
was restless, but not like my father had been. I was restless from
waiting. Waiting for the questions to be over. Waiting for the investigation to close. Waiting for permission to take my father away.

I decided not to take him too far. Anna just listened as I worked it out, sometimes out loud, for her, but really for me, and when I was sure she told me my decision was a good one. He loved Florida. I would come back once a year, the way we always had, to see my father. The place we found looked out on the ocean. The waves were breaking hard that day. The dirt I put over my father's coffin was mostly sand. It slid through my hands too easily.

Instead of driving, we flew back. I didn't hate to fly, even though I'd never flown before. And Anna had grown up on a real island, had flown her whole life. The flight was smooth, only a little turbulence before we landed in New York. He would have been fine.

I didn't know what to do with my days. I didn't know how to do them. Time still seemed drunk. Some mornings I woke and didn't know if I was in Miami or New York. Some mornings I didn't know if my father was here or not.

I started school in another school. At Stuyvesant it would have been too strange. They would have looked at me like I had come back from the dead. Anna knew the headmaster at one of the good private schools and I spoke to the track coach, who took me outside and held a stopwatch while I ran a mile. I was admitted as a second-semester junior so I wouldn't lose any time. Over two weekends, Anna helped me pack up our apartment. There wasn't much to pack. My father's Spartan existence was too clear without the two of us there. We sold most of the furniture and what we didn't sell we left out on the street to disappear, like before had disappeared.

I spent some weekend nights at Anna's apartment. She would cook dinner and we would rent a movie or take a long walk somewhere. There were photographs all over her apartment, blown up, taped to the walls, some of them framed. One night she gave me an envelope that had hundreds of pictures of my father. I looked through them all, slowly. I recognized all the streets in the background. The Village streets. The Miami streets. The streets in Key West. He looked beautiful in her photographs, the light always in his eyes. I took a stack of photographs taken in New York and held them together, tight, and then I let them flip between my fingers, fast, like stills from a movie. My father moved as if he were alive, as if he were the star, at the peak of his career. In the last photograph his hat was tilted all the way back and he was smiling at the camera, looking straight into the lens.

Most nights I stayed in student housing near the school. I had a small room with a bed, a chair, a desk and a bookshelf. A public bathroom was down the hall. A dining room was on the first floor. I met a few kids, but I kept to myself. I didn't feel like talking about my past. I kept it vague the way my father had done. That silence helped me understand my father. Maybe he'd gone through something that he wanted forgotten, burned like an old piece of film so it would never be seen, not by anybody. He kept quiet and I kept quiet. I decided not to go searching for the past before my father. It would disappear that way, the way my father wanted it to disappear. My past with my father was different. I kept that vague because I wanted to keep it sacred. He was my father. Our past was ours. Just ours.

I ran all the time. Miles and miles and miles of running, when all alone was not only acceptable, but right. Instead of running along the river I ran in Central Park along the horse path that meandered around the reservoir and past the Great Lawn, easy on the feet, dirt instead of pavement, some parts of the park so green it didn't feel like the city at all. My mind would go far away, in time, my father counting his money at the table, my father putting his hand on my shoulder, my father running with me. When I ran it was like magicing the past. It came to me. But he didn't come to me. Nobody was that mighty.

One afternoon, I left the park and kept running. Past Columbus

Circle. Down Fifth Avenue. Over to the West Side Highway. The Hudson River looked almost clean. There were no barges carrying goods, no cruise ships with passengers doing parade waves. Stuyvesant was in the distance, but it was late enough that no one from school would be around.

I recognized his slow walk from a distance. I didn't stop running, didn't stop moving forward, didn't turn around. His face came into view, his mouth, his lips not as chapped in the warmer weather. I slowed my pace and stopped in front of him.

Michael looked at me and then looked away. He'd been so steady when we'd met, so sure, and I had been young, but now I felt not so young. I'd been away and I'd come back. I'd slept with a man. I'd lost a father. I just stayed looking at him, forcing myself to show nothing, the way I'd been taught. There were power plays in every relationship and sometimes the power changed.

My legs were strong. I was in shape again, almost as fast as I had been. But standing in front of Michael, my legs felt heavy. I could have kept running, miles and miles, but I couldn't.

"Why did you do it?"

It was the question I'd been waiting to ask him. Waiting and waiting. In the hospital. After the hospital. Driving down to Florida. On the bus to Key West. In the man's room when I was so drunk, so hurt, so angry at my father for his running away, so hurt at Michael for his running away, that I did something I had waited so long for in a bad way. Waiting and waiting. Why. Why. Why. All the questions distilled into one.

"What?" he said.

"Tell me."

"Tell you what?"

"Why did you do it?"

"I didn't do anything."

"You did nothing."

He couldn't hold my eyes.

"Where did you go?" I said.

"I'm still around."

"I see that. Don't act stupid. Where did you go? I heard you coughing and then you were gone."

"I got hit and I ran."

"Do you know what they did to me?"

"I know."

"How do you know?"

"I read about it," he said.

He was looking at his feet.

"I wouldn't have run," I said. "I would have tried to help."

"There was nothing I could do."

He looked almost sad standing there. Not so sure. Not so calm. He had run and that would never disappear. I wanted to hold him the way he'd held me, to kiss his lips, to see how they felt in warmer weather, but I also wanted to hit him. Of course, life had gone on for him. Of course, he hadn't thought about me. I was old enough to know that.

"I understand that you were scared. I was scared too. But afterwards, when there was nothing to be scared of, you could have found me. You could have found me just for a moment. To see if I was okay."

"Are you okay?" he said.

I almost said I was fine. But I didn't.

"I'm sorry," he said. "Are you okay now?"

"Now? Now I run."

I said the word to hurt him.

"I run and run."

"I'm sorry."

"I'm almost as fast as I was before," I said.

I looked at him and past him at the same time. But more than

273

that. I looked at him until I didn't really care. If he kissed me, I would put my hands on his waist and gently push him away. Like my father. Before Anna. And that was fine. He wasn't the person I wanted him to be. He wasn't breathless anymore. I would have to wait for my all or nothing and that was fine. That was fine.

"I'm going to finish my run," I said.

"It's nice to see you."

"Nice," I said.

I nodded my head once. For him. For me. Then I started running.

I ran to Stuyvesant. I ran past Stuyvesant. It was the route my father and I had always run, runs I might talk about when I was ready, when time turned more sober. It was not so cold that my breath turned to smoke, not so cold that my father would breathe into his hands. I got to Battery Park and turned around where we'd always turned around.

I ran. Past where the World Trade Centers had been. Past Stuyvesant. Past the FedEx garage, the arrowed-logo on a parked truck pointing me forward. I started to sprint toward Christopher Street. That's when my father looked like a runner, when he sprinted, his stride opening up, his head high, his eyes looking straight ahead, moving fast.

Maybe it was all part of his plan. Maybe he had all the details in place and when the time came, when the moment happened, he was ready. Like an understudy who gets his chance. It just so happened that I was the catalyst, but I had to let go of that. My father wouldn't have wanted me to feel guilty. He put his back to the wall completely, at the bottom tip of the States, the final wall long and blue, shore-to-horizon thick.

Sometimes when I sprinted, I broke down. Even as my legs kept moving, I would cry, catching my breath hard between the sobs. My eyes would fill with tears and I could almost pretend he was running next to me. I was running hard, past the quarter-mile marker, a final push to Christopher Street. I was running hard but my breath was steady. I was almost back in shape. Back to before. Almost.

I was running.

I wasn't crying. I didn't hear the sobs.

I ran past Christopher Street, past the line where we'd started so many runs and finished so many runs. I slowed my pace, my stride open even when I wasn't sprinting, and I kept running, uptown, running within myself. Breathing steady. Breathe and breathe.

I lifted my thumb, moved it once across my lips and then kissed the air in front of me.